Lady at Last

Annabelle Anders

Lady at Last
Annabelle Anders

Copyright © 2019 Annabelle Anders
Print Edition

CHAPTER ONE

A MIRACLE.

It had taken a miracle to change Penelope Cross's mind about spinsterhood, but her mind had changed, nonetheless.

Penelope wrinkled her nose. Had it been a miracle? It was simply a baby. A birth. The creation of life.

Perhaps it *was* a miracle, after all. Penelope placed her gloved hands atop the sturdy fence post, leaned her head forward, and pressed it against the wood. The air was crisp; the sun bright. A bit of snow remained in the shaded areas of the meadow.

It ought to be a perfectly normal February evening.

But it was not.

After thirty-six hours of labor pains, her dear friend, Lilly, the Duchess of Cortland, had finally given birth to a tiny, red-faced, wiggling, and wrinkled human. He was all of two hours old.

Penelope had witnessed the entire event. And oh, what a spectacle it had been. One would think at the ripe age of eight-and-twenty that nothing could change her mind about what she wanted in life. But this...

Seeing a child enter the world...

Well, it had.

And the craziest thought had developed as she'd assisted the midwife in cleaning the squirming, slimy little creature before handing him over to his exhausted mother.

I want one.

Which, of course, changed everything.

Because Penelope had long ago given up any hope of capturing the attention of her one true love. And if she could not have him, she didn't want anybody else. She would never marry; she had decided so just this past fall.

And now this!

This bodily need—this hunger—had hit her so very unexpectedly. An emptiness had opened up inside of her, an emptiness that could only be filled by making her own little screaming human.

She smiled and covered her mouth with one hand, tears flowing down her cheeks. The look on Lilly's face, in her eyes, when Penelope had handed her the blanketed bundle. Total fulfillment.

Penelope swiped at her tears and sniffled.

Lilly's husband, the Duke of Cortland, had been in awe—of both his wife and his son. For theirs was a marriage of love. Not only did the duke have his heir now, but he and Lilly and that miniature human were a family now.

Penelope did not begrudge them. In fact, most of the girls who'd befriended her when she'd first entered society were now married. Not only married but happily so. Even Abigail! The least likely of them all to wed!

Again, the image of tiny little hands, tiny little feet and toes, tiny little everything, clouded her vision. And again, she experienced the hunger.

I want one!

But how? Well, the answer was obvious. Penelope sighed. *I'll have to find myself a man! A husband to be exact.*

As Penelope marched back toward Summer's Park, the duke's large country estate near Exeter, she mentally calculated which gentlemen of her acquaintance she'd be willing to tolerate. Since *he* was most definitely not interested, she was going to have to find somebody else. Somebody she could bear for the remainder of her life—or his, whichever the case may be.

She could always set her sights upon one of his brothers. But Penelope quickly dismissed the notion.

If she could not have *him,* then she most definitely did not wish to become a part of his family.

No, she would have to find some other lucky gent.

Hugh Chesterton, the Viscount of Danbury, was the most obvious choice. Except Danbury had eluded marriage for as long as she'd known him. Nearly ten years, in fact!

Ouch. This fact reminded her that the next London season would be her tenth. Most would consider her firmly upon the shelf. At eight and twenty, she could never hope to take the *ton* by storm. She'd become something more along the lines of a drizzle. She personified London itself—in the form of a woman. Had she really participated in a decade of seasons?

Not to be distracted by these negative thoughts, Penelope enumerated to herself the reasons Danbury would be a good choice.

Proximity, first and foremost.

He was, at this very moment, lounging in Cortland's study consuming copious amounts of celebratory scotch. For this was where the gentlemen had spent the past twenty or so hours awaiting the news of a safe delivery for the duchess and their little marquess.

Tolerability as well.

Hugh, as a friend, could very possibly be molded into a tolerable husband. He was pleasant, had a fine sense of humor, and wasn't a complete idiot.

Neither was he hard on the eyes.

And ah, yes, suitability. As a viscount, he was born of a fine lineage. Her parents would not find any fault in him whatsoever. Which wasn't really an issue for Penelope, but it would make things easier.

Availability.

Hmmm… this was an uncertainty. Not that Danbury was actually attached to any other female of her acquaintance, but he had certainly been successful in escaping wedlock thus far.

The debutantes who'd set their sights upon Viscount Danbury had gone about attempting to capture him in all the wrong ways. They'd endeavored to seduce him with their frills, sighs, batting eyelashes, and empty-headed opinions.

But Penelope had an advantage. She *knew* Hugh.

She knew him for what he was. A bit of a rogue. He preferred a turn of the ankle to a pretty blush any day. He preferred cleavage to lace, passion to infatuation, and he also preferred…

Red hair.

How did she know this? How could she *not* know this? Every demi-mondaine he'd ever appeared with had had red hair. Quite honestly, he must have worked his way through piles and piles of the stuff. And why had Penelope noticed this tendency?

Well, she had red hair herself. Not the brassy, deep-colored red hair of Danbury's lady friends, but a sun-kissed sort of red, closer to blond, but definitely red.

This could come in quite handy.

And, she reasoned with herself, Danbury needed to marry eventually. He was halfway through his thirties, for heaven's sake. He might as well marry her. They got along well enough. Aside from some occasional bickering, that was.

She was a baron's daughter and tolerably pretty when she put forth an effort. She had a decent-sized dowry, and she was smart as a whip.

Well, perhaps he would not appreciate the last attribute in his wife at first, but eventually, he would be forced to admit that such a characteristic made for a considerable asset in the woman one married.

With her as his wife, he would not beggar any of his estates, nor would he cast any unwise votes in Parliament.

Yes, Danbury could use such a guiding hand as hers.

The cool air sent a shiver through her as she entered the large open foyer of the ancient castle. It reminded her of entering a cathedral—or a museum. The large home at Summer's Park certainly boasted enough artwork and sculptures to rival either. She handed her coat, bonnet, and gloves to the stoic butler and then commenced climbing the long curving staircase to the upper floors.

Would Danbury still be in the study?

Would he be alone?

Penelope stopped to glance in a mirror at one of the landings and pushed a few tendrils of hair behind her ears. She then removed her fichu and tucked it into her skirt. Shimmying her shoulders a bit, she leaned forward and plumped her breasts upward, so they were nearly coming out of her stays. Ah, yes, a bit of cleavage was just what she needed. She bit her lips to plump them up as well.

Much better. Studying herself again, she untucked the hair from behind her ears and pulled out a few hairpins. The released strands made her look softer... less the spinster she'd been for several years now.

Her eyes were shining, and her cheeks were a bit reddened from the cold outside. Penelope bit her lips one last time and smoothed her skirts.

If Danbury was to be the father to her child, she'd best get to work now.

She spun on her heel and marched purposefully toward

the masculine study, her plan to land a husband underway.

Later, she would consider that perhaps she ought to have slept on the matter first—allowed herself a few days to consider the matter practically. One didn't always make the wisest of decisions when they'd gone two days without sleep.

*H*UGH LEANED BACK and swung one leg over the armrest of the ancient leather chair he preferred while visiting Summer's Park. He was more than a little foxed. Cortland had deserted him over an hour ago to go to his duchess and newborn son, leaving Hugh to his own devices. The two men had paced the study for ages before receiving the news of Lilly's safe delivery. Well, Cortland had paced anyhow. Hugh had languished on the comfortable settee, sipping scotch—liberal amounts of it. And now, even though he had every intention of retiring to the guest chamber he normally used, his body refused to obey. He really must cut back on the spirits.

Guilt groused at him. He ought to be traveling north. He needed to investigate rumors of tenant unrest at his estate near Manchester. He'd only detoured to Summer's Park to consult with Cortland before addressing the situation, but then Lilly had gone into labor, and he could not leave his oldest friend at such a distressing time!

That had been two days ago.

Tomorrow, he would depart.

Hearing footsteps approach the corridor, Hugh glanced toward the door, expecting to see Cortland. He would be strutting like a peacock, no doubt, having sired a son first time around. Preparing for another toast, Hugh reached for the decanter of scotch but then stopped when he saw that it was not Cortland.

Definitely not Cortland.

Rather, it was a disheveled Penelope Crone. The good old girl was one of the rare single ladies with whom a bachelor was safe to find himself alone. As an unmarried viscount, he remained vigilantly mindful of ambitious mamas and debutantes. He enjoyed his bachelor status far too much to risk it for a peck and a feel.

No, Penelope, a confirmed spinster, was as reluctant to marry as he.

Except, this evening, there was something different about her.

As she entered the room, her hips swayed in a manner he'd almost consider beguiling. Very unusual. Penelope was pragmatic about all things. Was she ill? Was *she* foxed? Holy hell, he must have drowned in his cups, because damned if Practical Pen wasn't looking as though she wanted to seduce him!

Surely, he was mistaken.

Her cheeks flushed crimson, and her lips tilted upward in a secret sort of smile. Soft tufts of reddish golden hair framed her face. Hugh also could not fail to notice that her breasts were very close to spilling out the top of her bodice.

He pulled his leg off the chair and sat up straight. "Pen," he nearly choked when she leaned forward, giving him an even better view of her…, "I trust all is well with mother and babe?"

Hugh had known Penelope for ages and being alone with her was not something he'd normally find concerning. She was like a cousin to him, practically a sister! Obviously, assisting the ladies with the long birth had brought about her unusually disheveled appearance. She'd most likely not slept in over twenty-four hours. This sensuality in her gaze was surely an aberration—the concoction of her tousled appearance and too much scotch on his part.

And then she turned toward the window, raised her hands up and behind her neck, and stretched, like a feline soaking up the sun. Her position thrust her chest forward and emphasized the long, swanlike column of her neck. Her skin was the color of porcelain except for a few delicate freckles sprinkled here and there. Hugh gulped as he watched the edge of her bodice.

She then turned her head toward him and gave him *a look*.

This could not be reality, for Hugh knew women, and that look was the look a woman gave a man when she wanted him. "Lilly and the little marquess are perfect." Her voice sounded breathy as she floated toward him.

Hugh's body stirred.

Jumping to his feet, he ignored the unwanted sensation of lust. Where had his manners gone? A gentleman always rose to his feet when a lady entered the room.

"What a day, eh, Pen, old gal? Join me for a toast?" He reached for the glass he'd been going to pour for Cortland, tipped a few fingers of the amber liquid into it, and held it out toward her. He struggled with his balance but managed to avoid spilling any of the liquid onto the table. His hand barely shook as he handed her the drink.

Penelope stepped closer to him. Closer than necessary for her to retrieve the drink. "I've never tasted scotch before." She wrapped her fingers around the glass, covering his, her voice low and velvety.

Hugh wanted to release the drink, but fragile fingers had captured his own and, for the life of him, he could not figure out why he would ever want to be free. His mind was unusually distracted by her lips, which parted temptingly when Penelope lifted the glass, along with his hand, so that she might take a sip.

Watching the aromatic liquor flow into her soft, wet mouth, held him in an enchanted trance. After taking a long and steady sip, she closed her eyes and tilted her head back. She licked her lips and swallowed the strong spirit.

"Mmm..." She surprised him by not coughing. And then she lowered her chin again and opened her eyes. Emerald eyes that he'd never really noticed before. With her hair not pulled back so tightly, they appeared wider. Her lashes were lightly colored but lush and thick. Studying them for the first time, he noticed little blue flecks. Why, her eyes were nothing short of spectacular!

She stood intimately close to him, her hand still covering his. Hugh glanced down to her bodice and pleasantly noted how proximity gave him quite an eyeful of cleavage. His groin tightened when she again lifted the glass.

To *his* lips.

He watched her over the rim as he swallowed. She then took another drink for herself before returning it to the table. What in the hell was going on?

And then Miss Penelope Crone, the original wallflower, bluestocking, queen of all spinsters, pressed her body up against him and wound her arms around his neck. She was tall, not as tall as Hugh, but tall enough that when she spoke into his ear, her breath heated his skin.

"We ought to celebrate, don't you think?"

Of their own volition, Hugh's arms wound themselves around his fantasy. That's what this was, a dream, a drunken hallucination. He might as well enjoy it!

One hand reached for her bottom, and the other wrapped around her waist. With no hesitation whatsoever, he tightened his grip, pressing her against his torso and groin. "Damn straight we should," he growled in agreement before claiming her lips.

*T*HIS WAS GOING to work. This was actually going to work! The thought had barely registered in Penelope's mind when Danbury covered her mouth with his. Encouraged by such enthusiasm, she parted her lips and allowed his very capable tongue free reign. In her mouth!

She'd known he was something of a womanizer. She'd known he was experienced and would be well-versed in the aspects of physical love.

She had *not* known how it would affect her.

Her control slipped slightly, but she had no cause to be concerned.

Because, the thing about a true gentleman, even a roguish one like Danbury, was that he would never dally lightly with a woman who was a *lady*.

For if he were caught dallying with a *lady,* he could be forced to marry her. And if he refused to make the poor girl an offer, his honor was compromised.

And Hugh Chesterton, Viscount of Danbury, was nothing if he was not honorable.

And technically speaking, Penelope was a lady.

First and foremost, an unwed lady had her virginity. A gentleman had his honor.

Did she feel guilty for presuming upon Danbury's honor? Ouch, yes, she did. A little.

But really, she reasoned with herself as his hand reached around to claim her breast, he was going to get a great deal out of this as well. When she'd entered the room, she'd only intended allowing him to compromise her in the most innocent sense. But—she couldn't stop the moan from escaping past her lips—that felt delightful. Was he pinching her? Oh my!

Hugh moved to her other breast and she was able to return to her train of thought. Oh yes, if she allowed him even greater liberties, then the end result would be far more expedient.

She would give up her virginity, and Danbury would act honorably. She'd have her husband and then her baby.

She moaned again as his lips left her mouth and found her neck. Good God, this felt wonderful. The sensations soaring through her had absolutely nothing to do with wanting to make a baby.

No, she thought, as her fingers ran through Hugh's springy chestnut hair, these sensations were far more primitive. She found herself writhing against him, wanting to be closer.

Danbury growled and lifted her in his arms. As he carried her to the long settee, Penelope congratulated herself on having the foresight to lock the door behind her. She lay back against a pillow, and he held himself above her. His gaze travelled downward and she startled to realize her modest bosoms were no longer covered by her bodice. And then his mouth was on her again. On her shoulder, her neck, and oh, God, on the tip of her breast.

Penelope gripped the sides of his head tightly as he did amazing things with his lips and teeth. She arched her back, reaching, wanting more. And with no thought at all, her thighs fell open and his weight bore down upon her. She hadn't truly thought things would go this far, had she? She'd entered Cortland's study with the thought of flirting with Danbury, tempting him. But could that have been enough to extract a proposal for marriage? Most likely not. Others had tried. All of them had failed. When she'd seen how foxed he was, forgetting even to stand when she'd entered the room, she knew this was her chance.

She must carry out this deed if she wanted him to offer

for her. She'd deal with the aftermath later.

Hugh stroked the length of her leg. He then pushed her skirts aside and slid his hand up to the very sensitive skin on the inside of her thigh.

Heat pooled at her apex. She hungered for him. His fingers teased her, drifting from one leg to the other, and then to her abdomen, just below her stays.

Penelope thrust herself into his hand. "Touch me, Hugh," she demanded. She had never experienced anything like this. There had been nights that she'd awakened, alone of course, and touched herself. She'd brought herself satisfaction even, but that had been entirely different.

She was allowing another person, *a man* to touch her intimately. She knew what he felt. The curling hair that concealed her womanhood, and then the plump creases of skin beneath it. She opened her thighs wider, and his hand took her possessively.

This was so very different than touching herself.

Penelope's breath hitched when he slid one finger inside. Havoc spiraled within as her need grew.

"You're so wet for me," Hugh breathed, "so very ready for me."

And then his hand was gone. Penelope opened her eyes to find he was undoing his falls. A sharp stab of regret threatened to engulf her, but she would not allow it. If not now, when? If not Hugh, then who?

She barely caught sight of his manhood, protruding from a thatch of dark hair, before Hugh leaned forward again.

His breath was warm, the fumes of the scotch he'd consumed nearly overwhelming.

Suddenly, the setting for losing her virginity was horribly, horrifically wrong! They were on a settee, in the Duke of Cortland's study, for God's sake. And Hugh was drunk out of his mind. Was she insane? Alarm bells sounded in her head but there was no turning back.

He was pressing into her. She wanted to pull away, but she had nowhere to go.

It hurt.

The pushing, the invading, oh, God, the tearing. Penelope couldn't stop the scream that suddenly pierced the late afternoon quiet of the study.

CHAPTER TWO

*H*UGH WAS AWAKENED early the next morning by Chester, his valet of over a dozen years, to read an urgent missive sent from his mother. Splitting head aside, Hugh knew Chester took enjoyment insisting his master rise early. He'd said the courier had declared the correspondence to be urgent. And the damnable thing of it all was, Hugh loved his mother.

Swinging his legs over to the side of the bed, he unsealed the note while Chester threw open the heavy curtains. The bright sunlight was punishment, surely, for the previous day's overconsumption of brandy and scotch. Hugh rubbed his forehead with one hand and attempted to decipher his mother's handwriting. It was atrocious, as always—barely legible.

Hugh,

I've purchased new capes (drapes?) *for the foyer. The old ones are not allowing enough sunlight in to chase the cold of winter away. These new ones will be made of a lighter fabric and consist of a yellow and green floral print. I'm thinking of having a dark green egging* (edging?) *added so they aren't overwhelmingly feminine. This is your estate, after all. For I would never guess. It has been so lonely* (long?)*, my dearest, since you have spent any time here.*

Your dodder (sister?) *is departing soon to participate in the season, but I am considering forgoing*

14

Town to stay at home. What with having to fight off this scarlet fever and all.

Anyhow, I would simply ask that you keep an eye on your sister while she is there and offer her your lemon (escort?) *on a few occasions.*

Love,
Mother

It took a moment or two for the words to penetrate the fog of his brain. He had to read through the entire missive in order to ascertain that he was not mistaken. Even then, he was not entirely certain.

Scarlet fever? Good God, why had no one contacted him sooner!

"Chester, we'll be departing for Land's End immediately. Why did no one see fit to inform me that my mother had contracted scarlet fever? Damn me, I've been told nothing of it. Is there an epidemic at the estate? In the village? Do you know anything of any of this, Chester?" Hugh was near panicked at the thought of his mother's mortality.

"I'm certain I do not, my lord," Chester responded uselessly as he pulled one of Hugh's large traveling trunks out of the dressing room and began folding clothing into it. "Might I suggest you journey ahead of the traveling coach on your mount instead of waiting? The weather looks fine, and you'd make quicker time that way."

Hugh rubbed his hand through his hair and nodded in agreement. Of course, what was he thinking? He could be back at the estate in half the time. Oh, hell, he simply wished his head would stop pounding. He'd not be imbibing again anytime in the near future. "Of course, of course." He glanced around in frustration. "Where are my damn riding boots?"

Less than half an hour passed before Hugh and Dicky, one of his outriders, rode off the estate together. The sun had barely yet risen. Glancing over his shoulder, Hugh knew Cortland and the duchess would not take offense at his quick departure. He'd left word of the situation and adamantly instructed nobody follow. He needed to verify the facts of his mother's letter first.

His conscience niggled, however, as though he were forgetting something very important. He searched his memory to the best of his ability before dismissing the thought. Whatever he'd forgotten would most likely be taken care of by Chester.

He had just over one hundred miles to travel before reaching Morrow Point, his estate near Land's End, located along the coast of the most southwesterly point in Great Britain. If he and Dicky changed out their mounts a few times and took very short breaks, weather permitting, they could arrive late tomorrow night. His heart raced at the potentially devastating situation he might be heading into.

And what of his sister, Lavinia? Surely, she would not leave Mother at such a time. Surely, she was not that selfish. She'd not been the same woman since losing her husband a few years ago, but she was still quite level-headed. In fact, she'd never been like other frivolous ladies of the *ton*. This entire situation made no sense.

The question of an outbreak of scarlet fever at Morrow Point, nonetheless, was nothing to ignore. He pushed his horse a bit harder. As Summer's Park disappeared behind him, he again dismissed the thought that he was forgetting something.

*P*ENELOPE'S FIRST THOUGHT upon awakening was that she was not in her own bed. She was at Summer's Park.

Lilly had given birth to the most adorable baby boy yesterday. A smile spread across Penelope's lips as she pictured the screaming, squirming bundle of innocence.

And then other memories swept her thoughts of delight aside.

Merciful Heavens! She heaved the bedclothes over her head and groaned. She'd truly gone and done it last night. She'd made the most spectacular mistake of her entire lifetime.

Or perhaps not.

The seduction of Viscount Danbury. She'd lured him in and then, well… She didn't even wish to think about what they'd done.

It had been horrible. Well, part of it anyway—that end part, when it had hurt so much—and then again, when Hugh had gone and passed out.

Yes, she'd given herself to the scoundrel, and he'd barely had the courtesy to stay awake through it all.

Burying her head under her pillow, Penelope groaned with mortification as she remembered how she'd shoved Hugh off of her. After she slipped out from beneath his hulking form, he'd snuggled back into the cushions and begun snoring softly.

And then she'd realized there had been blood! She was lucky none had gotten on the settee. But her bloomers and petticoat were both stained. She'd done her best with a small handkerchief to clean herself off, and God help her, to some extent, Hugh.

She'd then pulled his britches back together, tossed a blanket upon him, and raced for her room. Thank heavens Rose, her maid, could be trusted. Penelope had rinsed the offensive garments out herself and hung them on the screen to dry, but Rose would not be fooled.

In spite of having not really slept for nearly two days, it had taken quite some time to fall asleep. She had lain in bed forever, questions and guilt swirling about her mind. Would she be with child? Would Hugh hate her forever? Would he offer for her? And the most frightening thought of all: would he even remember what they'd done?

She'd heard stories of certain people not recalling events that occurred while they were inebriated.

Ought she to have left him undone, so when he awakened, he would be forced to remember? But then anybody could have walked in on him. Hugh would have been mortified. For all his swagger and roguishness, he prided himself on being a gentleman. He was a good man. She could never have allowed him to be embarrassed so horribly.

She would face him today and, of course, he'd offer for her.

She climbed out of bed, ignoring the unfamiliar twinges between her legs and dressed in a simple gown. Rose would have something to say about all of this later.

Bracing herself for the possibility that she could run into Hugh at any moment, she marched downstairs to the morning room where a scrumptious-smelling breakfast had already been set out upon the sideboards.

Cortland, Lilly's husband, was seated but pushed back his chair and rose when he saw Penelope in the doorway. He was a man who looked quite satisfied with his life. He was alone.

Penelope gestured for him to sit down again—they had been friends for several years now—and she turned to fill a plate for herself. "Lilly is well this morning? And the babe?" she asked.

Cortland chuckled. "Both of them are catching up on

their sleep. What a red-faced little screamer, was he not? When he welcomed himself into this world?"

Penelope found a seat and organized the shining silverware around her plate. She then nodded at the hovering footman and waited as he poured hot tea. "He was at that," Penelope agreed. "I am glad Lilly is resting. She did marvelously, don't you think?" Of course, the duke would agree with her. He doted on his duchess.

Penelope watched as the duke again took on that funny, happy expression that had first appeared yesterday afternoon. "She was amazing. Proudest moment of my life."

Penelope took a careful sip of the hot tea and watched him over the rim. She then, oh-so-casually asked him, "Has Danbury seen the little marquess yet? He was awfully deep in his cups when I found him."

At her words, Cortland took on a more serious demeanor. "He left at first light. His mother has taken ill."

She blinked a few times in confusion. Unwilling to believe he'd do this too her and then barely contained a snort of incredulity. That scoundrel! That oafish ape! He was running away from her! *His mother taken ill, my foot!*

"He is returning to Morrow Point then? Delaying his trip north?" She'd known he had important business to attend to. Tenant unrest was becoming something of a problem for many of the nation's landlords. "I'd thought his business up there was rather urgent."

Cortland poured himself some more tea before answering. He would be used to discussing such worldly issues with Penelope by now. She was no simpering miss. "He was quite concerned about her health. Didn't leave any details but specifically instructed that nobody follow him in case it's catching."

"Is his sister well?" Penelope was stunned. Perhaps he

wasn't being a blighter, after all.

"He didn't say. We will simply have to await his news. I'm hopeful that his mother has merely exaggerated the seriousness of her malady. She's done so in the past."

"Oh, I hope so, too." Penelope wasn't sure what to think.

As she dug in to her breakfast more heartily, she decided she'd worried the entire situation too much already. She needed to take responsibility for her actions and move forward without dwelling on possible regrets.

One, she had given her innocence away to an old friend who'd been barely sober enough to accomplish the deed.

Two, he had then disappeared and was possibly putting his own life into imminent danger.

And third, she might very well this moment be with child herself, with the father on death's door.

She mustn't overthink any of this.

Be reasonable. She did not know for certain that she was with child. She was expecting her monthlies in a few weeks and could not do one whit about it.

Hugh had departed, and she could not do one whit about that either.

She was a grown woman. She was not one to give in to a fit of vapors.

But she could not eat a single bite more. Taking a final sip of her tea, she made her excuses to Cortland and then headed upstairs to check in on the baby. He was so very adorable! She wondered what her own would look like...

The nurse was quite happy to hand the little lad over to Penelope. Lilly had just fed him and was already resting again. The babe, however, was wide awake and alert and gazed back at her with curious eyes. Cradling him in her arms, she sat in the rocking chair and cooed at him. "Such a beautiful boy you are, aren't you, my love?" What was it about babies, about *this* baby, that made her feel so empty inside?

Knowing her actions last night had been foolish and reckless to the extreme, Penelope found some justification for them.

As she'd come of age, she'd devoured all available books on history, politics, philosophy, and anthropology. In doing so, she'd had the epiphany that women of her time were raised and treated as second-class citizens. And if they married, they were at even more of a disadvantage.

She'd only marry if she found true love.

And she thought she had, except that it was unrequited. Roman Spencer, Viscount Darlington and heir to the Earl of Ravensdale, was never going to think of her as anything other than a clever friend.

She adjusted the bundle of warmth so he was upright against her shoulder and rubbed his little bum lovingly.

The last time she'd seen Rome, at Lady Natalie and the Earl of Hawthorne's wedding breakfast, the love of her life had been attached to another lady. She was a simpering little thing who had obviously just made her come out. Why did men allow themselves to behave so ridiculously when it came to much younger women? And how could she, Penelope, continue to hold him in high regard when he was so easily enthralled by a mere infant?

And Rome had been enthralled. That fact had been painfully, yes, *painfully* obvious to Penelope. Rome had never looked at *her* with such a tender expression. He'd never been obsessed with watching *her* as she'd danced with other eligible gentlemen.

He'd never loved her, and he never would. The epiphany had been staggering.

And so, Penelope extinguished any hope she'd had for a happy marriage and left London the very next morning with just her maid. In her father's coach, of course, with a driver and two outriders. She wasn't a fool, after all.

First, they'd gone to Bath where she stayed with some friends of her parents. She took the waters, attended theatrical performances, and shopped to her heart's content. There was never an abundance of eligible men in Bath. In fact, most of the folks she visited with were well past the age of fifty. She could ignore her single predicament quite easily while surrounded by other spinsters and widows. But after a while, the sheer boredom of it sent her packing.

She'd returned to her parents' home for the holidays, just long enough to become aggravated with them, and then traveled farther south to be with Lilly for the remainder of her confinement.

Which had been satisfying and enjoyable overall but made her even more aware that she was the last of her set to remain single.

Penelope hadn't minded when Betsy had married, years ago, and gone on to give birth to half a cricket team. And she'd not minded when Lilly had married nor when Lady Natalie had gotten herself engaged.

But then, even Abigail had gotten herself hitched—and quite happily, too! Abigail was to have been her sole companion through spinsterhood and old age. But now Abigail was married, too—to the Duke of Monfort no less!

Penelope was all alone.

Heartbroken and all alone. She practically snorted at such self-pitying thoughts.

Everything ought to have been all fine and well. But then she'd gone and watched Lilly give birth to this tiny little creature.

And now, after the events of last night, thoughts of Roman Spencer could be put to rest forever. She was going to have to wait for Hugh's return.

She hated waiting.

CHAPTER THREE

"*T*OLD YOU HE wasn't coming," Rose, Penelope's mutinous maid, blurted out after Penelope had sauntered into her bedchamber and thrown herself upon the bed.

After three weeks, Danbury had still failed to return to Summer's Park. In addition to this unfortunate fact, obtaining information was becoming more and more difficult. Penelope had pestered the Duke of Cortland so often as to the wayward viscount's whereabouts and health, it was quite possible suspicions were already roused.

She'd never been overly interested in Danbury's whereabouts in the past, so what cause would she have to do so now? What cause indeed?

"Cortland received a missive from him today. Thank heavens he'd misread his mother's missive and she is quite well, apparently." But then she frowned. "He bypassed Summer's Park, however, in order to make quicker time up to Manchester. Oh, Rose, what am I going to do?"

Rose had been dabbing some of Penelope's new perfume upon her wrists but set it aside at Penelope's moaning. "Men will be men, the whole world over. Surely, you've heard 'why buy the cow if you can get the milk for free?' You *gave* the viscount your milk. Poof, he's gone. Simple as that."

Penelope glared at her maid and sat forward on the bed. "But that's the problem. I don't think he has any memory of *taking* the milk! Danbury is not only a gentleman but an honorable one! He's a scoundrel, I'll give you that, but I refuse to believe he would have abandoned me like this had he remembered our... evening of... physical joining. Good Heavens, Rose, he was too bosky to remember anything. I ought to have taken this into consideration."

Rose reached for some lip rouge and dabbed some on herself. "Either way, Penelope, you're in an awful pinch."

Penelope barely kept from moaning out loud again. She was now officially six days late. And even more worrisome was the biliousness she'd begun feeling in the mornings. She pondered her situation rationally. Nothing was going to be achieved by staying at Summer's Park with Lilly and Cortland. As adorable as the baby was and as delightful a friend as Lilly was, Penelope would go mad if she didn't track Danbury down soon. Watching the two lovebirds crooning over their tiny marquess was becoming trying as well. Not that she didn't love them all, but really! Enough was enough.

And then Rose pulled a small pouch from her waistband. "In case you have need, I had Peters take me three villages over and met with the apothecary there."

As recognition of what Rose was saying hit her, Penelope swallowed hard. She knew exactly what the small pouch contained. "Pennyroyal?"

Rose nodded. "I figured that in case he refuses you or does not believe you, you need to have a backup plan."

Penelope was already shaking her head. She did not judge women who turned to such a drastic action when necessary but now, knowing a child grew inside of her, the love for that life was greater than the fear for her situation. "I won't be needing it, Rose." But she was not angry with her maid.

Penelope had first educated her maid as to the concept itself. Over the years, Penelope had been slowly, in secret, collecting the tomes of Mary Wollstonecraft. And she'd shared them with Rose. They'd largely influenced Penelope's own assertions that marriage was a Bastille-like institution, that a woman ought to have the choice as to whether she was willing to sacrifice her body, and possibly her very life, in order to become a mother.

She'd known of more than one perfectly healthy lady who had died in childbirth. It was part of why she'd come to assist Lilly.

But suddenly, none of that mattered. The image of Lilly's little marquess jumped into Penelope's mind. She wanted this child. She would find Hugh, and all would be well.

"Put that away," she said more forcefully. Rose nodded and tucked it back into her skirt. "And take a care with it. It's poison. Please, Rose, I don't want it anywhere near my belongings."

"I'm not going to throw it out, but I'll put it in a safe place." Rose tilted her head back proudly. She did not really appreciate being scolded in any way. Ever.

"We'll have to travel up to Manchester," Penelope informed Rose.

Rose studied her skeptically. "Are you up to it? I've noticed you've been a trifle green in the mornings."

This time, Penelope did moan. She also threw herself face down on the bed. "I'll have to be, Rose. Good God, do you realize what will happen if anyone discovers what I've done? My parents will go into an apoplexy. I could never show my face in London again. Not that that's such a horrible thing to contemplate, but I do appreciate the shopping and the theatre occasionally. And most of my friends are members of the *ton*! How many of them would continue to acknowledge me?"

"You should have married that one gent, your second

year out. What was his name?"

"You mean Betsy's brother? Miles Harris?" Penelope was all astonishment.

"Yes. I will remind you that I told you then that you would be the one in control of everything in such a marriage. You would hold the purse strings. You would decide when and how many children would come along. Lord Harris would give you free rein. But did you listen to me?"

"You do remember, on occasion, anyhow, that *you are my maid*, don't you?" This argument had begun over a decade ago and would continue far into the future. But Penelope would never give Rose up. They'd been friends as children, and when Rose's father had threatened to send his only daughter away, Penelope had convinced her parents to hire Rose on as her maid. Both girls had barely reached the ages of ten and six at the time, but the Crones had found the situation tolerable.

And so, Rose had gone from being friend, confidante, and playmate to being Penelope's lady's maid overnight.

Rose really didn't always have the temperament of a maid, but that did not matter to Penelope. Most of the time.

"Miles Harris is a milksop. Was back then and continues to be so today." Penelope remembered the last time she'd seen him, at Lady Natalie's wedding breakfast. Miles had lost a great deal of hair and gained a great deal of weight. He was, as of yet, unmarried.

"You might keep him in mind if the viscount continues to be elusive."

At Rose's words, Penelope shuddered. But she had a point. "No, we've got to track down Danbury. And he's going to have to marry me right off." And then a wave of nausea washed over her. Oh, Lord! What had she done?

*H*UGH'S MOTHER WAS well, except for a mild cough. And although the impromptu journey had caused him to fall even farther behind in his responsibilities, Hugh was relieved to see his mother's good health in person. She'd had a touch of fever the previous week, and she corrected Hugh's interpretation of her chicken scrawls easy enough. She'd meant to have written *darned fever.*

"It was plain as day," she'd told him.

Ah, well. With his mind at ease, he'd stayed just a few days and then turned back from where he'd come. Rainy weather and a lame horse had delayed their travels, but at last they were nearing Hugh's northernmost estate.

As he and Dicky rode the last few miles into Manchester, the strangest thought persisted in nagging at his conscience.

Before leaving Summer's Park, he'd had that incredibly vivid dream about Penelope Crone. Surely, it had been a dream. He'd drank too much of Cortland's liquor and passed out in the study. And when he'd awakened, he'd been fully clothed and bundled up in a blanket.

Had a servant covered him? Cortland? Or had Penelope stopped into the study on her way up to bed that night?

Impossible.

She was the last woman in the world he'd ever consider bedding. As a baron's daughter, she was not to be dallied with. He'd never wanted to dally with her anyway.

She was domineering, opinionated, and too damned independent for his liking.

When Hugh married—for eventually, he would have to—he was going to marry a silly young chit who would not deign to question any of his decisions. He did not want a managing wife. He wanted a *manageable* one. Ha! Penelope Crone was the last person any bachelor would credibly wish to marry. Any sane bachelor, anyhow. Good thing she had no desire to find a husband, or else they'd all have to leave the country.

He chuckled ironically to himself. If Penelope Crone ever set out to land a husband, he would be on one of the first packets out of Dover. Because Penelope Crone was unlike most women. She didn't suffer in silence waiting for her wishes to be granted. No, that minx was not afraid to go after what she wanted, and she then usually got it right away.

He had enough to worry about with his mother's persistent matchmaking. Once again, during this last visit, she'd announced that she'd located a bride for him. She said that her dearest friend, Mrs. Iris Merriman, was going to sponsor her nineteen-year-old niece this spring for her debut season. And the niece was a dream of a girl. She was sweet yet not overly so. She was biddable yet not empty-headed. His mother had already promised Mrs. Merriman that Hugh would be of the utmost assistance to her. *But, of course,* Hugh would escort them to the first event of the season. *But, of course,* Hugh would lead the niece out for her first dance at her come out.

He forcibly pushed all thoughts of matrimony from his mind as he turned up the drive to the estate he'd not visited in over twelve years, since before his father's death. Fencing was falling down, gates hung at odd angles, and there seemed to be no order to the landscape whatsoever. As he neared the house, he realized that the manor was not in much better condition.

Cortland had told him that the steward was most likely swindling him. For Hugh knew rents were high. There ought to have been enough funds to keep Augusta Heights in near perfect condition.

No groom greeted him as he rode toward the stable, and no butler gaped out the door to see who was arriving. Hugh had intentionally not given word of his impending arrival. He'd wanted to catch the estate on a normal day. Well. Not a very auspicious beginning.

When he rounded the corner of the stable, he could see right into the interior of the building. For some reason, the doors had been removed. Likely, they'd fallen off their hinges and not been repaired. He could see that the floors needed sweeping, but at least hay was available and apparently being used to provide for the cattle inside.

A young lad leaned lazily on one of the bales of hay with a piece of it sticking out of his mouth. "That's a fancy horse you got there, mister," he managed to speak without removing the straw from his mouth. "But you must be in the wrong place. We ain't had no visitors here never." The boy barely moved a muscle, so very relaxed he was in his reclined position.

"Where's your stable master, lad?" There was a man being paid to perform such duties. Hugh knew this by reading reports sent over by the steward, a Mr. Periwinkle. Or perhaps an even better question was, "Where's Mr. Periwinkle?"

The lad leaned back and closed his eyes, in no hurry to be of assistance. "Mr. Periwinkle lives up at the big house. We ain't got no stable master—no master at all, come to think about it."

Hugh easily dismounted his horse and strolled over to this servant of his. Reaching forward, he snatched the piece of hay from the boy's mouth and glared straight into his suddenly alert eyes. "You've a master now, lad. And I suggest that if you wish to keep your position in this house, you give my horse a good rub down. Then there are floors that need swept and stalls to be cleaned. You do wish to continue eating, don't you?" Hugh was disgusted. Not with the boy so much as with himself for leaving this property mismanaged for so long.

But the boy wasn't ready to give in yet. "Who are you to be telling me what to do?"

Hugh studied the dirty bare feet of this little mongrel and then the long greasy hair and stained clothing. "You do know something of horses, don't you?"

The boy nodded, belligerently. "What matter is it to you?" He practically spat the words out.

Turning on his heel, Hugh responded without looking as he marched away, "I am Danbury, that's what matter it is. Now get to work!"

No butler greeted him as he entered the house. No evidence of a housekeeper, either, if the layers of dust could be counted on to make such an assumption. He wondered if there was even a cook to be found in this dilapidated, rundown, and dusty old mansion. Hugh guessed where the liquor might be. In the study.

Which was exactly where he would find Mr. Periwinkle, no doubt.

Before Hugh even entered the room, he was assaulted by the odor of stale cigars.

His steward looked quite comfortable, lounging in an elaborate chair with his feet resting most comfortably on a large antique desk. Behind him, tall windows ran the entire width of the room.

Cortland had urged him to be hard-hearted with the man, which was something Hugh had struggled with in the past.

"Periwinkle, I presume?" Hugh broke the silence in a hushed tone, leaning nonchalantly against the very solid doorframe.

The overweight man jerked forward, then backward, and then disappeared altogether as he toppled backward completely. Grunts and curses emitting from beneath the desk assured Hugh that the man was not seriously injured. Pushing himself away from the door, Hugh strolled across the room to peer at the man lying on the floor. "Can I take that for an affirmative answer then?"

Blood must have been rushing to the man's head, as his face and scalp turned a blotchy red color. "I am Mr. Periwinkle," the man blustered. There was not much dignity to have, however, when a man's feet were propped above his head and the rest of his person was caught in a most demeaning horizontal position.

Hugh reached out to assist the man up but found the supine gentleman's fists already occupied. One with a half-burnt cigar and the other with an amazingly intact tumbler of scotch. Admittedly, Hugh had some respect for a man who protected liquor so assiduously. If only Periwinkle had protected the rest of his possessions with half as much diligence.

"Danbury, at your service, Viscount, that is." Hugh relieved the man of both the cigar and the tumbler and set them on the desk before turning back to assist his steward to a more dignified position. "There now, won't you come and sit over here? That desk, I presume, is reserved for me?" With these words, he lifted one eyebrow lazily. Hugh was an easy-going fellow most of the time, but he found these circumstances quite unacceptable.

As Periwinkle lumbered around to find another seat, Hugh propped his hip against the desk, crossed one ankle over the other, and folded his arms across his chest. "Tell me about the progress that has been made since the last report you sent to London. Tell me of the thriving fields and diligent staff you've added to the payroll. For I'll have to hear of it from you, most assuredly, as I've yet to see any of it with my own eyes."

The cornered steward's gaze flashed toward the papers on the desk, lending credence to Hugh's suspicions. Leaning backward, Hugh snatched the account book and glanced down at the open pages. "Ahh... a second set of books." Licking his index finger, Hugh turned a few pages and casually perused them. "Fascinating, Peri, old man. Much more compelling than your fictitious works."

And suddenly, Hugh found himself not such an easy-going fellow after all. This man, no, this *blackguard* was stealing from him! Where had the funds that had been allocated for a butler gone? For a stable master? For a housekeeper, for God's sake! The estate was meant to support numerous servants and tenants. No wonder tenants were migrating overseas.

Periwinkle was not a small man, but this did not keep Hugh from grasping him by the collar and lifting him at least a few inches off the ground. "You will gather your belongings, and by that I mean yours and not mine, and be gone from this estate within the hour. If you are caught lifting so much as a spoon, you'll find yourself swinging from the end of a noose in the blink of an eye. Do I make myself clear, *Mister* Periwinkle?"

But the man could not speak as he was, instead choking from the manner in which Hugh held him, so Hugh was forced to loosen his grip.

Once released, Periwinkle rubbed his neck and blathered, "I was just doing my job to the best of my ability, my lord. No reason to be accusing a person of anything dishonest. Besides, where would I go?" The man was pitiful.

Hugh studied his hands. They shook from his anger. This was not like him. He normally abhorred violence.

Glancing back at Mr. Periwinkle, Hugh wondered if perhaps he wasn't being hasty. The steward was the only person in residence who knew what was going on here. Periwinkle was a liar and a crook, but until Hugh figured this mess out and found a replacement, perhaps he ought to keep the old man around a little longer.

Contemplating his options, Hugh walked over to one of the shelves behind the large desk and ran his index finger along the surface. When he withdrew, his fingertip was covered with a gray grimy material. The manor was filthy.

He then picked up a small model of a ship, and with one quick breath, blew a cloud of dust off the helm. "You think I ought to allow you to remain, Mr. Periwinkle?"

Before Hugh finished his question, the man's head was bobbing up and down. "I do, m'lord," he answered eagerly. The man was still rubbing his neck. "Caught us on a bad day, is all. You should have given me notice you were coming. I would have spruced the place up for you." Hesitating a moment, he added, "M'lord."

Hugh let out a heavy sigh and placed the small ship back upon the shelf. This situation was quickly becoming more and more overwhelming. He hadn't put much effort into anything of substance for years, and he was beginning to feel more than a little guilty about it. When he'd first inherited, Hugh hadn't yet reached his majority. That had been justification enough for him to allow the running of his estates to be done by solicitors and stewards. But that excuse no longer applied. He was in his thirties, by God!

Not sure where to begin, Hugh ran his hand through his hair. "Very well," he relented reluctantly, "you shall remain here on probation. For now, you are to return to the steward's quarters. We'll go over these books tomorrow."

Periwinkle went to casually collect the black leather tome from the top of the desk, but Hugh pressed his own palm down upon the offending item first. "Tomorrow, Mr. Periwinkle."

Periwinkle was obviously reluctant for Hugh to have access to what appeared to be the more truthful version of estate accounts. The man paused and then rubbed at his bottom lip thoughtfully. "I've some entries I'd like to finish today, m'lord, if you wouldn't mind." Again, he reached for the book, but Hugh had already picked it up himself.

"No hurry, Mr. Periwinkle. Now, good day to you." Hugh sat down in the chair that had overturned earlier and opened the book to begin perusing it himself. When he did not hear the steward exit, he glanced up dismissively. "Leave me now, sir."

It didn't take long for all of Hugh's suspicions to be confirmed. This book was, in fact, the real accounting of the estate. And the figures far more detailed and concise than anything he'd been sent. If Periwinkle hadn't been so criminally inclined, he would have made an excellent steward.

But where ought he to start? Catching a glimpse of the bottle of scotch Periwinkle had been enjoying earlier, Hugh decided this quandary would have to wait until tomorrow. He walked over to the cabinet and poured himself a hearty amount of the aromatic spirit.

And then that memory again. Of Penelope covering his hands with hers and lifting the drink to her own lips. This recollection was not hazy, nor dreamy, nor did it feel in any way like something of his imagination. No, he remembered he'd suddenly noticed the blue specks of light surrounded by her otherwise emerald eyes.

He shook his head and drank the liquid in one long swallow.

The warmth filled him almost immediately. He closed his eyes. Of course, it had been a dream! Good God, the alternative was unthinkable!

CHAPTER FOUR

"*I* SO WISH you could stay longer, Penelope." The Duchess of Cortland, Lilly Redmond, did not look away from the babe in her arms as she spoke. Breaking ducal tradition, Lilly had decided she would not have a wet nurse for the child. She was determined to feed the child of her own body. "You can do it, little Edward," she told the baby now as she encouraged him to suckle. Her endeavor had not been an easy one.

Penelope leaned forward and watched as the tiny infant turned his head from side to side, eluding his mother's fingertips. He then let out a few disgruntled cries, causing Lilly to lift him to her shoulders and pat his little bum. "What will I do without you, Pen?" Lilly asked, looking over at her this time.

Penelope smiled reassuringly at her friend. In spite of the challenges the duchess experienced as a new mother, Lilly was more beautiful than ever. Her unusually colored golden eyes looked a little more tired than normal, but her hair was done up in an elegant twist and her clothing was, as always, immaculate. "You'll do just perfectly, Lilly. Look at him. He's plump and healthy. I don't think there has ever been a happier baby." She said this in spite of the grumbling sounds coming from the cherub.

Lilly glanced back down at the baby and sighed in agreement. Her smile widened when the little marquess let out a satisfying burp. "He is, isn't he?" And then a frown of concern marred her forehead. "But what is it, Penelope? You haven't been yourself since Edward was born."

Penelope sat up straight. What did Lilly see? Was her condition so very obvious? "I—well, er, I'm just feeling a little restless, that's all."

A familiar odor suddenly began filling the room. Oh, not the biliousness now! The nausea she'd felt upon waking had gone away after nuncheon. It was not supposed to come back! Lilly mustn't learn the truth of Penelope's situation! For she would be inclined to tell Cortland, who was Danbury's best friend. Penelope nonchalantly lifted her hand to her mouth and inhaled the fragrance of her soap from earlier.

She need not have been concerned. Lilly had become aware of the odor as well and rose from the rocking chair. Her concern for Penelope temporarily forgotten, she laid the baby down on a padded dressing table. "At least we know he's eating enough! Right, little man?" She cooed to the infant and then glanced back over at Penelope. "As long as you know you're welcome anytime. I don't ever want you to feel as though you're not wanted here."

Lilly's words, simple though they were, suddenly had Penelope on the brink of tears, and she glanced out the window. The hills were a deep green and the sky ominous. Was a snowstorm approaching? That would not be advantageous at all! In an attempt to ward off her weepiness, Penelope forced herself to think of anything but her apparent situation. She'd felt unusually emotional throughout the past week. This was unacceptable. *I am not a watering pot!*

She discreetly wiped at her eyes before turning back to Lilly. "Oh, I know, Lilly. You and Cortland have been kindness itself." The baby gazed adoringly up at his mother. "I'll most certainly miss playing with little Edward. But I probably ought to go home and spend some time with Mother and Father before the season, for I'm contemplating forgoing London this year." The season would kick off in a little more than a month. She most definitely needed to get a few things ironed out before then. She couldn't have Danbury trolling through the young debutantes now! Not when she was carrying his child.

Penelope stood up abruptly at the thought. "I've told Rose to get everything packed today so that we can leave first thing in the morning."

"Then we should do something special tonight," Lilly said while wrapping the infant tightly in his soft blanket. "Wait a few more days, Penelope, and I will plan a going away supper for you! I'll feel horrible if you leave without a party first."

Penelope shook her head. "You have far more important things to concern yourself with than a silly dinner party for me. Besides, I think I'm going to try to get to sleep early tonight." She couldn't stand the thought of having to be civil to a roomful of Lilly's guests. Normally, Penelope enjoyed socializing, but this was not a normal time for her at all. She already longed for the cool sheets of her bed. She'd never realized that her current condition would cause her to feel so tired. A nap just now sounded heavenly. And if she were left alone, she could have a good cry as well.

Lilly looked disappointed but not overly so. Right now, all Lilly's energies were focused upon being a mother. She did not really wish to hold a dinner party. She was simply being kind.

A mother.

The thought was nearly enough to summon those tears again.

She desperately needed to find Danbury.

Later. She would track him down and all would be well.

But first, she needed that nap.

THE ROAD HEADING north was not a well-maintained one. And with the intermittent snowflakes along the way, the driver seemed to move at a snail's pace, making the journey more exhausting than usual. Even Rose's spirits flagged by the time they drove through Manchester.

They had been traveling for just over a week and the inns they had stopped at had not been nearly as comfortable as the lodgings Penelope usually patronized. She'd never traveled this far north, so, not trusting her driver to obtain the best directions, she'd discussed their route with every innkeeper along the way. Aside from riding up top with her driver, however, she was forced to trust that he could get them to Danbury's estate. She would not relish having to travel additional miles unnecessarily.

She'd not heard any positive comments about Augusta Heights. The recent years' crops had gotten smaller and smaller, and the estate itself now employed few villagers. Penelope's understanding was that the steward had gradually put them all off, either by failing to pay fair wages or failing to pay at all. Sitting in the open dining area with Rose the evening before, Penelope had collected all sorts of information by merely eavesdropping.

Viscount Danbury's massive estate ought to have been a positive economic force for the small villages nearby. Augusta Heights, it seemed, was instead a scapegoat for all that was wrong.

She was more certain than ever that Danbury required her assistance.

The coach jerked as they turned onto a long drive. The smaller road had even more ruts and holes in it than the road before. Penelope slid across the bench into Rose as the carriage tilted a little and then righted itself.

"Thank God," Rose echoed Penelope's own sentiments. "I don't believe I could have tolerated another day on this godforsaken road."

Penelope peered out the window. Even during the tail end of winter, it was painfully obvious that the landscaping had been completely overcome by wild vines and shrubbery. The road had nearly been overtaken as well.

And then there was the manor in the distance.

It was... slightly lopsided. Yes, that was the problem. Danbury was going to need an engineer to come and take a look at the foundation. It desperately needed repair.

Broken windows riddled the upper floors, and one of the chimneys appeared to have caught fire sometime in the past.

She could only imagine what condition the interior was in.

They rolled along for a few more minutes, bouncing and creaking, until at last they came to a stop in front of the crumbling steps leading up to the main house.

Penelope did not wait for one of the outriders to set down the step for her. She pushed the door open herself and jumped out onto the ground. Rose waited graciously for the groomsman to pull out the step before accepting his hand as he assisted her down from the conveyance.

Penelope was looking about curiously when a potbellied gentleman opened the front door and ambled down the steps. The man's skin was a sallow yellow color, and his jowls swayed from side to side as he walked. He did not look happily upon the new visitors.

"Are you lost, madam?" he shouted as he approached her. "You must have taken a wrong turn a ways back."

"I am not, and no, we have not taken a wrong turn. Who might I ask are you, sir?" If this man was Danbury's steward, it would explain the comments she'd heard about the estate. He was puffed up full of his own self-importance and yet his shirt was soiled, and his pants needed mending. The yellowness of his skin indicated he imbibed more than was healthy and the additional flesh on his person that he ate more food than his share.

"I am Mr. Matthew Periwinkle, steward of Augusta Heights. Who might you be, madam?"

Penelope lifted her chin and narrowed her eyes at the pitiful man. "I am Miss Penelope Crone, daughter to Baron Riverton. My driver and outrider will be utilizing your stable." She glanced over at the tumble-down condition of the building in question. "And my maid and I shall require superior accommodations as well. Please inform the viscount that we are arrived."

The end was all bluster on her part, but it was obvious that this man needed to be put in his place. She was of half a mind to sack him herself, for when he'd gotten nearer to her, she smelled whiskey on his breath.

Which, considering recent events, was more than a little unnerving.

Gathering her gown about her, she lifted it out of the way so that she could climb the disintegrating steps safely. She was forced to open the heavy door herself, as there was no butler in evidence, and then remove her own wrapper and bonnet. She brushed the dust off a nearby chair and draped her belongings over it.

The foyer smelled of mildew and decay.

"Hello!" she shouted. Her own voice echoed back mockingly.

A shiver ran through her. Perhaps she ought to have kept her wrapper on.

"Hello!" she shouted again.

This time, she heard a door open and close upstairs and

then footsteps approaching the landing.

A rush of emotion swept through Penelope when Danbury paused at the top of the stairs. The last time she'd seen him, he'd been... Oh, Lord. It had been just over one month since she'd been with him, since she'd lain with him.

And now here he was, his shirt hanging out of his trousers, no cravat or waistcoat, and at least three days' growth of whiskers on his face. "What on earth has happened to you, Danbury?" she asked, forgetting the rehearsed greeting she'd planned over the past few weeks. "Good Lord, you look like death warmed over."

The man standing above her pinched the bridge of his nose and then rubbed his eyes. "Penelope? Penelope Crone, is that you? What in God's name are you doing here?"

Ignoring his questions, she beckoned him to come down the stairs. "I thought you were coming up here to take matters in hand! Where is your butler? Do you even have a housekeeper? And your steward, he's got to go, Hugh! That man is robbing you blind."

Danbury shook his head. Blinked several times, and then descended the stairs cautiously. Perhaps because he was uncertain as to his own stability or perhaps because he was just a little bit frightened of her.

After stepping off the bottom step, he grasped Penelope by the shoulders and looked searchingly into her eyes. "They do have blue..." he mumbled nonsensically. And then, getting ahold of himself, he addressed her again. "Why are you here, Penelope? Has something happened with Cortland? Did my mother send you?"

Penelope could not look him directly in the eyes. His proximity, after... Well, she was more than a little flustered. Did he not remember *anything*? How could a person not remember doing *that*? He had been, well, inside of her! She bit her lip and lowered her gaze from his to stare at the floor.

"I, um. Well…" A tiny gray creature peeked out from beneath the settee. "Oh, good Lord, Danbury, there are mice running about this place! Did you not stop to think that you might need a little assistance after ignoring this estate for over a decade? Did you not think that perhaps a friend might feel inclined to come to your assistance?" She finally worked up the courage to meet his stare again. "I'm here to offer my assistance. God knows you need it."

Danbury shook his head, as though trying to wake himself out of a dream of some sort—or nightmare, whatever the case may be. "You… have come all this way… to help me with the estate?" He looked somewhat incredulous at the thought.

"Do you think that because I am a woman, I do not know how to go about running an estate? Do you not wonder how my parents have prospered so well? Did you really think that my *father* was responsible for doubling his assets over the past decade? Do you not know *me*, Hugh Chesterton?"

"But, Pen—"

"Don't Pen me, Danbury. Now, let's take a look at your books. And then we'll need to find a replacement for that Periwinkle fellow, and we most definitely need to find you a good butler and a housekeeper. It ought not to be a problem, though. There are dozens of people in this area looking for work."

CHAPTER FIVE

As a gentleman, Hugh suddenly felt all of the responsibility of Penelope Crone fall squarely upon his shoulders. A lady did not travel over one hundred miles without a chaperone. It simply was not done! What was the baron thinking, allowing his daughter to gallivant all over the country alone?

And now this managing female was making herself comfortable in his home, ready to tackle the problems he'd been contemplating for over a week.

He ought to send her packing. Confirmed spinster or not, her presence here put his bachelorhood in definite peril. She was craning her neck around at all the disrepair as she led them both toward his study.

"This place is filthy, Hugh! How have you been living here?" She pulled a handkerchief out of her skirt and began wiping down any visible surface on the ancient wooden desk. As she did so, she appeared to be organizing papers and envelopes into various piles. "That Mr. Periwinkle is a crook if I ever saw one. Look at this, Hugh. I'd be willing to bet this is a second set of books. It's most likely completely different than the reports he's been sending you."

"I already—" Hugh began.

"If you've already discovered his thievery, then why is the man still lurking about?" Penelope interrupted him. Glimpsing more receipts on the floor, she turned and bent down to retrieve them, giving Hugh an unusually disturbing view of her rounded derriere.

Disturbing because he hadn't before considered the shape of Penelope's body—well, he hadn't for a very long time. Like most men, Penelope's bluestocking tendencies had extinguished any spark of interest he'd ever acknowledged for her. He must have been up here alone too long because his hand suddenly itched to caress, squeeze, and lightly slap...

"And I'll bet the man has finished off most of the contents of your cellar by now. Did you not notice the yellow color in his eyes or the tint of his complexion? Ah, yes!" She held out a piece of paper with several scrawls upon it. "Take a look at this. These bills are long overdue! It seems as though your steward has swindled nearly every shop in town!"

Hugh grabbed the papers out of her hand. "Not nearly every shop, Penelope. Every single one." He dropped into the settee. "The estate owes a fortune in funds, and I've no idea what Periwinkle has done with them. This mess isn't going to be cleaned up any time soon." He'd put some feelers out to locate a new steward, but these things took time.

Glancing up, he realized that Penelope was watching him strangely. She looked different, somehow, softer perhaps. "Is it boredom that has driven you to travel all the way up here, Pen? Because to be frank with you, if anyone of consequence discovers your presence here, we're both doomed."

Penelope grimaced and then walked over and sat down beside him.

"Damn me, Pen, why is it that I always forget my manners when I'm around you?" He had a vague recollection of failing to stand before when she'd entered a room but could not pinpoint exactly when that had been. When she sat down, Hugh got a whiff of her scent and felt a stirring of...

something. He'd not noticed Penelope's scent before. It was clean, not cloying, but pretty.

Penelope looked over at him with wide innocent eyes. Yes, by God, there were blue flecks flickering around in the green.

"Nobody knows I'm here." She shrugged off his concern. "What we need to do is go through all of this paperwork and put together an accurate set of books."

"Your maid knows. And what of your parents? Where did you tell Cortland you were heading when you left Summer's Park?"

"My parents think I'm in Bath, shopping or visiting friends; they don't really bother to keep track of my whereabouts any longer. I'm nearly thirty, you know!"

"And what of Lilly? Surely, she was curious as to your destination."

Penelope swiped her hand in the air dismissively. "Lilly and Cortland are so wrapped up in each other and that little marquess that they wouldn't have cared if I'd said I was leaving for the moon!"

But why had she come here? Was boredom really the reason or could there have been something else? "How long do you plan on staying? The season begins in less than a month, you know."

If Penelope Crone planned on staying six months, Hugh very seriously doubted he could do anything to change her mind. She was that stubborn.

"Just long enough," she answered enigmatically. "And lucky for you, might I add."

This entire appearance of hers was enigmatic, really. For although they'd known each other for years, they hadn't ever done anything to seek one another out. They were more than acquaintances, yes, but nothing that would warrant her traveling all the way up to Augusta Heights.

"Are you in some kind of trouble, Pen?"

And there it was. She bit her lip and turned away from him.

"You can tell me, Pen. If you've done something ill-advised, it doesn't matter to me. I can help you if you'd like, but I can't do anything if you don't tell me what the problem is."

She sat up straight and seemed to shake off her melancholy. "I'm just bored, that's all, Hugh. I figured you could use a little help. Now, do you want it? My help, that is? Or would you prefer to tackle this decade of neglect alone?" Ah, here was the prickly girl he'd come to know.

Who really was—dare he think it?—smarter than most men.

"Of course, I'd like your help." Perhaps she was just what he needed right now. If she wished to stay up here and straighten out the mess Periwinkle had created, then so be it. Perhaps he could even get back to London sooner.

He stood up and walked over to the desk and Penelope pulled over one of the high-backed chairs. Without further ado, they began sorting receipts together. He read off the information, and Penelope wrote it all down on a new ledger, creating an accurate account system. Periwinkle's black book had mysteriously disappeared from the desk two days ago. Working with Penelope, for the first time, he felt he was beginning to see a clear picture of the estate's circumstances. After what didn't seem like very long at all, Hugh glanced up at the clock and realized they'd been at work for nearly three hours.

He set down the envelope he'd been about to open and took a moment to study Penelope's bent over form. Watching her, he was surprised again to discover that he was feeling oddly attracted to her. And his body responded in kind. Soft tendrils of her hair had escaped her plait and now caressed the tender skin around her face and neck. And when he glanced at her neck, he couldn't help but notice that the bodice of her dress emphasized her bosom a bit more than usual. Funny that, he'd never really considered Penelope to be very well endowed.

"I think I'm beginning to realize why you haven't sent Periwinkle packing, after all." She set down her pencil and nodded somewhat respectfully at him. "He's obviously embezzled a great deal of money from the estate and you hope to discover its whereabouts before giving him the boot. Am I right?"

Leave it to Penelope to be completely unaware of the fact that she had just spent over three hours behind closed doors—with a man who was not her brother nor her father. Unchaperoned.

Hugh pushed his inappropriate thoughts out of his mind and contemplated what she said. At first, he'd allowed Periwinkle to stay on the property out of some misplaced sense of duty to an old retainer. But upon further consideration, he'd realized that he owed the man nothing. In fact, it was Periwinkle who owed him. And the way Periwinkle had been prowling about, Hugh guessed that some of what Periwinkle was hiding was actually inside of the main house.

"I can see it in your eyes that I am right!" Penelope was suddenly much more animated than before. "Tell me, Hugh. What are your suspicions?"

Should he tell her? How could he not?

"There ought to have been several thousands of pounds in the safe." He indicated with a jerk of his head toward a large painting. "At first, I had all intentions of calling the magistrate in but unfortunately," he winced as he completed his statement, "the magistrate is already here."

"You?"

"Yes," he said, "unfortunately."

"You already said that," she reminded him.

"What?"

"That it is unfortunate that you are the magistrate."

Hugh narrowed his eyes at her but did not comment on her smart mouth.

"Why don't you think he's spent the money already? Why do you think he is still in possession of it?" Hugh could see in her eyes that she was already working the details out. "He wears clothing that is shabby and fraying. He has nowhere to go, as he has most likely pleaded with you to stay on, and he doesn't appear to own much of anything. Furthermore... He no longer has unfettered access to this house. The man no longer has free run of... Of the master suite! Hugh, that's it! It must be in your suite, or most assuredly Periwinkle would have taken everything and gone off on his own!"

Hugh jumped up. Of course! Since he'd arrived, he had spent a great deal of time in his suite. And Periwinkle had never been far away. "That's got to be it!"

Penelope sprung to her feet as well but just as Hugh turned to head for the door he heard a thud.

What in the world? Where had she gone? "Penelope?" And then he saw her lying on the floor. The old girl had fainted!

Penelope Crone.

Fainted!

Impossible.

What was the matter with her?

Hugh knelt on the floor beside her and patted her cheek gently. "Penelope? Penelope?"

Her lashes fluttered but she did not answer.

"Pen?

And then she opened her eyes. Having such close proximity to her, as she lay on the floor, Hugh had to admit to himself that she truly did have incredible eyes.

Dancing across the bridge of her nose was a smidgen of freckles. Just below her rebellious little nose, her lips were pink and plump.

"Hugh?"

He was still kneeling over her. "You are unwell. Penelope, you need to tell me what's wrong!"

For a full three seconds, he thought she would 'fess up to whatever was going on with her. But then she raised her hands up and pushed him away. "I'm perfectly fine, Hugh Chesterton. Why would you think that just because I…? Well, because I slipped, yes, I fell, you think that something is wrong?" But her eyes were hiding something. "Now help me up. We need to find that money in your chamber before Periwinkle lays siege to it!

Reluctantly, Hugh helped her to her feet. She *was* pale. Much paler than her normal pale self. And her hands were cold and clammy. She swayed slightly once she was on her feet again, but Hugh refused to mention it. If she needed his help than she was goddamn well going to have to ask him for it. And if she didn't want his help, then so be it. Once he was certain she wouldn't collapse on him again, he dropped her hands and turned for the door.

They'd been in the study for nearly four hours. He hoped Periwinkle hadn't been so brazen as to enter the master suite while he was in the house. Not bothering to see if Penelope was able to keep up with him, Hugh dashed up the stairs, two steps at a time, and rushed toward his chamber.

STILL IN THE study, Penelope waited for Hugh to disappear before sitting back down in the chair she'd just occupied. But that wasn't good enough. She laid her head down on the desk and rested her cheek against the cool, smooth wood.

She *had* fainted.

In all her life, growing up and then spending nearly a decade in cloyingly warm ballrooms, Penelope had never once succumbed to such a ridiculous malady. In fact, she speculated that most of the girls she'd seen faint had actually feigned it. Which allowed her little, if any, empathy for the swooning debutante in question.

Except for Abigail, her cousin, who Penelope knew for certain did not fake it when she fainted. Because when Abigail went down, she did so like a ton of bricks. She had also, on occasion, clobbered her head on something before hitting the ground. And once Abigail was on the ground, she normally lay there for several minutes, eventually either drooling or snoring softly.

Nobody was idiot enough to pretend the type of fainting Abigail experienced.

Penelope was pretty certain that she'd only lost consciousness for a few seconds—just enough time for Hugh to rush around the desk and crouch over her. When she'd opened her eyes, his face had been inches away from her own. For the briefest of moments, she'd imagined she'd gone back in time and been on the Duke of Cortland's settee. The memory of willingly giving her innocence away to a drunken buffoon, all too vivid. Thank God she'd come to her wits before saying anything too revealing...

Nothing was going as planned.

An apparently naïve part of her had believed Hugh remembered everything. She had hoped that he had merely fled Summer's Park out of shame and guilt for what he'd done. That upon seeing her, he would fall down onto one knee and propose marriage.

Another part of her characterized by the most ridiculous feminine vanity—of which she'd believed herself rid of long ago—had felt insulted and hurt that he did not remember what they'd done. It wasn't every day a woman lost her maidenhead, for heaven's sake!

Was she truly that forgettable?

Penelope turned her head so that her other cheek rested on the cool wood. She should not be saddened by the fact that she'd made no impression on him whatsoever. She'd never done anything before in order to capture a gentleman's interest. In fact, she'd gone out of her way to be sensible and prudent. Even when she'd thought she was in love with Rome Spencer, she'd made it a point to always be herself around him. For as much as she'd thought he was *the one,* she knew in her heart she could never pretend to be something, *someone,* she wasn't.

When other debutantes had fluttered their lashes and listened raptly to the ramblings of some Lord or other in order to capture a husband, Penelope had staunchly stood her ground in regard to marriage. It was unwise for a woman to marry a man who might not care as much about her well-being as she did. Marriage was an institution that primarily benefited men.

Penelope was fortunate though.

She would never have to worry about having a roof over her head or putting food in her mouth. It had been horrifying to learn that many of her friends, many young women of her acquaintance, had no choice in the matter. Or so they said.

There was always a choice. Unfortunately, the options did not always present people with the choices they wanted. Penelope closed her eyes and moaned to herself.

After years of condemning the notion of marriage, she herself was on the hunt for a husband. Not just any husband but a husband who was currently London's most confirmed bachelor.

He had not been happy to see her. When he'd realized

who it was who had traveled all those godawful miles to see him, his main concern had been that no one know she was here.

What had she been thinking? *Fool, Penelope!* And now, when she ought to be searching Hugh's chamber with him, she sat here like a slug, doing nothing.

She opened her eyes and allowed her gaze to lazily travel around the stuffy room. So much dust, ah, and yes, a century's worth of cobwebs. From the angle in which she lay, she could see that virtually every book on the enormous shelves was covered in a thick layer of dust and its own lacy web.

Except four or five on the right-hand side of the top shelf. Those books looked like they'd been handled recently. In fact, those books were wiped completely clean.

Slowly, this time, so as not to swoon again, Penelope rose and pulled the slide ladder so that it leaned just below the books she'd spotted. Not wanting to be interrupted by anyone, either Periwinkle or Hugh, Penelope closed the door before returning to investigate that top shelf. She hesitated a moment. If she fainted while on the ladder, it would not be a good thing at all.

Not only would she likely hit her head and be injured, she could possibly injure the baby growing inside of her.

Which did, in fact, give her considerable pause.

She raised her hand to her abdomen and pressed against it gently. Was it protruding just slightly? That was impossible! Women didn't begin to show until they were several months along, did they? She'd not suspected that Lilly was with child until her friend had told her, and that had been three or four months into the pregnancy.

But whereas in the past, her abdomen had always been somewhat concave, it felt different now. It swelled outward just slightly.

Impossible! Penelope dropped her hand dismissively

and inspected the ladder.

It was quite sturdy and had rails on both sides. More of a staircase, actually. She would be fine. That spinning, ethereal feeling was gone, and she felt more her normal self.

Satisfied that she wasn't risking her baby's life, she lifted her skirt with one hand, took hold of the railing with the other, and carefully climbed until she could lift her arm and take hold of the books that had been disturbed. She grasped the largest one and pulled it down to peruse. It was rather weighty for its size.

Except it wasn't a book.

No, when she opened the cover, it revealed a secret compartment filled with coins and banknotes.

"Ah hah!" she said softly. Suddenly concerned that someone would find her, she replaced the one book and examined the others. They contained more coins but also what looked to be several bank notes and important documents. Here were the former contents of the safe.

She jumped when she heard the sound of furniture scraping the floor overhead.

Hugh must be trying to look behind a wardrobe or something. Penelope scrutinized the room for just a moment before discovering what she needed. An old cloth-lined basket filled with knitting needles and yarn was stuffed against the wall behind a large wing-backed chair. It was covered in dust, and she wondered how long it had been since any knitting had been accomplished in this room.

She removed a few of the balls of yarn, stuffed Hugh's treasure deep into the basket, and then returned the now-empty books back to the top shelf in the same order she'd found them.

She'd been sitting on the settee knitting for several minutes before the door opened and Hugh stood in the opening, looking frustrated.

CHAPTER SIX

"*I* THOUGHT YOU were going to help me," Hugh's voice dripped in sarcasm. His hair sprung out from his head, roguishly, and dust smeared liberally across his face and hands. He had donned a banyan, however, in a belated attempt at maintaining his manners with her.

Penelope inserted one of her needles under the loop on her thumb and pulled the strand snugly.

"Decided to knit me a scarf instead?" He dropped onto the wing backed chair and threw one leg over the arm casually.

Penelope smiled and then spoke without thinking. "Just thought I'd make a blanket for the baby." She was quite pleased with herself.

"I'd imagine the little marquess will appreciate it." But he was scowling.

"The marquess? Oh, yes, of course, little Edward." That hadn't been what Penelope had been thinking at all!

"Aren't you going to ask me if I found anything?" He continued to scowl but Penelope was finding him somewhat adorable. Hugh was a clever man. He'd achieved high marks while at Oxford and on occasion had expressed his regret at not being allowed to make a career out of scholarly endeavors. She found it substantially satisfying to have outmaneuvered him.

"What did you find, Hugh?" she asked smugly.

Whereas her nonchalant knitting had not captured his attention, her tone of voice did.

Finally, took him long enough.

"You know very well that I found nothing." His eyes narrowed as he dropped both feet to the floor and leaned toward her. "What have *you* found, Penelope?"

And then Penelope did something she'd never done before.

She fluttered her eyelashes.

Hugh looked at her sideways. "What *have* you found, Penelope?"

Dropping the knitting into her lap, enjoying his consternation completely, Penelope goaded him further. "Do I look like I've found something?" She shrugged and indicated her dress. "I've no pockets—no purse. Where would I put it? That is, where would I put *anything,* if I had in fact found it?"

She jumped back when he lurched over to the settee, practically on top of her.

Leering with exaggerated ferocity, his fisted hands pushed deep into the cushions on each side of her. She was trapped. Then he waggled his eyebrows threateningly, trying to appear menacing. "Hand it over, you minx!" he growled, but amusement lit his eyes.

"There is nothing on my person, Hugh," she laughed. The scent of his cologne invited sensations she'd do well to ignore. She remembered it from before and had an urge to pull him closer.

"You have obviously found something, wench," he said through gritted teeth. "And I'm going to discover it eventually, so fess up now, woman." He was doing his best to contain the laughter threatening to overcome him. Although he held most of his weight off of her, he did not appear to strain at all. She could not keep her gaze from straying to the dark hairs at the opening of his shirt. She remembered she'd flicked her tongue along them before.

And then his full weight dropped, pinning her, and one

of his hands was running along the length of her body.

Oh no! She couldn't prevent the half giggle, half screech that tore from her lips when she realized his intent.

He was tickling her!

"Stop, Hugh. Stop." She tried freeing her hands so that she could cease his relentless torture. "You brute, I'm too ticklish, Hugh. Stop! Please!" Was she still laughing, or had she began to cry? She wasn't sure, but she felt a few tears roll down her cheek.

Something in her voice caught his attention and he stopped suddenly. Both of them breathed heavily from their exertions but neither moved. Instead, Hugh gazed down at her with a funny expression.

"You really have the prettiest eyes, Pen."

Penelope swallowed.

Hugh just kept looking at her and then added, "I never did understand you. So set against marriage, determined to emasculate every man you've ever met. Don't you ever wish you didn't have to be so... different?"

As his words penetrated the temporary insanity that had overcome her, she used all of her strength to form a mighty shove, which resulted in Hugh sprawled on the floor.

"You... You... bacon brained, nitwitted, beastly maggot!"

How dare he criticize her independence! Why did everyone in society think that all women needed to be the same? Why was it that there was this notion that an ideal woman was one who dressed prettily and kept her opinion to herself? Why was it that a woman was only considered useful in that she could provide her husband with children?

Women had brains, too!

Well, she did anyhow!

He'd told her the very last thing she ever wanted to

hear from a man, from anyone.

He'd told her he thought she should change.

Penelope primly arranged herself on the sofa once again, and retrieved the knitting. She had been just about ready to turn her findings over to Hugh, before he'd insulted her.

He hadn't insulted her hair or her dress or her face. No. He'd insulted the very essence of who she was. It took all of her concentration to keep tears from falling.

Hugh sat on the floor and simply looked at her, dumbfounded. "It was just a question!"

Penelope blinked hard so that she could see what her needles were doing. There really wasn't enough light in here to knit properly. "I am who I am," she replied.

She did not look up but sensed Hugh's continued contemplation of her.

"You think I am insulting who you are?"

"I don't wish to discuss this." Penelope was already far too emotional these days.

Hugh pushed himself up and returned to sit beside her. She scooted away from him, deliberately avoiding his touch.

But he would not let this go. "I did not insult who you are, Pen. I was merely wondering if it was necessary to be so different in order to be you." Now his voice was cajoling, sympathetic. Dash it all, her eyes burned again.

She'd always been different.

For if she was the same... she would lose... herself.

"It's the way of our world, Hugh," she said, realizing she'd just created a bungled knot of yarn rather than a proper stitch.

"So, you truly believe that if you ever dressed up a little, flirted a little, married and had children, you could not live by the values you believe in?"

The question threw her into even more turmoil. For when she'd made that blasted decision to have a child, she'd compromised her own position on women and the potential of womanhood in general.

"What of you, Hugh? Would you wish to marry a woman who was of her own mind? Would you marry a woman who disagreed with you and was not afraid to say so? Would you marry a woman who didn't laugh at all your jokes? Or look at you adoringly in wide eyed innocence? What if she were smarter than you? Could you marry a woman like that?"

"We aren't talking about me," Hugh said stubbornly.

"But we are, Hugh, for you represent the typical London Gentleman Bachelor. You are titled, you own land, you are of a good family, and will eventually have to set up a nursery. Tell me, Hugh, what kind of woman do you foresee as your wife?"

This was crazy. Why was she goading him so? Soon, very soon, she was going to take away all of his options. How was she going to feel when she knew he wanted somebody who was completely opposite from her?

Even if he truly needed a strong woman by his side—a strong, *smart* woman.

Hugh was considering her question, however. "Honestly, Penelope, I'm not looking for a certain 'type' of woman." He'd leaned forward, resting his elbows on his knees and was staring at his hands. He sounded pensive, almost melancholy. "Against common practice, against the advice of my mother and my sister and pretty much all of the *ton*, I foresee marrying a woman I can love. As besotted as Cortland is, I want what he has finally found. I want a woman who is a friend to me, who is a lover to me. I want to marry for love. Did you think I had avoided marriage all of these years because I wished to shirk my responsibilities to my title and my family?"

Penelope was stunned. *Oh no, no, no!* What had she done? Hugh and she had discussed numerous subjects over the years they'd known each other. They'd discussed politics, society, fashion, and gossiped about common friends even. But they had not ever discussed the desires of their hearts. And now here he was, declaring that he had simply been waiting all this time to marry because he hadn't yet found the right woman.

He'd not yet found the woman he wished to marry.

But here she was. Ready for him to marry her, desperate for him to marry her, in fact.

And she was not the right woman.

Oh, hell.

*H*UGH LET OUT a long sigh and leaned into the cushioned back of the sofa. Why was he having this conversation with Penelope Crone, of all people?

And what was he blathering on about the "right woman" to her for? He'd not really even admitted such to himself. But as he sat next to this termagant, he concluded to himself that it was exactly why he'd not given into his mother's matchmaking. He'd not ever felt... interested enough in one woman to the point that he could consider spending the rest of his life with her. In fact, the mere idea of pledging himself to any of them was enough to send him as quickly as possible in the opposite direction. The debutantes he'd met were almost always only slightly more entertaining to him than... a new pair of boots. He frowned. Some, not even that, for a pair of good or bad fitting Hessians could make or break a gentleman's day.

Indeed, he'd learned quickly not to dally with a debutante unless he wished to be netted.

Chorus girls and dancers could not net themselves a gentleman. Upon which thought, Talia came to mind. He'd been her protector for nearly two years, the longest attachment he'd ever allowed himself. But Talia had received an offer from a French gentleman and actually left him. She'd given him an ultimatum, the impertinent chit, said if he'd see fit to marry her, she would turn the Frenchman down.

Hugh had sent her one last gift along with a letter wishing her well in France.

He'd been slightly regretful but had quickly replaced her with less permanent arrangements.

But he'd never fallen in love.

He'd found it easy enough to live without a permanently attached female.

Upon this thought, he turned his attention back to Penelope. "Why *are* you here, Penelope?" Was she trying to 'net' him? The thought was preposterous, but so were her actions.

Penelope reached for her knitting and began moving the needles furiously. "Can you not simply accept that I am here to help you, Hugh? Must there be some ulterior motive you've concocted in your mind?"

These were not the sentiments of a woman on the hunt for a husband. She did not simper, nor hang on his every word. She was not flirtatious in any way. Except…

She had fluttered her eyelashes at him a few minutes ago. He'd thought it was because she'd discovered something but… Wait a minute.

"Did you find the contents of the safe?"

Penelope looked up at him then and bit her lip. "No, I was just teasing you."

So, she *had* been flirting with him! She was here to net a husband! Hugh jumped to his feet as if he'd suddenly found himself sitting beside a snake.

She'd turned her feminine wiles on him and he'd quite nearly succumbed.

To Penelope Crone!

Good God, in jest, he'd lain atop her—pressed his body down upon hers.

And enjoyed it.

He'd even thought for a moment that he might kiss her. Yes, by God, he'd been staring into her eyes and for an instant—a mere second, really—had wanted to know her in a different way.

But then she'd gotten offended by his question and shoved him onto the floor. Thank God for that!

He was in grave danger of losing his bachelor status. The Baron Riverton, Penelope's father, must never discover that she was here with him alone.

If she was not going to depart, then he would have to. He would most likely be much safer in London, with his mother's friend's niece. At least in London, he knew how to play the game.

Sitting here with Penelope, he didn't even know what game they were playing.

CHAPTER SEVEN

*P*ENELOPE COVERED HER face with both hands after Hugh left the library. This wasn't going at all as she'd planned. He was suspicious of her motives. She could see it in his eyes when he'd made some vague excuses and left her alone. She was handling this entire situation poorly. She never should have acted so quickly on her sudden compulsion to enter motherhood. Her actions had been entirely out of character. She was normally a very rational girl, logical—reasonable! How could she have done something so utterly stupid?

But no.

She mustn't think this way.

She dropped her hands back into her lap and took a few deep steady breaths.

In, out.

In, out.

Slowly in.

Slowly out.

Much better. Her heart no longer raced, and the desire to burst into tears subsided. She opened her eyes and glanced around the room.

Hugh needed a housekeeper. She would discuss that with him tomorrow, after having a good night's sleep.

As if Penelope's thoughts had beckoned her, Rose knocked on the door and peeked inside.

"What did you say to him? Did you tell him? Ye Gods, Pen, this place is a pigsty." Rose was wearing one of Penelope's day dresses and had done her dark hair into a neat chignon.

"I didn't tell him, Rose. He's in an awful predicament with this estate, though. That horrible Mr. Periwinkle has been robbing him blind and letting this beautiful manor fall to pieces. Are there any manservants about that we could send into the village to announce available positions?" Without waiting for an answer, Penelope walked over to the desk and started writing out a list. "We'll need a butler and a new housekeeper. I don't care if there is one in residence already; if there is, she'll need to compete for the job with any new applicants. And once we've located people to fill those two positions, we will be looking for maids, footmen, a cook, scullery staff, houseboys, and stable lads."

Rose took the list as Penelope handed it over and scrunched up her nose. "There is an old man in the kitchen and a dirty little urchin making it look as though he's cutting wood out back."

Penelope held her finger to her chin. "Send the urchin. The old man will see his position as threatened and most likely toss my advertisement into the trash. Tell the urchin to spread the word that applicants are to appear on the morrow promptly at one in the afternoon." Slipping her hand into the large pocket hidden in her skirts, she pulled out a shilling. "Give this to the boy and tell him he will receive another tomorrow if any of the applicants are suitable."

But Rose didn't rush off right away. "And what of the other, Pen? The real reason we've traveled all the way up here to the middle of nowhere?"

There were times when Penelope wished she had a normal lady's maid, one who didn't question her at every turn. Rose was most definitely not a normal maid.

"I must tell him at the right time. It's going to change

his entire life. I cannot simply blurt it out. Besides, he's already dealing with the quagmire of this estate. I plan to ease his burden a bit before hitting him with the other."

Rose's eyebrows rose doubtfully. "Very well, Pen, but don't wait too long." She glanced meaningfully at Penelope's midsection, "You're already looking bloated. I imagine Danbury will be happier with the idea of marrying you if you don't look like a whale."

"Go," Penelope said through clenched teeth. She did not enjoy the criticism of her waistline.

After Rose disappeared, Penelope gathered up the knitting basket and went upstairs in search of the chamber Rose would have laid siege to for the two of them. She found it easily, as the doorway was open, and a cool breeze drifted into the corridor. Her trunks were piled at the end of the bed.

Stepping inside, Penelope understood immediately why the room was being aired out. It smelled as though it hadn't been cleaned or used in over a century. Most likely, she would not find any acceptable linens about, what with the current slovenly state of the rest of the house. Luckily, Penelope was something of a fussy sleeper and never traveled without her own bedding.

She placed the knitting basket beside the bed and went in search of the outriders she always traveled with, Mokey and Peter. If she was going to sleep in here, it would take more than herself to make the room inhabitable.

Well into the evening, Penelope assisted Mokey and Peter as they beat the rugs and heavy drapes outside, scrubbed the floors, and polished every surface inside of her chamber. By the time the sun had set, Rose had finally returned to make up the bed and unpack her clothing.

Peter lit a fire in the grate, and Mokey located a tub for her bath. The old man in the kitchen had grudgingly sent up stale bread and cheese, along with some ale, for an informal dinner. By the time she was done eating, it took every ounce of Penelope's energy to bathe and then climb onto the large canopied bed.

Ah, but the cleaning had been worth it.

As she inhaled the scent of her own pillow, Penelope let out a deep sigh of relief. She hadn't seen Hugh since he'd hightailed it out of the library. A twinge of concern pierced her drowsiness, but she was too tired to give it consideration.

She would speak with him tomorrow. They would set Augusta Heights to rights and then she'd sit him down and tell him her situation. As that daunting thought flitted through her mind, she drifted into a troubled sleep.

"PENNY! PENNY! YOU have to wake up!"

Penelope moaned and turned away from Rose's voice.

"You have to wake up, Penelope! The viscount is gone!"

"What viscount?" Penelope mumbled as she attempted to snuggle deeper into the soft bedding.

"Danbury! Penelope, Danbury has left Augusta Heights!" Rose's voice was annoyingly shrill this morning.

And then the meaning of what was being said penetrated. Penelope rolled over and opened her eyes. "What do you mean he's left?"

Rose held an opened missive in her hands, "He left you a note." And then she read it aloud. "'Miss Crone,' he says. 'Upon consideration of the strict standards set by polite society, and in order to preserve your pristine reputation, I must vacate the premises immediately and allow you to enjoy your holiday here at Augusta Heights for as long as you please. As a gentleman, I felt this was the best course of action. I could not turn you away when you so obviously are in need of a retreat, but I do not wish to bring a rain of judgment down upon you if it were ever discovered that you and I were in residence, alone, without proper chaperonage. Please make yourself at home. Stay as long as you wish. I shall be in London for the season and will perhaps run into you there. Felicitations, Hugh Chesterton, Viscount Danbury.'"

Rose threw the missive on the bed and began pacing. "I told you so, Penelope. Didn't I tell you? You should have given him the news right away!" And then she dropped into a nearby chair and slumped dejectedly. "This journey has all been for naught! We'll be on the road again for another week now!"

But Penelope had rolled onto her side and propped her head up on one hand. "No, we won't be leaving right away." She was a lady. She had Hugh's permission to make herself at home. She would go about righting the estate on her own and then she and Rose would travel to London to see Hugh. On a rueful note, she figured that at least she would make her parents happy. It seemed as though she would participate in yet another season after all, well, part of one anyhow. And her parents would be even happier when she finally got herself married.

"You plan on staying in this rundown estate longer than absolutely necessary?" Rose asked. But upon seeing the gleam of challenge in her mistress' eyes, she moaned. "Not more cleaning!"

"We won't be doing the cleaning, Rose. We're going to staff this place properly. And they shall do the cleaning. But first," she paused, "we need to get rid of Periwinkle."

"DANBURY, AS I live and breathe! I thought you were up in Manchester overhauling Augusta Heights! I'm all astonishment that you have been able to accomplish so much from such a distance. Excellent to see you, my good fellow."

Hugh glanced up from the broadsheet he was reading, slightly irritated that his business was such common knowledge to all and sunder. Gerald Cokeburn, Earl of Pinkerton, had never been one of his favorite people and his comments today made him even less so. And what did he mean by 'accomplish so much from a distance?' Reluctantly, Hugh set his paper aside and rose to his feet. Taking the older man's outstretched hand, Hugh forced himself to be sociable.

"Pinkerton, what a special treat it is to run into you. And yes, one can accomplish a great deal what with the mail and a few good solicitors." He was deliberately vague. It wouldn't be the thing to ask after his own business. What had Penelope done up there?

"Don't play the innocent with me, young man." The older man gained a few extra chins as he held his head in mock consternation. "Stealing away one of England's best land stewards. I don't know how you did it. Michaelson's father and grandfather before him were both more than happy to look after my northern estates for me. You must have offered him a fortune!"

It took all of twenty seconds for Hugh to formulate a reply. "Well, er, one does what one must." *New land steward? A fortune?*

It had been nearly three weeks since he'd abandoned Penelope Crone on his estate. But it had been done for his protection as well as hers. She would be just as unhappy wed to him as he would be wed to her. He hadn't really thought she would remain there for very long after he'd departed. But apparently...

New land steward? What had she done with Periwinkle?

"And I'll tell you, my neighbor was none too happy to lose his housekeeper. She'd been working for the family forever."

Hugh was flummoxed. Hiring good help required funds. Where had the funds come from?

She had discovered them in the library that day! She must have. There was no other possibility. She'd discovered the monies, sacked Periwinkle, and gone about setting his estate to rights.

Oh, bollocks.

He'd been utterly wrong about her. He'd assumed she'd been flirting with him. Penelope Crone! He chuckled to himself at his own tomfoolery.

He'd never have assumed she'd been setting her sights upon him if it hadn't been for that dream. Had it been a dream? Of course! Why else would he have thought of her in such a light?

She was the most abrasive, managing bluestocking of a female he'd ever known.

Not that there was anything wrong with a woman being capable. It was just that, well, a man liked to be the manager of his own affairs.

He ought to take her to task for assuming the responsibility of Augusta Heights after he'd left. He ought to speak with her father—tell him his daughter needed to be taken in hand.

He smiled as the doorman held open the door to the club for him to exit. She was a damn smart woman. Not only that but a damn smart *person*. She truly could hold her own against any man intellectually.

Most likely, Augusta Heights was in the process of becoming one of the most lucrative estates in the country. He had known that Penelope was the brains behind her father's success. That had been no secret amongst the gentlemen of the *ton*. Again, he smiled ruefully to himself. Men gossiped just as much as women. Only instead of nattering on and on about balls and hair ribbons, they gossiped about horses, gambling, and ladies. Mostly the disreputable kind.

And, on occasion, they discussed the marriageable ones.

On that thought, Hugh's mind turned to Mrs. Merriman's niece, Miss Louisa Redcliffe. Upon meeting her, he'd initially thought she was exactly the same as every other London debutante he'd ever met. She was of average height, slim, fair-skinned with brown hair, usually done up in ringlets and cunningly coy.

Mrs. Merriman was sponsoring her niece because there was no other woman in her life to do so. She had only her father.

Who happened to be rich as Croesus. Word had spread that she came with one of the largest dowries in recent memory.

Hugh had, in fact, escorted the ladies to the first ball of the season, a lavish affair, and stood up with the niece for her first dance. She was all of seventeen and sweet as a peach. She was delightful in that she listened to him with wide fascinated eyes and never failed to laugh at any of his jokes. She never failed to mention what a handsome and respected gentleman he was and how much she had enjoyed spending time with his mother at Land's End.

She gave him pause to think.

Marriage to her would fill his coffers for generations to

come.

And he could perhaps enjoy her for a while. When he'd tired of her, he supposed he could tolerate her company for the occasional visits to London. She would most likely want to be set up at Land's End for most of the year. Although she was by no means a country bumpkin, she had mentioned her preference for the simple life.

She was not a redhead, however.

She would not surprise him, or manage him, or do any of those things gentlemen resented. He would have a well-ordered life and at last his mother would be satisfied that the title would not go to a distant cousin.

He would finally set up his nursery. Any girls would be left to his wife to raise, and he would send his son off to Eton, just as he had been.

Would his daughters turn out as insipid as their mother? He hoped not. For some reason, he hoped to have intelligent daughters. Perhaps he would have to guide his daughters' educations, as well as his sons.

If Penelope Crone ever had daughters, he suspected she would direct them to be better educated than even she had been. What a novel idea that was! Educate his daughters so that they did not become mere pawns of society.

But then, as the Baron of Riverton was, would he be saddled with them for life?

Poor fellow. Except... Penelope was no financial burden to her father.

And, Hugh considered, she had most likely deepened his own pockets as well.

The thought lightened his steps considerably. Perhaps he'd play a bit of cards tonight.

CHAPTER EIGHT

ROUGHLY TEN WEEKS had passed since the little marquess had been born to the Duke and Duchess of Cortland.

Penelope and Rose had arrived in London, much to the delight of the Baroness Riverton, after missing only a few weeks of the season. Her mother had been so pleased that she'd insisted on taking Penelope to her favorite *modiste* in order to bolster her only daughter's wardrobe. She'd told Penelope that it would be extra important to look her best this season, since next year there would be no hope.

For when the season rolled around next year, Penelope would be only one year shy of the ancient age of thirty.

Rose was delighted, as well, with the prospect of Penelope acquiring several new gowns. For she knew that Penelope would only be able to wear then for a short while, and they would then be available for her own exclusive use.

Standing on the pedestal as the seamstresses fussed and measured her, Penelope could only wonder at the fact that her midsection was already expanding. Her bosom had increased in size as well. She winced as a tape measure wrapped around that tender part of her anatomy. Rose was right. She had to find Hugh and extract a commitment for marriage from him before she became any more bloated than she already was.

She was going to wear more vibrant colors this year. It had been decided that since she was no longer a young miss, she could wear some deep blues, olives, and perhaps even something red. Her mother had insisted that she order multiple gowns, made up of the finest muslin, and even satin and silk. It was to be the most striking wardrobe Penelope had ever owned.

Catching sight of herself in the large looking glass on the wall, Penelope examined her person. One could not really see any differences in her appearance yet. She looked the same as she always had.

Except perhaps for the fact that her face looked softer. Her normally prominent cheekbones were somewhat less defined, and her hair looked... duller.

Frumpish and boring.

"Mama," Penelope said to her mother, who was perusing some fashion plates on the other side of the fitting room, "I think I'd like to do something different with my hair this year."

The Baroness Riverton nearly went into raptures. It was the most wonderful thing her daughter had ever said.

"NOT... SO... TIGHT... Rose!" Penelope nearly swooned as her damnable maid pulled the laces tight on her corset. Good Lord, when was the last time she'd worn the ridiculous garment? And why did she continue to expand even though she could hardly keep down any food in the mornings?

"It's gapping at least an inch more than it ever has before."

"I don't care," Penelope said, holding tight to the bedpost. "I won't be able to speak to the man if I cannot breathe. And surely, it cannot be good for the baby. Loosen it, Rose." Penelope leaned her forehead against the round wooden post. She would hopefully run into Danbury tonight. She knew he was in Town. Her father had mentioned in passing that he'd shared a drink with him at White's earlier that week.

"Ahhh... much better." Penelope inhaled deeply as her lungs were able to expand normally once again. Some of her new gowns had been delivered earlier in the day, and she and Rose had decided on a low-cut gown of emerald silk with blue embroidery accents. And Penelope had gotten her hair cut into soft layers the day before. Instead of pulling it into the austere knot she'd worn for over a decade, Rose had curled it softly and then pinned several loops around the crown of her head. Swirly tendrils fell softly around her face and neck.

Penelope barely recognized herself.

"Do you think he'll be in attendance tonight?" Rose asked.

"Dash it all but I hope so. If not, I'll have to figure some other way to track him down. It's not as though I can simply arrive upon his doorstep." Doing so in Manchester had been one thing. Such a breach of etiquette in London would be beyond the pale.

"It wouldn't do to arrive at his residence," Rose agreed. "Perhaps you could send him a missive."

"Yes, I've thought of that. Hopefully, it won't be necessary, though." Penelope located her slippers and then allowed Rose to drape a silvery-green gossamer-like wrap upon her shoulders. Penelope reached up and touched one of the silk flowers in her hair. Rose had made certain her mistress was dressed to the nines tonight. It was in both of their best interests that Penelope not become a fallen woman and thus be ostracized from all of society. Rose would suffer as well if that were to become the case.

Sitting across from her parents in the carriage as they waited in the long line of vehicles to pull up to the entrance at the Helmer's ball, Penelope's nerves became even more tightly strung. The debutantes she could see already milling around looked fresh from the schoolroom. They wore pastels and whites and looked fresh and innocent.

None of them would ever do such a thing as she had.

If any of them guessed, or discovered…

That wave of panic that was becoming all too familiar swept through her once again. She had lain with a man who was not her husband. She had done so while he'd been intoxicated, and he did not even remember. And now she was increasingly increasing!

She was *most definitely not* fresh and innocent.

The door was swung open by a neatly uniformed footman, and Penelope exited the carriage behind her mother. As she did so, the fine silk fabric of her dress caressed her legs. It was just the reminder she needed to boost her confidence.

She would be fine. Everything would be fine. She mustn't think the worst.

They climbed the steps and entered the crowded foyer to wait in the receiving line. Penelope nodded in the direction of a few familiar faces. She noticed a few second glances sent her direction. Her appearance was a bit startling, even to herself.

And then she saw him.

He was not alone.

Hugh, confirmed bachelor, had only ever attended *ton* events with his mother and sister or alone. The woman on his arm was neither his sister, nor his mother.

She was one of those simpering types, dressed in a dusty-rose pastel gown that matched the glow on her cheeks. Unlike many debutantes, the pastel shade did not cause her to look colorless and bland. No, the color suited her perfectly. She was darling.

Hugh tipped his head in the direction of his partner so

that he could listen more carefully to what she had to say. Whatever she said caused him to chuckle and pat her hand fondly.

Panic shot through her. What on earth was he doing? Had he finally found *the one*, after all?

*H*UGH WAS ALREADY tiring of the season. As he stood in line, he wondered how he had allowed himself to be corralled into escorting the two women to yet another event.

Mrs. Merriman was reeling him in for her niece, that was how. With each passing day, Hugh found himself more and more thrown into the company of Miss Louisa Redcliffe.

Tonight, he'd promised the lady two dances. Although, neither was a waltz. Miss Redcliffe hadn't yet received the nod from Almacks.

But two dances!

It was nearly the equivalent of an engagement announcement!

He needed to make a decision fast, before it was made for him.

"Wouldn't you agree, my lord?" Miss Redcliffe had been speaking to him.

"Pardon?" He leaned down so that he could hear her. That was something else he was beginning to find quite annoying. The woman spoke in a voice just barely above the volume of a whisper. He was constantly having to lean toward her in order to hear her words.

He supposed that it wasn't too horrible of a thought to have a wife one could not hear.

"This foyer would look lovely with a few Grecian statues. It's rather bland, wouldn't you agree?"

"Ah, yes, I suppose, although where would the guests stand if the room were crowded with effigies?" Really, who gave a damn about such nonsense? He glanced around. The foyer seemed fine to him. Grand columns and molded archways were tastefully placed in useful positions. What more did a foyer need?

And then, he caught a glimpse of red.

Not scarlet, as in a dress or a flower. But that particular golden-red hair, silken and curled.

The lady's hair was set off most advantageously by an emerald gown with hints of blue, rather like some eyes he'd been remembering. Hugh's gaze traveled the length of the lady's shapely form and then settled on her face.

Green eyes glared at him.

Good God, the lady was Penelope!

After the shock of seeing that this beauty who'd caught his attention was none other than Penelope wore off, Hugh quickly excused himself and strode across the floor. First greeting the Baron and Baroness, Hugh then turned toward Penelope and raised one eyebrow. Remembering Pinkerton's words from earlier, he dismissed his momentary attraction and leaned close to her ear. "What the hell have you been up to?"

Her head snapped up at his words. "And such a pleasure it is to see you, as well, my lord."

Oh, hell, he never seemed to exhibit any manners whatsoever around her.

"My apologies," he said before bowing in her direction. As he did so, Penelope curtsied. He could not remember her ever doing any such thing before.

And as she curtsied, Hugh was given a rather pleasing eyeful of some delightfully plump cleavage. Penelope looked to be fuming when he finally met her eyes.

In that moment, he did not know which of his urges was the strongest. The one to press her body up against his own and deliver her a punishing kiss, or the one to drag her off into some private room and demand an accounting of her actions in up north.

The baron raised his brows at him, apparently sensing Hugh's conflicting inclinations, whereas, the baroness was looking quite pleased with her daughter, which as far as he could remember, was something of a first.

Hugh cleared his throat. "Miss Crone, will you do me the honor of saving me a dance?"

In an un-Penelope-like demeanor, she dipped her chin in assent. "Of course, my lord" and then lifted her arm.

Hugh pulled a pencil from his pocket and took hold of her dance card. As he did so, he noticed for the first time how delicate her wrist seemed, and as his hand brushed against hers, above her short gloves, how soft and fair her skin was. It was even paler than Miss Louisa Redcliffe's, only Penelope's was not flawless. Tiny freckles dotted the back of her arm, as though even her skin wished to mock the dictates of society.

Dismissing his ridiculous musings, he wrote his name next to a waltz. He did not wish to attempt a discussion with her in between circling other partners and across the line.

On impulse, he added his name to a second dance. The supper dance. They had much to discuss.

And then he did something he hadn't planned. He raised her wrist to his lips and held it there a moment. As he inhaled her fragrance, strange memories troubled him. He'd been close to this clean floral scent before. In fact, he was certain he'd tasted it.

As though burned, he dropped her hand and stepped

back. It seemed lately, that whenever he was in Penelope's presence, he felt like he was losing his mind. "I'm looking forward to our dance," he managed, before turning away from her and returning to Miss Redcliffe and her aunt.

"Who is that, my lord? I haven't yet met that lady, and I've met hundreds of people since I arrived in London!" Miss Redcliffe placed her hand upon his arm. She had an amazing grip for such a petite little thing.

"She is the Baroness of Riverton, there with her husband and unmarried daughter." Miss Redcliffe had sharp nails. It was a good thing the fabric of his jacket was a sturdy wool, or it was quite possible she would have drawn blood.

"It was most generous of you to single the daughter out. I noticed you placed your name upon her dance card. A spinster of such advanced age most likely had all of her dances to choose from. You did remember which ones you've promised me, I hope, my lord?"

He was beginning to feel more than a little annoyed at her possessiveness. "How could I forget, Miss Redcliffe? I have claimed a waltz with Miss Crone." He smiled at her but did not allow it to reach his eyes. Her grip loosened somewhat. "And the supper dance," he added.

The woman must have realized she had overstepped her claim to him and so she once again became the timid London miss. Summoning an attractive pout, she looked up at him from under her eyelashes. "You are such a kind gentleman. If I were in her position, I would be so very grateful to not be a wallflower for the entire night." And then she giggled into her hand. "It's a good thing you claimed your dances with me when you did, my lord, since my dance card is nearly full!"

Hugh made a tight smile and was relieved to see they'd reached the receiving line. Lord Helmer shook his hand jovially and welcomed him. Lady Helmer used her fan to chastise him for being absent from her ball last season. The elderly couple were close acquaintances of his mother's. He knew that his appearance with Miss Redcliffe would be duly relayed.

After the majordomo announced them, Hugh, promising he'd return in time for the first dance, made a vague excuse and escaped the suddenly cloying company he'd found himself in. He wished he could escape altogether, but that would not do. And if he did that, he would miss his opportunity to interrogate Penelope.

Where was that minx, anyhow?

"Danbury!" He turned at the sound of his name. It was Garrett Castleton, the Earl of Hawthorne. Up until last summer, the Earl had been considered something of a rake and womanizer. But Hawthorne had surprised everybody after the death of his father and become quite respectable, marrying one of the *ton's* most sought after debutantes, Lady Natalie Spencer.

At the time, Hugh had been a bit put out. When Lady Natalie had jilted her fiancé, the Duke of Cortland, he'd thought for a time he'd set his cap for her himself.

"Hawthorne," Hugh returned. "How fares married life?"

At his question, the formerly brooding gentleman grinned. "Well, very well indeed. I hear you're considering taking the leap yourself. Word is you are days away from offering for Miss Louisa Redcliffe."

Hugh decided he might become the brooding type himself. He'd been careless. Best to step back from Mrs. Merriman and her niece, lest he truly was ready to make an offer.

He shuttered.

"Rumors, my friend, mere rumors. How is the countess?" he asked, happy to change the subject.

Again, that grin. "Natalie is in her element. Construction is well under way at Maple Hall, and she has taken responsibility for details I hadn't even considered."

Last spring, Maple Hall had experienced a disastrous fire, and the former earl had died. "So, the estate is coming along, then?" He could not help but note that Hawthorne was more than happy to give up some of the rebuilding decisions to a woman. There was no way in hell Hugh would ever trust Louisa Darling with anything so important. The only woman of his acquaintance that he would trust with such decisions would be...

"It is, magnificently, might I add. I've realized one has less negotiating to do when one's wife wins them over first. Several of our old tenants have returned, and we've a marvelous crop planted this spring. Of course, it will be years before the estate is in the black again, but I'm pleased at the direction it's taking."

Hugh chatted with the man for quite some time before Hawthorne excused himself to find his countess. "She always saves the first dance for me," Hawthorne said, winking as he turned, and the he added, "And the last, of course, too."

Which reminded Hugh of his own obligations.

CHAPTER NINE

WITH EVERY INTENTION of locating and then planting herself in the wallflower section, Penelope entered the ballroom behind her parents.

And then the most unusual thing happened.

Gentlemen began seeking her out in order to place their names on her dance card. Initially, it was a few older, titled gentlemen, but gradually, some of the younger men approached her, and a few of them were sought-after bachelors. Such a hoot!

At first, she was suspicious. What was this all about? Was it a joke? But as the compliments piled on, and her card filled, she gradually realized that her changed appearance was amazingly causing something of a stir.

In any other circumstance, she might appreciate the irony of her situation. For she was not an eligible maiden as her parents believed her to be. No, she was not a maiden at all.

If the truth of her situation were to become known, nobody would dare meet her eyes, let alone speak to her. Glancing down in awe at her nearly full dance card, Penelope did not see the latest man to approach. She recognized his voice, though.

"Miss Crone." The well-modulated masculine tone sent shivers down her spine. She raised her gaze from her card to look into eyes the color of a February sky. Eyes she'd mooned over for most of her adult life. Blinking in surprise, she dipped into a well-practiced curtsey.

"My lord," she said. Viscount Darlington, Rome Spencer, stood before her. Where was the emptyheaded blonde he'd been courting last year?

"Please don't tell me you've already promised all of your dances this evening." He cocked one eyebrow and tilted his head slightly. "Surely, you've saved one for an old friend."

This was most unexpected. "You wish to dance with me?" Oh, that was stupid. That was what he'd said, wasn't it? But she was used to him speaking to her like one of the fellows. Perhaps this was just a ruse to discuss the price of corn or the latest bills presented in Parliament.

Except that recently she had not kept as current on Parliamentary matters. She'd been caught up in fashion and husbands and babies and such. If he did wish to discuss current events, he would be sorely disappointed.

Rome did not answer her question. Instead, withdrawing a pencil from his pocket with one hand, he raised her wrist with his other. "Ah, delightful. I was hoping you had a waltz left." And he claimed her last available dance.

"This one is mine, I think." One of the older gentlemen who'd approached her first stepped between them. What was his name? Oh, yes, the Earl of Pinkerton.

Penelope looked apologetically at Rome. "It will be an honor, my lord." Turning toward the earl, she placed her hand upon his arm and allowed him to lead her out to the opening set. Luckily, it was a simple country dance. She would not have to be close to her partner very often.

Standing in the long line of revelers, she was staggered by the fact that Rome Spencer had put his name on her dance card. It made her feel all of seventeen again. She'd been in love with him forever, it seemed. But she'd given up on him.

Yes, and she'd seduced Hugh Chesterton.

Who was now standing across the way from her, just to

the right of the earl.

Hugh really was a very good-looking man. Or perhaps the inferior looks of Lord Pinkerton merely caused him to benefit from the comparison.

She noted Hugh's soft brown eyes, just a few lines on their outer edges from smiling, and something warm blossomed inside of her. He was not smiling now, however. No, he grimaced slightly as he bowed toward the lady on her left.

On the other side of Pinkerton stood Rome.

Rome was not looking at his own partner, rather he was watching *her*.

Penelope did not recognize the lady on her right, the lady who was to partner Rome. The music began, and her partner pulled her from her thoughts as he took her hand and proceeded to turn her about the circle.

"My dear Miss Crone, why is it that I have never danced with you at a ball before?"

Penelope merely smiled at him as he was forced to release her and dance with another lady.

Hugh caught her hand just then and placed his other on her waist. She resisted the urge to shiver. She felt slightly giddy, however, when his breath touched her ear. "Watch out for Pinkerton, Penelope. He's had four wives and is on the hunt for another. Heavy-handed bastard from what I understand."

Penelope glanced at Hugh sharply. "It's only a dance!" she said as he twirled her back into Pinkerton's grasp.

"You've not answered my question." Pinkerton leaned his head down and spoke near her face so that she would be sure to hear him over the music. "Have you been locked away in a castle somewhere for most of your life?"

Oh, good Heavens. The man was an utter fool. She'd been at nearly every ball held for the past ten years. "Not exactly," she answered, turning away from him. His breath was nauseating; onions and garlic and, ugh, cigar smoke.

He released her, and Rome caught her in a turn. "Natalie said you had planned on foregoing the season this year. I have to admit, seeing you here is a pleasant surprise." Lady Natalie Castleton, recently married, was Rome's only sister and a friend to Penelope.

Rome's scent was clean and musky, his grasp warm and firm. "I changed my mind," she said, feeling breathless.

And back to Pinkerton again. Penelope tried to hold her breath through the steps, afraid of what would happen if forced to inhale. "Funny," the older man said. "I've known your father for years—never knew he even had a daughter."

Oh, that was complimentary. "Well, he does," she said on an exhale and was then handed off to Hugh again.

"You look a bit green," Hugh said, looking concerned. His hands were strong as he guided her along the length of the hall. Luckily, it was time for a long promenade. The twirling had not been a good thing. "Breathe through your mouth."

She allowed him to guide them through the steps, all the time wishing she could simply lean into him and stop moving. But she did as he said, and by the time he passed her back to Pinkerton, she felt a little revived.

She kept her face averted from him as much as possible as Pinkerton continued to bemoan the fact that they'd never met and was then thankfully handed back to Rome.

"I barely recognized you, Pen," he said sheepishly as he pressed his palm against hers and they turned a circle. His palm was firm and his clothing impeccable. Rome Spencer had always been one of the most respectable bachelors she'd ever known. He'd never been very rakish, spending much of his time assisting his father in the management of their numerous estates.

She remembered on a few occasions how he'd seemed to disapprove of Hugh's lifestyle.

But what had happened with the lady from last year? She was certain he must be betrothed by now. She glanced over at him from under her lashes and smiled tentatively. He was not asking her about crop prices, nor was he seeking her opinion on Parliamentary laws.

And back to Pinkerton. Unfortunately, she pulled in a lungful of his odor before remembering to breathe through her mouth. Waves of nausea rolled around inside of her. In, out, in, out. Step, turn, step, step, step...

Pinkerton pulled her closer than was necessary, his clammy hands digging possessively into her waist. She contemplated giving him a facer.

If she didn't get sick on him first.

The man was saying something to her, but she could not focus on his words.

Air. She needed to get out of here.

When Hugh pulled her alongside him, she could have cried in relief.

Except that this dance seemed as though it was never going to end. She closed her eyes briefly as Hugh's arms held her up.

And then, all of a sudden, the air on her face was cool and the litany of smells she'd been experiencing turned to a wholesome scent of grass and flowers. As she opened her eyes, she realized she was outside on the terrace and being led to a concrete bench.

Hugh, the ornery, obnoxious, womanizing drunkard, was sitting her down tenderly and smoothing her hair away from her face. Penelope slumped against him as he murmured soothing words over her head.

"It's all right, Pen. Take deep breaths. That's a good

girl." He'd tucked her in beside him and was rubbing her arm lightly.

For the first time in weeks, she felt safe.

SOMETHING WAS VERY wrong with Penelope Crone. Hugh should have known when she arrived at Augusta Heights uninvited and unchaperoned. She was just so damn proud. Far too independent for her own good.

But not in this moment. He tucked her head beneath his chin and continued rubbing her arm. He heard a sniffle and a muffled whimper.

"Are you crying, Pen?" he asked softly.

Another whimper. "No," she said.

She *was* crying.

Free-thinking, fearless, outspoken Penelope Crone was crying in his arms.

And it felt right.

Not that she was crying, but that he was the one she trusted enough to let down her guard.

Hugh was quite certain she'd nearly fainted again in the ballroom. A lady who'd never so much as even considered carrying smelling salts.

Yes, there was definitely something wrong with Penelope. Was she ill? Was she being blackmailed by somebody? What would cause a lady to travel halfway across the country for no reason and begin having fainting spells?

"Won't you tell me what is upsetting you? Please?" He bent forward and tipped her chin up so that she was looking at him.

She was no longer pale. A little splotchy-looking now, actually. But her eyes looked even greener than normal and again, he noticed the tiny blue specks. The look of hopelessness on her face was heartbreaking. "Ah, sweetheart, nothing can be that bad."

"Oh, Hugh," she sniffed and buried her head back under his chin.

"I mean," he said casually, "I realize that ladies are required to accept a gentleman's invitation to dance, and you could not refuse Pinkerton, but really, was dancing with him as bad as all this?"

A broken laugh escaped her. "He smelled awful!"

"Ah, I see." He chuckled at her comment. Pinkerton may be an earl, but she quite had the right of it. How his valet held his head up amongst his peers, Hugh would never know.

Without thinking, Hugh kissed the top of her head. Why had he never realized what a gorgeous color her hair was?

She did not smell awful. She smelled feminine and soft, just as a woman ought to smell.

He'd always thought of Penelope as being pointy and sharp, but she was neither of those things. She felt soft and rounded. She was, in fact, curvy everywhere. Her shoulders were nicely rounded, and her waist dipped inward, just so. On impulse, he put one arm under her legs and lifted her onto his lap. She moved to protest but it was short lived as he wrapped her in his arms and tucked her head down on his shoulder.

No, Penelope was not pointy nor sharp. When had she become such a... woman?

She wiggled a little, as though to edge off his lap but Hugh held tight to her. "Stay put, Pen. I demand you tell me what is troubling you."

"I—I—"

"Don't tell me it's nothing. You did not travel to Manchester due to boredom, now did you? And you did, in fact, faint that day in the library. Just now, in that ballroom, you nearly fainted or worse, again. Now tell me what it is."

She didn't say anything for a few moments. He assumed she was either gathering her courage or trying to formulate a fictional answer. He waited.

"You are going to hate me, Hugh." She let out a deep sigh but turned her face to look at him. He could see a smattering of freckles sprinkled across her nose and under her eyes. She had a bit more color now. Their positions suddenly felt very intimate.

"I don't think I could ever hate you, Penelope." The bow of her mouth suddenly held his gaze captive. Dusty pink, that's what he would call her lips. They looked plump and sweet and tender. He leaned in and tasted. And when he did, there was no denying that he'd been thinking of doing so for quite some time now.

There was no need to coax her. She was as ready as he. Their tongues dueled, engaged, and then danced before she surrendered and allowed him to explore.

He unfurled a low growl before tightening his arms, drawing her closer. At the same time, one of her hands reached up and fluttered along his ear and cheek. She was hampered by her gloves. He wanted to feel her skin touching him.

He wanted to taste *her* skin.

Turning his head, he grasped the fabric on the end of her index finger with his teeth and tugged with a wicked snarl.

The satin material slid off easily. But it wasn't enough. He wanted to undress more than just her hand.

And now her fingers were in his hair.

Hugh trailed his lips along her jaw.

"Hugh," she murmured. "Hugh, we mustn't. I mustn't.

Anyone could come out here."

In spite of her words, he could feel that her heart was racing, and her breaths were uneven. But she was right. He halted his journey along her collarbone and waited a moment to slow his own racing libido. It would be disastrous if they were discovered.

Wouldn't it?

Penelope wiggled again, and this time, he allowed her to work her way free. She stood before him, smoothing her dress.

She did not look pale now. Not at all. In fact, a delightful flush had crept across her neck and cheeks.

"Miss Crone? Miss Crone, are you out here?" Pinkerton called.

Damn!

Hugh ran a hand through his hair and then tugged at his cravat, ensuring it was still tied properly. Considering what they'd been up to just moments before, he felt they looked rather respectable now.

"Ah, there you are, my dear. Whatever happened? I went to reclaim the lady I'd led onto the floor and was prevailed upon to lead Danbury's partner instead. Danbury, are you out here?"

"I, ah, was not feeling well. Lord Danbury was kind enough to escort me outside. The, ah, room was..." She ought not have to explain herself to this pompous ass.

"The lady needed some air, Pinkerton, I'm surprised you didn't notice. She was pale as a sheet. You're welcome, by the way. It was my pleasure to escort your partner when she needed it." Oh, hell, he'd forgotten all about Miss Redcliffe. He was definitely going to have to do something to distance that connection.

The earl narrowed his eyes but apparently was unwilling to press the issue. "Well, yes, yes, thank you,

Danbury." And then he winged his arm to Penelope. "Are you ready to return, my dear? I will escort you back to your mother."

Hugh realized he was, once again, sitting in the lady's company while she stood. Why did he only ever do this with her? He rose and searched her expression. Was she going to be all right with Pinkerton for the few moments it would take to return to the baroness?

She nodded in assent as though he'd asked the question aloud. Pinkerton pounced upon her unusual docility and pulled her toward the door. "You really must take better care of yourself, Miss Crone. A lady could lose her reputation by disappearing in the middle of a dance." The man continued to harangue her as the two disappeared through the terrace door. Hugh wondered if Penelope would set him down in her normally abrasive manner. But somehow, he doubted it. She was no longer quite the same girl he'd thought he knew.

Which reminded him. He'd never gotten an answer out of her.

CHAPTER TEN

*T*HANKFULLY, PENELOPE'S MOTHER hadn't noticed her momentary absence. And the earl was apparently less interested in her now than he'd been earlier. One less thing to worry about. She didn't think he'd seen anything on the terrace. Surely, if he had, he was not the sort to keep quiet about it.

Except upon reflection, she realized that had she and Danbury been discovered in their embrace, it would have solved her current problem. A hysterical burst of laughter nearly erupted at the thought. She would have been compromised by Hugh Danbury at the Helmers' ball. She had a great appreciation for irony but really, that would have been unreal.

She'd almost told him. She doubted she'd be presented with a more perfect opportunity.

But they'd gotten distracted.

Penelope sat beside her mother and fanned herself slowly. Her heart raced at the mere thought of how Danbury had held her. How his lips had felt on hers.

She'd been with him that one time, yes, but this experience had been oh, so very different. He'd been tender, soothing; his touch had felt meaningful.

She'd not wanted to stop him. She'd not wanted to stop herself, but years of attending *ton* functions had created a strong awareness of how society worked. There were eyes everywhere. And behind those curious eyes were suspicious minds and flapping mouths. Yes, Penelope understood what titillated the *ton*. She'd had no wish to become the on-dit of the evening. Even if Lady Helmer would have appreciated the notoriety.

Her lips still tingled from his kiss though.

"You look flushed, dear," Penelope's mother interrupted her thoughts. "It's nice to see you with a bit of color. You've looked so wan lately—more so than usual."

Penelope waved her fan rapidly. "It's warm in here." A believable explanation for her flushed face, since the room was lit by literally hundreds of candles. She was amazed at how a mere quarter of an hour ago, she'd thought she might faint from dancing; she'd barely been able to keep herself standing upright. But now, after a few minutes in the company of Hugh Chesterton, she suddenly seemed filled with energy.

Which was a good thing, for seeing Rome Spencer moving in her direction, she glanced at her card upon her wrist and was pleased that it was he who'd claimed the next set. And it was a waltz.

What would it feel like to be held by the man she'd thought she'd loved for over a decade? Why did he wish to dance with her tonight, of all nights? In the past, he'd taken time to converse with her, much the same as he had with her father, and other gentlemen. Had she really made such a great change in her appearance? Or was it something else? Had her condition altered her demeanor? She'd lain with a man. And now she carried a child.

She couldn't help but remember Hugh's question. *I never did understand you. So set against marriage, determined to emasculate every man you've ever met. Don't you ever wish you didn't have to be so... different?* He'd said the question wasn't an insult. *I was merely wondering if it was necessary to be so different in order to be you.*

She'd been so certain she had all the answers, not even

three months before. So much had changed. She was experiencing a tumult that was causing her to question her very essence. Who was she now? Not a mother—yet. Heaven help her, she wasn't anyone's wife yet either. But she was no longer intent upon spinsterhood.

She'd never been afraid to be alone before. But now... Being an outcast loomed ominously.

"Miss Crone." Rome Spencer bowed in front of her and then presented his arm. It was only a dance, and yet, Penelope felt herself blushing as she rose to take it. His smile had always been captivating. It was unnerving to have him turn his charm upon *her*.

And he'd yet to have asked her about the price of corn. "My lord," she murmured, dipping into a gentle curtsey.

He led her to the center of the floor and turned her to face him. As the musicians raised their instruments, Viscount Darlington placed one hand on her waist and took hold of hers with the other. She placed her palm on his shoulder and waited for the fluttering to commence.

There was pleasure but no butterflies. No tingling awareness...

He expertly steered her around the room with long graceful steps. It was almost magical. It *should have been* magical.

Last fall, at his sister's wedding ball, Penelope had watched him as he'd danced with Lady Eliza Frost. Rumor had been that there was an understanding between the two families. They were to have become engaged upon the holidays.

"Are you affianced?" she asked for no other reason than curiosity.

"I am not." He gazed at her with some intensity. Was that a meaningful look in his eyes? Surely, she'd imagined that. "Are you?"

She raised her brows. "Is there any reason you would think that I might be?"

"You are different," he responded, and then added. "I simply wondered…"

This was *not* happening. Unsure of how to respond, Penelope laughed nervously. The indifference with which he'd always treated her before was absent tonight.

"How are your northern estates faring? Has the tenant unrest continued?" They'd discussed these issues last summer.

Rome twirled her expertly. She was a little breathless when his hand settled on her waist once again.

"The estates are the same." His mouth pinched as he spoke but then he seemed to shrug off any tension. "I understand you assisted Danbury with Augusta Heights last month. Sounds like you've achieved quite a coup in landing him such a sought-after steward." Another twirl. When he took her in his arms this time, he was smiling again.

"Merely good business," she said noncommittally.

"You never answered my question." He leaned in and spoke close to her ear. Rome Spencer's scent was masculine and clean. She found herself comparing it to Hugh's, which was similar, yet different. Danbury's was muskier, darker. The thought of it caused her to shiver. Rome looked satisfied at her reaction.

How should she answer his question? *My lord, I'm increasing and hoping to bring Danbury up to scratch as soon as possible. And no, he knows nothing of the entire situation. In fact, he does not even remember bedding me.*

"I remain, of course, unattached," she said instead. It was the answer he would expect, was it not? It was the only answer she'd ever expected to give to such a question.

"Ah, my good fortune then."

How should she deal with this sudden interest from

Rome? What if Hugh refused to marry her? Would it be prudent to encourage Viscount Darlington in case Hugh didn't come up to scratch?

No, no, no! She could not do that to Rome. She would not do that to any man! What she'd done to Hugh was bad enough! Regardless of what happened, she must, above all, hold onto her self-respect. If everyone in the world turned against her, at the very least, she needed to like herself.

She would most certainly *not* attempt to pass another man's child off as Rome Spencer's heir. Rome was due to inherit an earldom. In addition to that, he was a good and decent person. She would not do such a thing to him.

Even if she wanted to, she was far too advanced for it to be believable.

She was no longer even a maiden! Rome Spencer, or any gentleman for that matter, might be disappointed, or perhaps even disgusted, to discover they'd married a woman who was not chaste.

It would be Danbury or no one.

"What of Lady Eliza?" Perhaps she could turn Rome's thoughts in another direction.

He frowned. "Lady Eliza," he said through pinched lips, "is now Mrs. Blackwell."

Penelope raised her brows. A woman who would give up Rome Spencer, a man due to inherit a prominent title and vast wealth, to become a mere Missus, must have been very much in love, indeed.

"The lady and her husband eloped just before the new year." Rome had been considered one of London's most eligible bachelors for years. Surely, he had not expected that when he did finally choose a woman to offer for, she would prefer another instead.

"*Were* you betrothed?" She knew it would be inappropriate for him to discuss this with her, especially here, surrounded by other dancers, in the middle of the ball-room, but really, they'd known each other for simply *ages*.

Rome took in a deep breath and then let out a long sigh. "Not publicly. No announcement was made, but yes. I asked, and the lady accepted." He looked pained. "I'll expect your confidence on this matter, of course. The lady's reputation is at stake, that and her family's."

"Of course," she answered automatically. Penelope did not gossip.

So, while she'd been pining away for him in January and February, he'd been recovering from a broken engagement. Poor thing.

Rome would not want her sympathy.

No, apparently, he wanted something else from her.

"Lady Eliza is very young. I hope she knew what she was doing."

He grimaced. "I believe she is happy." A sadness entered his eyes that she'd never seen there before. Suddenly, the affection one might feel for a brother rose up inside of her. Not jealousy.

She did not wish to extend platitudes. "You will be happy again," she said sincerely and looked into his eyes.

Rome tilted his head back and gathered his pride once again. She was certain he'd revealed far more to her than he'd intended. The rest of the dance was completed without any further conversation. He returned her to her mother's side and bowed formally.

As the evening progressed, Penelope realized she was both looking forward to and dreading the supper dance. He'd also signed for the last waltz. She hoped she could last that long.

What would she say to him? At least the supper dance was not another waltz. She'd not be forced into such intimate proximity so soon after their... whatever it was.

What had it meant? Had he felt something for her? Gentlemen didn't really go about kissing ladies of the ton for no reason, did they? For a girl of such an advanced age, she really did lack understanding of the nuances of courting. Hellfire, she might as well be one of the tender debutantes for all she knew on the subject.

But tonight was the first time she'd ever found herself the object of such masculine attention. And not from only elderly gentlemen, but younger ones too. And all the while, she danced.

She danced with gentlemen she'd known most of her life but also several she'd just met tonight. She'd never remember all of their names. She barely remembered their faces.

She hoped she wouldn't run into any of them again soon. Social niceties had never been a strong suit for her.

And then it was time for the supper dance.

Her mother was the first to see him approach. "My lord, I certainly am going to miss your mother this season. I was tempted to forego it myself when I read the letter she sent to me stating that she would be staying at Land's End."

Penelope was able to study him, unfettered, as he directed all of his charm toward her mother.

"She caught a bit of a fever earlier this spring. Although it isn't anything serious, she said she'd rather not travel. When I visited a few months ago, her cough persisted. She assured me it was nothing serious, but one always worries when it's one's only parent."

Penelope frowned. Cortland had said Lady Danbury was in good health. She'd always considered the viscountess one of the more indomitable dragons of the *ton*. But of course, her son would not be in London for the season if his mother was in decline.

"Yes," Penelope's own mother broke into her thoughts. "She mentioned that in her letter, although it was a bit difficult to decipher. I've been corresponding with your mother for nearly fifty years, and I still require a magnifying glass to unravel what she's written." Winking up at the viscount, she added, "It's almost as though I'm a spy, interpreting a secret code."

Hugh laughed at her mother's outrageous comment and then turned his gaze upon Penelope. The force of his looks and charm nearly stopped her heart. When he smiled, he had these tiny little wrinkles around his eyes. He pushed back the lock of hair that never failed to fall forward and then bowed toward her.

"My dance, I believe." The piece of hair fell forward again. She'd always known he was handsome, but she'd never been so affected by his presence.

Physical attraction was a mysterious matter, indeed!

She rose and took the arm he held out to her. "You are correct, my lord." Both her manner and her words sounded incredibly docile in her own ears.

When they were several feet away from her mother, Hugh leaned down and murmured, "Shall we forego the dance and take a turn about the garden instead?"

Oh, dear.

Did he intend to pick up where they'd left off earlier? If she said yes, would that make her something of a brazen hussy? And then, for the millionth time that night, the irony of her own thoughts nearly gave rise to hysterical laughter. For of course she was a brazen hussy!

"I believe we have some unfinished business," he added.

Oh dear.

They could find some tucked away bench somewhere, away from the other guests. He'd planted a craving in her that she'd never expected.

Sexual desire!

Oh, dear.

She glanced over at him suspiciously. Was he reading her mind?

"You never revealed your secret to me. The reason you went gallivanting around England earlier this spring and the cause of your fainting spells." He looked just a little disapproving.

She needed to tell him everything tonight. She doubted she'd get a better opportunity. If she did not take him up on it, Rose would harangue her to no end.

Steering her expertly out through the same terrace doors she'd used before, Hugh took matters into his own hands.

The breeze was cooler now than it had been before. Spring had not arrived completely. Most of the flowers were reaching for the sky but few of them had opened yet.

A tremor ran through her. Hugh pulled her closer and they stepped off the formal terrace onto a flagstone path.

"Confession time, Miss Crone," he said softly as they strolled. She was no longer clinging to his arm. For it had somehow found its way around her shoulders and the entire left side of her body was pressed up against his.

He was warm and solid and, in that moment, felt like a safe haven.

"Well…" she began.

They took several more steps.

"Well?" he prompted.

How should she do this? She'd worked this conversation out in her mind a thousand times but never really come up with any satisfactory script for herself.

"You know that I have never been one to hide my opinion of the institution of marriage?" She glanced up at him.

His eyes sparkled, giving her cause to believe he was laughing inside. Was he laughing at her? She was in no mood to be laughed at. "Please don't find jest in this."

Her words brought about a more serious demeanor. "Of course not."

She picked her way over a few of the large flat stones before continuing. "Well, I had thought that I could only marry if I were lucky enough to find a person who could be the mate to my soul and vice-versa. I had thought there was one person. I had thought that I could only marry this one person, but he was never, well, he proved to be... not."

"You are speaking of Darlington, I take it. Ravensdale's heir."

Her head jerked up at his words. How did he know? Oh, this was mortifying.

"Pen, anyone who has ever known you has known you were infatuated with the Viscount."

"No! Please! Oh, this is humiliating!" She'd thought she'd been so clever. She'd thought she'd hidden her emotions so well. She'd never told a soul—even Abigail, her cousin and dearest friend.

Of course, she had discussed him with Rose. But Rose. Well. Rose knew everything.

Penelope attempted to pull herself away from Hugh, but his grip merely tightened.

Throughout the evening, she'd begun to feel attractive, feminine, sought after even. No wonder Rome had flirted with her. He'd wanted to soothe his wounds and figured good old Penelope was always there.

"Tell me he was not aware, Hugh, please?"

Hugh grimaced and shifted his gaze away from her.

"Oh, no!" She could not face him ever again. Thank heavens she'd not flirted back with him this evening! She turned her head and banged it against Hugh's shoulder.

They had stopped walking. Hugh turned and wrapped both arms around her waist.

"But I watched you with him tonight." *He'd watched her?* "You were not as entranced with him as before."

"Of course, I'm not, you fool!" The words escaped her before she could consider them more carefully.

A huge grin spread across his face. "No, you are not," he said in a somewhat satisfied tone. "But why would I be a fool for not knowing this?" The moonlight caught the white gleam of his teeth as he continued smiling down at her.

Why would he be a fool? Perhaps because she'd already given him her virginity and was carrying his child, that was why! Except that she hadn't yet revealed this rather pertinent information to him.

And then his hand was on her chin and his face was moving closer to hers. "Perhaps because of this?"

His lips did not need to coax hers for long before she opened her mouth to him.

He tilted his head and explored one corner of her mouth. "Or this?"

She was now pressed up fully against his chest and thighs... and other parts.

She let out a soft sigh when his lips moved along her chin and onto her throat. "Um." She sought some words to answer him, but she'd seemingly lost the ability to speak English.

He just went right on kissing her. On her neck.

Behind her ear.

He pushed down the sleeve of her dress and kissed her there.

On her shoulder.

"Um," she said again. What had been the question?

His hand had slid up her waist and located the ridge

along the edge of her stays. Just above there, his thumb grazed the sensitive skin of her breast. A low growl emitted from his throat.

"Penelope." He sounded as breathless as she was.

He'd pushed her dress down farther, and his mouth covered her where her dress had done so only moments before.

When he attempted to claim the tip with his mouth...

"Ouch!" She pulled back. Recently her breasts had been so tender that they pained her. His head jerked up, giving her the very brief respite she needed to draw on common sense. She hurriedly tugged the sleeves back over her shoulders, but she did so carefully. That had really hurt!

Hugh looked crestfallen.

Men!

This was why she'd once decided she'd never wed.

They really were a rather pathetic lot.

But then Hugh pulled her into another embrace. This one more tender and gentler than before. He reached up and tucked a strand of hair behind her ear. "I'm sorry, Pen." He looked so very sheepish in that moment. "Got a little too carried away. You've never done this before, have you?"

"Er..." She looked away from him. "Not really." What *could* she say? She didn't want him to think she was the harlot that she apparently was, and yet she really did not wish to dissemble with him any more than she already had.

"I may shoot myself tomorrow for saying this," his expression was tender, "but, I'm thinking that perhaps I ought to speak with your father." Was he going to say he'd fallen in love with her? Was that even possible?

"Speak with my father?" Her grasp of the English language had apparently escaped her completely.

"I've quite overstepped the bounds of common decency with you this evening. It's the right thing to do."

"I am nearly thirty years old, Hugh. If you have something to say, I suggest you say it to me." Ah, she could speak again. This was it. This was exactly what she'd wanted from him.

But whereas just a moment ago, her heart had been soaring, it now felt as though it had sunk low inside of her.

"Penelope?"

She looked up at him warily. "Yes?"

"Will you be my... estate manager?"

A storm of magnificent proportions began swirling around inside of her head as she stared at his grinning mouth. Had he really just said what she thought he'd said? Penelope pulled her hand away from his shoulder, clenched it into a fist, and without taking even a moment to think matters through, released it to make very solid contact with Danbury's nose.

CHAPTER ELEVEN

SHE STEPPED BACK in horror at what she'd actually done and Hugh bent over covering his nose with both hands. Large drops of blood appeared on the stone and in the dirt.

Penelope pulled out the handkerchief she'd tucked into her dress and went to dab at Danbury's face. But he was more than a little wary and turned his head away from her.

"God damnit, Pen!" he said just before spitting a large amount of blood onto the ground. He reached up and snatched the cloth out of her hand. "I was only joking with you! I cannot believe you actually did that." And then in wonder, or perhaps shock, he said, "My nose. I think you've broken it."

Oh, this was horrible!

"Let me see, Hugh, look up here." He stood up straight and removed another handkerchief from his own pocket. His head tilted back and she could see that his nose remained as straight and arrogant looking as ever. Dripping down his face, however, the blood looked black.

"I'm pretty sure it isn't broken." Not that it would mar his looks in any way. Penelope looked down at her hand and realized that she, too, was bleeding.

She must have caught it on one of his teeth.

Again, he said, "I cannot believe you did that." Blood flowed freely from his nostril. She looked down at her dress and realized that it had not escaped the splatter.

"It was not a very good joke, Hugh." It really wasn't. This was really his own fault.

Remembering a fountain they'd passed just before

stopping, Penelope swiped one of the handkerchiefs away from Hugh and turned to go back to it.

"You can't return to the ball looking like that."

Without looking back at him, she waved her hand dismissively. "I'm going back to the fountain. Stay here, I'll return shortly."

As she soaked the once pristine cloth, she saw that the handkerchief she'd taken was his. The crest embroidered on it must be that of his family. After swirling it around, rinsing out the blood, she squeezed it tightly and folded it into a careful rectangle. When she found Hugh again, he was sitting on a conveniently placed iron bench. She sat down beside him and turned his head so that she could dab at the blood on his lip and chin.

When she touched it to his nostril, she was careful not to press too hard, knowing he might be feeling some pain. He merely watched her from beneath shuttered lids.

"Is that really what you wanted to ask me, Hugh?"

He scowled but then caught sight of the cut on her hand. "You're bleeding."

She examined the scratch and shrugged. "It's nothing."

But he picked her hand up and examined it more closely. "You need to get it cared for though. A fellow at Gentleman Jackson's died of such an injury."

"Joking with me again?" *Really, Hugh.*

The look in his eyes was serious though. "No, I wish I were. There was a fighter a few years back whose fist came away with a tooth in it. Within weeks, the hand became putrid and he later died of fever."

Observing the stains on his cravat and the part of his lip that was already swelling, she smiled inwardly at his concern for her. But his story was a strange one. "Were you well acquainted with the man?"

His look became shuttered again. "I'd sparred with him

on several occasions." He scowled at the blood on her dress and then stood up and pulled her with him. "You can't be seen like that. Come with me."

Feeling like a child playing Sardines, Penelope followed Hugh as he carefully maneuvered her through the trees until they came up just alongside the terrace, hidden by some shrubs. The silhouette of a couple was barely visible, but their conversation carried easily across the protective hedges.

"I don't wish for you to overtire yourself. If you're unwell, we will leave. Lady Helmer will understand." It was a familiar male voice, but Penelope could not place it.

"I'm fine, Garrett." Penelope easily recognized Natalie Spencer, Rome's only sister and the newly married Countess of Hawthorne. "I just wanted to be outside with you, alone for a few minutes." Theirs was a love match. Lady Natalie and Garrett Castleton would have been considered an impossible match a year ago, but they had somehow, miraculously become the darlings of the *ton*.

"Hawthorne," Danbury spoke softly to attract their attention without alerting anyone else.

"What the...?" The earl moved in front of his wife protectively as he turned to see who was in hiding nearby.

"Natalie, it's me, Penelope. And Danbury."

Lady Natalie peeked curiously around the hedge. "Whatever are you two up to?" Seeing the blood, her eyes flew open wide. "Garrett, they are injured."

"Not really, but in need of assistance to be certain." Hugh gestured with his hands toward the blood on their clothing. "And Penelope needs her hand attended to. I don't wish for it to become putrid."

Lady Natalie looked to the sky in exasperation. "Do you mean to tell me that the two of you have come to fist-a-cuffs over your political opinions?" She lifted Penelope's hand to examine it more closely.

Garrett was grinning at Hugh. "She popped you a good one, eh?"

"Penelope, really!" Natalie shook her head as she took in the implications of their situation. "We need to get the two of you out of here without anyone seeing this blood-bath."

The earl looked over at his wife. "What would you like for me to do, my love?"

Natalie drummed her fingers along her chin for just a few seconds. "Order our carriage and then inform Penelope's mother that I am of need of her daughter for the rest of the evening. You may tell her, in confidence, the news that I am increasing. She will then understand my need to have her daughter with me. Meet us in the front then and we can deliver Penelope home."

"What of Hugh?" Guilt plagued Penelope when she saw that his nose was swelling and the skin around his eyes looked like it might bruise. His joke had not been funny at all but perhaps she'd overreactive ever so slightly.

"Danbury will be fine on his own, I imagine." The earl looked to Hugh questioningly who nodded.

And then Hugh caught Penelope's concerned gaze. "I'll be fine. Remember what I said about the hand though." And to Natalie, "You'll make certain she has it cleaned and dressed?"

"Of course, of course, now off with you both before somebody discovers us." Natalie shooed the men away and pulled Penelope alongside the house next to the hedges. "We'll wait over here until Charles brings the carriage around." From their vantage point, they could watch the front entrance without being observed. "I cannot believe you punched him, Penelope!" And then she laughed. "I imagine he deserved it. You ought to see the two of you! If

I didn't know both of you better, I'd assume it was a lover's spat."

"Of course not!"

But Natalie had far more fascinating news! "You are increasing? Oh, I am so happy for you! I was with the Duchess of Cortland when she was delivered of the little marquess. It was the most incredible thing I've ever seen in my life."

The Duchess of Cortland was Lord Hawthorne's first cousin. And Natalie had been engaged to the duke last year before marrying the earl. Surprisingly, they all remained in good standing with each other. Penelope knew they'd celebrated the holidays together even, at the duke's estate.

Natalie blushed and nodded. "We travelled down a few weeks ago. Before coming up to London. He is a darling!"

Unable to contain asking after Natalie's condition, wishing she could openly discuss her own physical maladies, Penelope blurted out, "Is the babe showing yet? Is it difficult to hide?"

Natalie giggled into her glove. "Not yet, it's only been about three months. Soon though, I can hardly wait."

Penelope froze inside. She wasn't yet eleven weeks along, and she already had a definitive bulge. "Does the babe make you feel ill?"

"A little swoony sometimes in the morning, and I'm feeling more tired than usual. But other than that, I'm fine. Garrett worries though. He's constantly hovering around me these days. I've had to practically force him out the door to go to his clubs while we're here." She smiled in confidence. "I love the attention, though, to be truthful. I love knowing he's as excited about it as I am."

A pang shot through Penelope. What had she done?

"Lilly told me you were not going to come to London this year. I am so glad you have come after all, and you look beautiful! I know you've done your hair differently, but you look absolutely stunning. The clothes, the jewelry... Have you decided to join the husband hunters after all?"

Penelope knew Natalie was teasing. Wasn't she? And then she remembered what Hugh had told her about everyone knowing of her former feelings for Natalie's brother. Did that mean Natalie had known as well? Oh, how embarrassing! She must think Penelope had come to chase after Rome?

But Penelope *had* come to London in search of a husband. Well, one man in particular.

Then Natalie confirmed her fears. "Rome remains unattached, you know."

Penelope moaned. "I'm not here to land Rome for a husband. Please believe me, Natalie. I merely grew weary of my old look, and Bath grows tiresome rather quickly."

The youthful countess looked disappointed but perked up again quickly. "Oh, well. I can hope, can I not? I must admit to you that I was not unhappy to see things fall apart between him and that poor girl. It was plain to me that she was being pressured into the match by her family. Poor Rome was so besotted that he didn't notice. He's been rather morose since then. When I saw the two of you dancing together, I rather hoped that..."

"I'm sorry to dash your hopes, but there is nothing there." She decided to explain further, "Perhaps in the past I held a bit of tenderness for the viscount, but that is where it remains, in the past."

Natalie sighed loudly. "Oh."

The two ladies waited quietly, each left to their own thoughts for a few minutes until the earl exited the front of the house and waved them over. The sound of hooves on pavement heralded the carriage approaching. The ladies dashed across the lawn and were quickly assisted into the privacy of the coach.

"You spoke with my mother?" Penelope asked the earl.

He nodded. "She wasn't thrilled that you were leaving, of course. Said you were committed to dance with half of the eligible gentlemen in attendance." And then he flashed a grin. Lord Hawthorne used to be a brooding mysterious rake. The change marriage had brought about in him was surprising.

Penelope glanced down at the dance card tied to her wrist with a thin silk ribbon. The only dance she was wishing for was the very last one. It had been a waltz, and she was to have partnered Hugh.

*H*UGH'S OWN TOWNHOUSE was not far from the Helmers' so he had walked over earlier. Oh, yes, and he'd then escorted Mrs. Merriman and her niece.

Striding along the sidewalk, he contemplated that it was probably for the best that he let down Mrs. Merriman and Miss Radcliffe now, rather than later. They would both be disappointed when he did not appear to partner Louisa for their second dance. More than disappointed... but he'd not feel overly guilt-ridden.

Their expectations had risen too high, too quickly. Admittedly, he'd given them both cause. He'd taken the young lady out for a drive through the park on more than one occasion within the last two weeks and singled her out at other balls and a few garden parties. But tonight, even before seeing Penelope, he'd begun feeling stifled by her possessiveness.

The lady had become bold, and perhaps she was entitled to be, what with such an enormous dowry. It would have come in handy, of course, but Hugh had never been a man motivated by the pursuit of great wealth. His weaknesses had always been women and spirits. He'd laugh at the thought, but as of late, he'd begun to recognize an unseemly pattern in his life.

And tonight... Hell, he'd nearly fallen victim to a very unexpected siren. Sober, no less.

Penelope Crone.

What in the world had come over him?

He dabbed at the tip of his nose and winced. He supposed it had *not* been an amusing joke to play on a lady when he'd only moments before had his mouth upon her breast.

At the thought of her plump, creamy exposed bosom, he had to mentally distract himself so as to not reawaken certain parts of his anatomy.

What baffled him the most was that he'd actually been on the cusp of proposing.

Proposing!

To Penelope Crone!

Ever since he'd left Cortland's estate, it was as though a spell had been cast upon him. Because, yes, it was when he'd first left for Land's End that those visions and fantasies began plaguing his quieter moments.

Perhaps something had been triggered in his mind upon seeing Cortland ecstatic beyond belief with his duchess and son. And Penelope had been the only other single lady in residence at the time.

Yes, that must be it. The sense of guilt that had been planted after his father's death for not setting up his nursery and assuring the title had finally blossomed.

And then Penelope kept showing up.

Yes, that was it.

He had rather enjoyed kissing her senseless. By God, he'd never expected to see the day when Penelope Crone couldn't form a rational sentence.

The question was, did he want to take the necessary steps in order to take Penelope's passion to its culmination?

He swallowed hard. He'd damn near made the commitment already.

What would her answer have been? As long as he'd known her, she'd adamantly professed her distaste of a society marriage.

Excepting, of course, to the Viscount Darlington. Of whom he'd not dissembled with her regarding the fact that all and sunder had been aware of it.

Was she really no longer interested in Rome Spencer? Darlington was heir to an earldom, the title of viscount being a mere courtesy one. He was highly respectable and, Hugh supposed, passably handsome.

Hugh had not appreciated the way Darlington held her on the dance floor. It wasn't that the man had done anything inappropriate, it was more the way he'd stared at her. The viscount had looked as though he was there to stake a claim.

Was Hugh willing to claim her first?

CHAPTER TWELVE

*F*OUR DAYS PASSED as Hugh contemplated the question of Penelope Crone.

When he finally did concede in his mind that he wanted to see her, to speak with her, he convinced himself that it was only so he could assure himself that her cut had not turned putrid.

The days that had passed had not been pleasant ones. His honor had required that he fulfill his commitment to escort Mrs. Merriman and Miss Radcliffe to a garden party, and then on another day walking in the park.

He'd had to step very carefully, as, on any number of occasions during these outings, he easily could have become ensnared in further commitments, and much lengthier ones as well.

His interest in Louisa Radcliffe had waned quickly. Every conversation with her was the same. They covered the weather, the latest fashions, and who attended what party when—and in that order. It was as though she followed a script. She only veered from it once when she chastised him for failing to partner her as promised at the Helmers' ball.

Hugh did not rise to the bait.

And although he'd caught her staring a few times, she'd not asked how he'd acquired the spectacular bruises around his eyes.

With great relief, he wished them both well after escorting them safely to their rented townhouse. Mrs. Merriman and Louisa had both laid out traps that he could have easily fallen into, but they did not know him very well at all. Hugh had spent much of the last decade dodging these snares. He was no novice. How did they think he'd managed to remain unwed for as long as he had? He was considered, he admitted most humbly to himself, something of a catch. The only reason they'd extracted any commitments from him at all was because he had decided it just might be time...

Upon meeting Miss Radcliffe for the first time, he'd not been uninterested. The lady had seemed soothing, of a sweet temperament and even attractive sexually. He'd thought he merely needed to spend some time in her company. If he did that, he thought, perhaps he could fall in love with her.

Seeing Cortland and Lilly with their newborn infant son had, in fact, made his own life feel rather empty.

Unfortunately, or fortunately, depending on how he chose to look at it, Miss Louisa Redcliffe was not the person he needed to fill it.

But could any woman?

Could Penelope Crone?

He'd known her for over a decade. Well, he'd thought he'd known her. On a few occasions, he'd even found her attractive, he recalled, almost surprised at the admission. But she had never flirted with him. He'd never seen her flirt with anyone, even Darlington. He didn't think she *knew how* to flirt. Penelope scoffed at coquettish behavior. And she'd always had such high standards for conversation.

She'd required it be intelligent.

Which the gentlemen did find attractive, when they wished to understand a particular bill more coherently, or hear predictions for the cost of corn, barley, or some other commodity. She was respected for having a keen mind.

Could any of these characteristics be an attractive trait

in a wife? As he entered his townhouse and handed his top hat over to the butler, Hugh knew the answer to that question.

He could discuss fashion, gossip, and parties with his wife for the rest of his life, or he could discuss virtually anything else under the sun.

There *was* something different about her. Aside from the mystery of her fainting spells and her showing up, uninvited and unannounced, at Augusta Heights, a subtle femininity had blossomed in her.

It was as though she'd finally admitted to herself that she was a woman.

And she looked at *him* differently now.

By Jove, that was it! She looked at him as though they shared an intimate secret. How did she learn such a thing? Was she hoping to land him for a husband? Was she, in fact, conniving to do so?

And even more importantly, was he willing to be landed?

He'd almost proposed marriage to her last night. He'd been very, very close.

Hugh dabbed at his nose and winced. *Note to self: do not make jokes to Penelope the next time you propose to her.* Because he would. Not quite yet, but he would. It just felt right. And somehow, a voice in his head whispered, it might be the best decision of his life.

ROSE FINISHED TYING the lace at the bottom of Penelope's stays and sighed. "I cannot believe he has failed to call upon you. Are you certain he remains in Town?"

"Lady Hawthorne said he was at the garden party she

attended yesterday." With a sideways glance, she added, "With Miss Radcliffe and her aunt. You don't think he could seriously be courting her?"

"I didn't—before. His absence, however, concerns me and it ought to concern you as well. If he is not in attendance tonight, you are going to have to seek him out intentionally."

Penelope had told Rose everything—the pertinent details, anyhow. She'd revealed that Danbury had kissed her. She had not mentioned how many times, nor the… other things he'd done. Knowing Rose, however, Penelope assumed her maid would fill in the blanks.

Penelope turned back toward the looking glass and tried not to feel panic.

She was certain he'd been about to offer for her. She should not have allowed her temper to take over so quickly. She ought to have known Hugh thought himself clever, but really, his thoughtless joke could not have been more poorly timed.

Had she not landed him a facer, would he have proposed?

Penelope winced. Natalie had also described the spectacular blue and purple bruises around Hugh's eyes.

She'd definitely overreacted.

She should have told him about the baby. She should have told him as soon as she'd arrived at Augusta Heights. Should haves… Too many of those lately. How many mistakes was she going to make where Hugh was concerned?

He would be at the ball tonight. It was to be hosted by Lady Hawthorne and Rome's parents, the Earl and Countess of Ravensdale. It would be a crush. Nobody who was anybody missed the Spencers' ball.

Penelope raised her arms as Rose assisted her into yet

another new ball gown. This one was made up of a deep red silk. A gold broach where her bodice dipped, long white gloves, and a matching velvet cape in rich crimson completed the ensemble. Rose styled her hair similarly to how she had a few nights ago. But it looked even better this time. Rose said she was *training* Penelope's hair.

"You must tell him tonight, Penelope. No more delays. If you don't receive an offer soon, your situation will become dire."

"Don't be so melodramatic, Rose." But there was truth in Rose's words. "Stop needling me. I'll tell him."

"Well, you haven't told him before. What else am I to think? What will become of me if you are a fallen woman? Would I then be consigned to a life in the country, shunned amongst my fellow ladies' maids and ousted from society along with you?"

"He very nearly came up to scratch. If only I hadn't…"

"And another thing, no matter what the man says, do not, I repeat, do not injure him in any way. Sissy, Lady Hawthorne's maid, says that one of Danbury's manservants told her that the earl's valet told him that Danbury says this sort of thing was why he avoided marriage. He says ladies are a dangerous breed."

"What is your purpose in telling me all of this?"

"Well, what if you'd knocked out one of his teeth? Then you would have a gap-toothed husband! Who knows what you might do next? A well-placed kick could cause serious complications indeed…"

"I won't kick him." But upon reflecting on the turbulent emotion that had swept through her when he'd asked her to be his estate manager, Penelope was not so certain. If he tried jesting with her like that again… She shook her head.

Hopefully he would refrain from any more ridiculously

ill-timed jokes.

She touched her abdomen. Dear God, she had to tell him soon.

THE SPENCERS' BALLROOM was considered to be second only to the regent's. It boasted intricately detailed artwork, an abundance of glass along an entire wall of terrace doors, and perhaps one of the most jewel-ridden chandeliers ever made. The parquet floor was shined to a high gloss, and hundreds of candles cast a golden glow upon the dancers and other inhabitants.

As had occurred at the previous ball, Penelope's card filled quickly once again. A little too quickly. Where was Hugh? She needed to save time to have their little... discussion.

Locating a pencil on a table nearby, Penelope scratched his name on the supper dance and a waltz later in the evening. She was going to have to pounce upon him as soon as he arrived to ensure he kept himself available for her dances.

Where was he?

As one set passed, and then another, and then more than she could count, Penelope realized the supper dance fast approached. Missing out on a dance didn't bother her. It was the thought that Hugh may not be going to make an appearance.

Penelope reached down to massage her ankles. She'd danced more this week than she had in her entire life. At least if Hugh didn't show up she could sit this next dance out.

"Would it be foolish to hope that you've saved a dance

or two for me this evening?"

He had come. She forced herself to refrain from scolding him for his absence over the last four days and smiled back at him. "Not foolish." But she had called him foolish just a few days ago. Right before...

She held out her wrist so that he could examine her card. "See for yourself!" And then he peered at it more closely and chuckled. When he looked back up, he winked.

"So, you are not angry with me?" The blues and purples around his eyes were beginning to fade to an ugly brown.

"I deserved it Pen. Are *you* angry with *me*?" That lock of hair had slipped out of his que and he appeared less jovial than usual.

She'd known him for so long. Why had she not ever noticed how his eyes crinkled when he smiled? Why had she not noticed that although he dressed conservatively, it enhanced the fitness of his physique and the strength of his legs?

She remembered how hard his thighs were, how solid his chest felt.

"No," she said around the lump that had suddenly formed in her throat. She cleared it. "I'm not angry with you."

He still held her hand. Before she realized what he was doing, he had drawn the long silk glove down her wrist and over her fingertips. With his index finger, he touched the outline of the cut, which was healing up nicely. There was one small puncture wound where his tooth caught her skin.

He looked somewhat satisfied. "It appears to be fine but continue to apply a salve."

Penelope snatched her glove back and proceeded to slide it back onto her hand and arm. What would people think? He was practically undressing her in the middle of an overflowing ballroom!

"It's fine." Tilting her head to get a better angle at his nose, she asked, "What of you? Does it still hurt."

Hugh touched the bridge of his nose hesitantly. That teasing glint appeared. "Not broken after all. Probably a good thing. A crooked nose would have ruined my perfect profile. But really, I deserved it. I'll do well to remember the pain whenever I think of saying something stupid, I'll remember that it may not be wise to make jokes—jokes where ladies are concerned anyhow."

Penelope sat up straight. She wasn't used to being teased. He *was* teasing her, wasn't he? "Very well." She sounded far too prim and proper. Flirting had not been something she'd ever set out to master.

So instead of coming up with a clever response, she sounded as though she were angry with him after all. "I'm glad I can help you out with that."

He was apparently not to be baited by the edge in her voice. He took her other hand and assisted her to her feet. "The orchestra is warming up again. Which will it be? A dull country dance? Or will you walk with me again outside? I hear Lady Ravensdale's prizewinning roses have begun blossoming this week."

It was exactly what she wanted, and yet, in that instance, all of her good intentions fled. She could tell him later. This was not the only set she'd reserved for him, after all. "A dull country dance." She smiled at his scowl. Taking his arm, she allowed him to lead her out to the floor. She knew that Danbury did not *really* mind dancing.

In fact, she did not either, when one had a pleasant partner—one who knew where he could appropriately put his hands, one who did not smell of onions, perspiration, and garlic.

This dance was a lively one. They lined up near the Earl

and Countess of Hawthorne and her longtime friend Betsy and her husband. She could never remember Betsy's husband's name. He was a rather nondescript barrister. Or had been. Penelope believed they were now living off of Betsy's inheritance. A distant aunt had recently passed and left Betsy an enormous portion. And what was Betsy's now belonged to her husband.

Who currently handed her back into the hands of Danbury. "You do not look faint," he said before twirling her off to his side. When she returned, he added, "You are well?"

"I am," she said quickly before being relinquished to take Lord Hawthorne's outstretched hand.

"No debates tonight?" Lady Natalie's husband teased her. "No blood or dismemberments yet?"

Penelope used her fan to slap him playfully on the arm. Who would have thought the earl could be so good natured? She laughed up at him before being passed back to Hugh.

A warm light glowed in his eyes. Or was it just the candlelight? She hadn't expected to enjoy this particular dance, but somehow she found herself smiling more than usual.

And then the dance ended and the doors to the supper room were thrown open wide.

Penelope found a seat with Natalie and Betsy while the gentlemen disappeared to procure their plates from the large buffet.

"You are not sitting at the hosts' table, my lady?" Betsy did not know Natalie as well as Penelope did.

"I am not the hostess. My mother is." She smiled pleasantly. There was a slight flush on her cheeks and forehead. It reminded Penelope of Natalie's condition, which had still not been made public.

And that reminded Penelope of her own condition.

It was one of the first evenings in a long time that she'd not experienced any dizziness or stomach upset. Oh, wouldn't it be wonderful if the sickness had come to an end?

"Speaking of being a hostess," Penelope remembered. "How is Maple Hall coming along?"

"It will be two years before we can consider living there. We're splitting our time between London Hills and the dower house at Maple Hall. Garrett wants me to settle down this summer, though, what with—" She placed her hand over her mouth and changed the subject quickly. "Will Monfort and your cousin be coming to London at all this season?"

"Not this year." Penelope had just received a letter from Abigail the day before. Newly married last fall, the duke and duchess were expecting their own little miracle in early June.

There must be something catching in England.

"They've decided to remain at Brooke's Abby." She leaned forward and whispered in Natalie's ear. When she sat back, she spoke out loud again. "Monfort is very protective of the duchess."

Natalie smiled smugly. She was convinced that it was she who had brought the duke and his new duchess together. "As he well should be."

"As Hawthorne is of you." Penelope added. She wanted to say something of Betsy's husband but his name persisted to elude her.

Betsy cleared her throat and then took the pause in conversation as an opportunity to regale the table with her eldest son's recent exploits. Penelope's mind wandered. Was she carrying a little boy? One with black hair and warm eyes? Or was it a girl, like her? She'd be happy with either, so long as the baby was healthy. Her baby. And Danbury's. Wonder of wonders.

Out of nowhere, a plate appeared in front of her and on it were all of her favorite foods. But how?

"I've known you since before the war, Pen. Of course, I know your tastes." It was as though Hugh had read her mind. As he sat down, her awareness of him drowned out whatever Betsy was saying.

Penelope ate with her left hand, and he ate with his right. The second time they bumped arms, he leaned near her. "Next time, I'll remember to sit on your other side." Penelope went to hand her fork into her right hand, but he stopped her. "You don't have to do that." He angled his chair and slid it backward somewhat. The next time they both raised their arms, his was slightly behind hers and they did not collide.

He adjusted his needs to mine.

The remainder of the conversation covered the latest on dits as well as upcoming affairs. A trip to Vauxhall was in the planning for the coming week and Penelope could tell that Betsy had figured out Natalie's delicate condition. The woman was mother to five strapping boys, after all.

On an alarming thought, she wondered if Betsy would see that she was increasing as well.

"We won't be staying for the entire season," Hawthorne said before giving his wife a loving look.

"But we'll be able to attend your party, Betsy," Natalie continued for her husband. "I haven't been to Vauxhall in ages!"

Betsy's husband was speaking to Hugh. "I've reserved a box not far from the large stage. Betsy would have nothing less."

Hugh glanced over at Penelope, "What do you think, Miss Crone? Will you allow me to escort you to Vauxhall next week?"

At Natalie's surprised glance, Penelope felt herself blushing. She never blushed! She was a cool-headed, fair-skinned redhead. She stabbed her fork into a tender shoot of corn. "You may," she said into her plate.

She realized that for the first time in her life, she was a part of a couple. It felt that way anyhow. Perhaps the others simply assumed that Hugh was being polite to ask to escort her. She'd always been included in their activities before, only then it had been as the token spinster, as one of the chaperones practically.

Betsy clasped her hands in front of her enthusiastically. "Oh, this will be so fun! Your mother's ball is a resounding success, of course, my lady," she said to Natalie, "But it will be so fun to take some activity outside."

The others agreed and as Penelope looked around at their faces, she realized that Danbury watched her curiously. A shiver ran up her spine.

She wished she'd opted to stroll outside with him earlier, after all. The large room that had been opened up for dining was clearing out quickly. Sounds of the orchestra tuning their instruments floated in through the giant open doors. She had promised the next set to some Rome. She was not interested in dancing anymore tonight. An overwhelming tiredness swept over her.

Oh, yes, and there was that queasy feeling again, thank you very much. She held a strawberry up to her nose and inhaled deeply.

Natalie smiled impishly over at her. "Mother cultivates them herself. She's managed to grow some amazingly sweet blackberries as well!"

Natalie then rose to her feet, followed by Betsy. After realizing the gentlemen were waiting upon her, Penelope rose as well, careful to keep hold of the tall back of her chair. She'd learned that when this feeling overcame her, she needed to move slowly. Sudden moves were not a good idea. It would pass. *Please let it pass.*

Placing her hand on his sleeve, Hugh steered her around a few tables and toward the ballroom. Once there, however, he kept right on walking with her, along the wall and outside onto the terrace.

Once he located a somewhat private alcove with an iron bench, he pulled her down to sit and looked into her eyes with the utmost of concern. "Are you dying, Penelope?"

CHAPTER THIRTEEN

$\mathcal{I}$T WAS THE only logical conclusion Hugh could come to.

The fainting, the paleness of her complexion, and all of the other changes that had come over her. She must be terrified of leaving this earth without experiencing the act of love and perhaps marriage. She must be looking at all of the experiences she'd missed out upon during her short adult life and decided to try to accomplish a few of them now.

"I know you've never set your cap for a husband. You've never included yourself in many of the feminine pursuits other ladies do. And you are afraid you'll miss out." He hoped he was wrong, but he could not think of anything else that would cause Penelope Crone to become so frail and delicate.

Except she did not look as though she were wasting away tonight.

"Oh, no, no, no! Hugh! Of course, I'm not dying. I'm healthy as a horse! Always have been." She smiled at him brightly but then bit her lip.

"Then tell me what it is." He was relieved to hear such conviction in her voice regarding her good health. Thank God she was not truly dying. As soon as the thought had entered his mind, he'd felt a darkness settle upon him.

But there *was* something. *I'm not an idiot.*

Her smile held for a few more seconds before fading away completely. "I am not ill, Hugh." She looked down at her hands and plucked at her gloves abstractly. "Something happened when we were at Summer's Park. Something happened after the baby was born."

Something had changed inside of him as well. Was it possible Penelope experienced similar feelings? "Seeing Cortland and his duchess with their newborn son changed something inside of me, too."

She glanced up in surprise. "It changed something inside of you as well? What did it change? Are you saying that it made you question your decision to remain a bachelor? I thought you said you were simply waiting for the right lady?"

And then he saw it in her eyes. A dawning recognition of what he'd been feeling. Hugh leaned forward and placed a chaste kiss on her lips. Such a delightful mix of intelligence and naïveté would need to be handled carefully.

And passion. Yes, Penelope had passion.

It rose to the surface when he deepened their kiss.

But this was not the right place for such activity, and he was frustrated from being interrupted. He pulled away and simply looked in her eyes.

"Since the day my father passed all those years ago, I've felt an intense pressure from all those around me to marry and secure the title." Penelope went to speak, but he placed a finger on her lips. "I've never felt any pressure from you. I'm speaking of my family, my father's colleagues, and eventually, my own friends and acquaintances to some extent or another." He smiled ruefully. "But never from you. In fact, one of the things I've always appreciated about you was your absolute honesty regarding your convictions and the way you've stood up to everybody in order to follow them."

"But I've changed—"

"—your mind. I know. I see things differently now as well. I see you differently, Penelope. It is as though there was a paradigm shift at Cortland's last February."

"And how *do* you see me now, Hugh?" Penelope bit her lip anxiously as she looked up at him.

This was the tricky part. Hugh had not reached the ancient age of thirty without knowing a trap question when he saw it. He would have to wade very carefully here. All the while remembering who he was talking to.

"I see you as an independent woman who has perhaps realized that she might one day like to become a mother."

Her jaw dropped but he went right on speaking.

"I see you as a lady of refinement and intelligence. A woman who is trustworthy and of an even temperament—most of the time."

"I thought you said you were waiting for the right woman," she reminded him.

"That's the devil of it, Penelope. It's very possible that that woman only exists in my imagination." Hugh tiptoed through this minefield. "And now that I've decided to marry, I've changed the criteria for what I'm wanting in a wife. You, Penelope, have caused me to realize what I really need.

"Augusta Heights was a mess when I got up there. In time, I'm certain, I could have brought it around to some of its former glory, but you accomplished significant improvements in the matter of just a few weeks. I've already received a few reports from the new steward that show profits in the future. And one of the neighbors sent me a letter thanking me for the wonderful changes I've made. He is ever so grateful that I've provided employment for so many." It was rather liberating to give her credit where credit was due.

"It was nothing." She shrugged.

Hugh took both of her hands in his. "But it wasn't nothing, Penelope. I'm a reasonably intelligent person but the difference between you and I, is that you are a doer.

You are gifted with a special talent for making things happen."

"I will not become your estate manager," she said through gritted teeth.

Hugh raised one arm and ducked behind it. "Of course not! Aren't you listening to me, Pen? I want you to be my wife!"

She looked at him and scowled. "So that I can manage your business affairs for you?"

"*With*, me, Pen. *With me*." Oh, hell, he was bungling this in a grand way. Hugh dropped to one knee in front of her, still holding her hands and looked up as earnestly as he possibly could.

"Penelope Crone, will you make me the happiest of men and consent to become my wife?"

But she looked disappointed. Surely, she'd not wanted him to spout romantic nonsense?

"Umm... Yes?"

Hugh tilted his head questioningly. "Not exactly the enthusiastic answer I'd hoped for."

She gave him a pained smile. "Not exactly what I expected either."

Hugh pushed off the ground and sat beside her again. "I've been lucky all these years, Penelope. Escorting Miss Radcliffe around the last few weeks has convinced me that one of these days my luck will run out. One of these days, if I continue as I have, I'm going to find myself saddled with one of those empty-headed debutantes and her mama. Forever! I can't do that, Pen. I mean, I actually *like* you." Oh, that painted it up spectacularly. Hugh ran his index finger along the length of her arm from shoulder to wrist. He watched as she shivered. "And now I discover that we have *this,* as well."

"I said I would, Hugh. I will, that is, marry you." She

sounded even less enthusiastic than she had before. "Thank you."

What was wrong with her?

"You won't regret this." He leaned in and kissed her again. But she seemed to have lost interest.

"When?" she asked.

"When?"

"When shall we marry? Do you wish to announce it this evening?"

Of course, she is a doer.

"Best to speak with your father first. I'll have a talk with him and after that, we can set a date. Is that acceptable to you?" Somehow, this wasn't playing out the way he'd imagined.

Speaking with her father, he knew, was a mere formality. She'd been making her own decisions for nearly a decade: her impromptu visit to Augusta Heights had been indicative of that. Most likely, her father would be ecstatic to relinquish any remaining responsibility he felt toward her.

She nodded.

"But you look as though your dog just died!" He through his hands into the air. She was exasperating. Did he really wish a betrothal with this woman? "If you don't wish to marry me, tell me now and we can forget this conversation ever happened."

"Oh, no, no! Hugh, of course, I wish to marry you. It's just that I'm a little overwhelmed, I guess. So much is changing so quickly." It was she who took his hand this time. "Of course, I wish to marry you." She leaned in and gave him a dry kiss on the lips.

As she went to move away, Hugh stopped her. Pulling her up against him, he found her mouth again with his own and coaxed the seam of her lips open.

"This matters as well, Penelope," he growled when he felt one of her hands reach up to his neck. After exploring the soft flesh behind her lips, and the smooth edges of her teeth, he moved to the corner of her mouth, and then along the graceful line of her neck.

Wisps of golden red hair tickled his nose and eyes. She had the most incredible skin, so pale and soft. Without realizing he'd even done so, one of his hands had found her left breast. Remembering how timid she'd been the night before, he drew circles around it gently. Nice, plump, perfect flesh hid beneath the material of her bodice.

Oh, yes, this mattered a great deal.

"The orchestra is playing again," she murmured. "I promised this dance to someone else."

"Who?" Hugh did not really care. She'd just promised her person to him.

"Um, I think it was…" She was trying to glance at the dance card tied to her wrist.

"Tsk, tsk, tsk, no cheating, Penelope," His mouth now trailed down her shoulder, along bared skin and then lower, along the silk of her glove. When he reached the dance card, he pulled at one string with his teeth and it dropped off her wrist and onto the ground.

"But he will be looking for me. What will he think?"

"If he saw you walk outside with me, he will know exactly what to think." Hugh grinned before sitting back and breaking their embrace. He supposed he ought to allow her to return. As long as he'd known her, Penelope had always avoided scandal. She'd been a very good girl up until now. He ought not to corrupt her completely.

Yet.

Penelope had retrieved the dance card and was attempting to tie it back around her wrist. "I'm to partner…" She squinted as she read the card. "Er… Darlington."

Rome Spencer.

Hugh confirmed as much as he tied the card for her. "Just so he knows…"

"Just so he knows what?"

"That you are no longer his for the taking." If Hugh had to have a discussion with the man himself, he would do so. He knew Darlington had been thrown over last winter. Hugh had watched as the man danced with Penelope before.

Ah, well, Darlington was too late.

CHAPTER FOURTEEN

PENELOPE THOUGHT FOR a moment that Rose was going to burst into tears when she informed her of the engagement.

"Oh, Pen, thank God! I've been so very anxious for us, for *you*!" She gave Penelope a firm hug and squeeze and then jumped up onto Penelope's bed and sat cross-legged. "Was he angry when you told him? Oh, I wish I could have been a fly on the wall, watching. Did he remember bedding you? Tell me everything!"

Penelope would have been happy to return to her room without having to suffer an inquisition from Rose. If she had any other maid, she could have done so.

"He is going to visit Father tomorrow before making any announcements." Penelope stepped out of her slippers and then turned her back on Rose. "Help me out of this. I want nothing more than to put on my nightdress and fall into bed."

Rose crawled off the bed and commenced assisting Penelope out of her dress. "You don't sound very happy for a newly engaged lady. Did you discuss the necessity for haste? Will he obtain a special license, then?"

"We'll discuss that tomorrow. We haven't made any plans yet."

"Well, you've made a baby, my friend, so Danbury had better get a move on." Rose could be intolerable!

Penelope snatched the night dress from her maid. Pulling the garment over her head, she mumbled into the fabric, "He doesn't know, Rose, He doesn't know about the baby yet."

Silence.

Penelope poked her head through the top of the night dress and watched for Rose's reaction.

Nothing.

"I tried," she said. "But it's very difficult to interrupt a person who is saying what you want to hear with something you don't really wish to say!" And that was the absolute truth.

"So, he proposed without even knowing about... all of it?"

"He wishes to marry me for my intelligence and because he likes me. He believes that if he doesn't wed me, or I imagine somebody *like* me, then he will be trapped into marriage to someone he doesn't even like by a determined mama." Which was precisely how she'd rationalized her actions a few months ago. She would not tell Rose about the physical aspect of his needs.

Although Hugh was right. That aspect mattered, indeed.

"Well," Rose huffed. She then disappeared into the dressing room with Penelope's gown for a few moments without saying another word. When she reappeared, Penelope had already climbed into the large bed that had been hers since childhood.

"Had he been drinking?" Rose finally asked.

Penelope shook her head. "No, I don't think so." She hadn't tasted any spirits on his breath. "He merely said the timing was right for him now. And so, I said yes. And then we—"

Rose's eyes narrowed. "Have you considered how he is going to feel when he discovers the truth? Will he believe you even? What if he thinks you're bringing someone else's child into this marriage?"

Penelope waved her hand, as though to dismiss such a concern. "He will believe me." Except, well, she hadn't really considered this new scenario through properly. Would he?

"You've got to tell him."

"What if he changes his mind about wanting to marry me then? What if he *doesn't* believe he is the father of my baby?"

"He'll hate you for the rest of your lives, Penelope. Do you want that?"

"Of course, I don't want for him to hate me! I'm marrying him, aren't I?"

But it was a legitimate concern. Hugh had fought against the notion of marriage for so very long, if he discovered that she had plotted to trap him from the very beginning, well... That was not a very happy thought at all.

Because she *had* plotted!

He was happy enough now, thinking this was all his idea, but how would he feel when he learned the truth?

Would he cry off if she told him before the wedding?

*T*HE NEXT MORNING, Penelope felt even sicker than normal. It must be the stress of all of this hullabaloo. She required two cups of tea and several small bites of dry toast before she felt well enough to climb out of bed. Rose dressed her slowly but carefully. They assumed Danbury would be making his visit sometime that afternoon.

He did not.

Nor did he come the next day or the next.

Where was he?

It was not until four days later that she realized she

wasn't out of the woods yet.

Anxious to have a word with the blighter, Penelope had been seeking him out at as many events and parties as she could attend. This had been Rose's idea, but Penelope couldn't come up with anything better. They'd both decided that Penelope would send him a missive if she could not locate him within one week. And if he did not answer that, she would be forced to present herself at his townhouse. She had no choice in the matter.

That afternoon, Penelope and her mother attended a lavish garden party hosted by Mr. and Mrs. Shufflebottom. The rain that had appeared all week had lifted, and it was one of those perfect spring days. But where was Hugh?

After greeting several clusters of guests alongside her mother, Penelope began resigning herself to the fact that he had not attended today either. This was not good.

Had he really changed his mind about marrying her so easily? Not good at all.

"Lady Sheffield says that your friend, the Countess of Hawthorne, is considering a house party, dear." Her mother touched her hand, knowing her daughter well enough to realized that Penelope was woolgathering. "Apparently, the couple owns a magnificent estate just outside of town. Has she mentioned anything to you about it?"

She had, but Penelope had not considered attending. Feeling her physical situation rather uncomfortably, she didn't wish to be in close confines with any more people than was absolutely necessary. Not for the first time, she was grateful that her mother was oblivious to most of what went on in her daughter's head. Good God, though, there would be quite the uproar if her parents discovered what she'd done.

Penelope ignored her mother's question and addressed

Lady Sheffield, who was Lilly, the Duchess of Cortland's, aunt.

"Have you seen the baby yet, my lady?" Penelope was happy to change the subject.

Lady Sheffield was a sturdy elderly *grande dame* and something of an icon within the *ton*. Her eyes crinkled up happily. "I managed to get down there before coming over for the season. He is simply adorable! And Lilly told me what a great help you were to her. Thank you, my dear, for being there when my niece needed you."

"Of course!" The miraculous event had not only changed the Duke and Duchess of Cortland's lives, but her own as well. And Danbury's. She could not leave him out.

Where is he?

"And Lilly said Viscount Danbury kept company with Cortland. Poor boy, I was so sad to hear about his mother's illness."

Poor boy, my a—wait! "Lady Danbury is ill?"

"She's consumptive. Her daughter sent word early this week. From my understanding, Danbury is trying to get to Land's End before it's too late."

Why had nobody informed her of this? Why had Hugh not sent word?

"Oh, that reminds me." Her mother tapped Penelope on the arm with her bamboo fan. "A letter came for you with Danbury's seal. I forgot to give it to you."

"When?" *Oh, Mother, how could you?*

Now she used the fan to tap against her own chin. "Hmmm, a few days ago. Maybe three. Most likely some political matter he wants your opinion on, if I know you properly, child."

When the dizziness and dark edges began appearing, Penelope used all the self-discipline she could muster to ward them off. She would *not faint*. She was not going to have a fit of the vapors at the Shufflebottoms' garden party.

"Most likely, Mother," she answered instead. She needed to see that letter!

Glancing around at the mingling guests, she mentally calculated how soon she could talk her mother into making their farewells. People were still arriving.

She would have to wait at least an hour.

A shadow heralded another arrival, and turning, Penelope curtsied to Rome Spencer, "My lord," she said politely while her mother cooed over the viscount.

The baroness was jubilant when he offered to stroll with Penelope in the sunshine. In a haze of stunned disbelief and panic, Penelope allowed him to take her arm and lead her away from the small groups of guests. There was nothing she could do in this moment, anyhow. She needed to read the damn letter and find out when Hugh planned upon returning.

He most likely did not know when.

She could not be angry with him. He'd doted on his mother for as long as she'd known him. Yes, he'd joked plenty about her incessant matchmaking but always with benevolence.

And the viscountess had always been friendly and warm to Penelope. To think of the woman coughing up blood at death's door was sobering, indeed. Without realizing it, she'd exhaled a rather loud sigh.

"You seem melancholy, Pen," Rome said. She was used to her male friends in the *ton* addressing her informally. She rather preferred it. This Miss Crone business felt rather awkward.

"I just heard about Danbury's mother. I had no idea she was ill." She admitted her sadness without editing her thoughts.

Rome reached up and patted her hand. "The end of an era, it would seem."

"So, you know the extent of it? There is no hope at all?"

Rome grimaced. "Not from my understanding. Word at the club is that Danbury's sister said she might pass any time. I hope, for his sake, he gets there on time. I believe he's finally settled on a wife. He certainly trailed after Miss Radcliffe a great deal. His mother's dying wish, I think would be to see him settled—or to know it was eminent anyhow."

Not that emptyheaded child! Rome was quite, quite wrong on that point.

"What of you? Are you feeling pressure from your family to wed?"

"I have three brothers, one who already can boast of a breeding wife. There is no urgency for me to set up a nursery."

"So, you became engaged because you wanted to." The statement was rather unnerving. She'd known him for years. She'd thought she'd loved him even, but in truth, she hadn't really known anything personal about him.

She'd thought she knew Hugh as well.

She'd thought matters would be so simple. Shame swept through her as the selfishness of her actions seemed glaring in that moment. Hugh deserved to choose his wife the same as she always insisted it was a woman's right to select her own husband—if she wanted one, that was.

Except she'd taken the choice away from him.

"I thought I did," Rome responded, both of them seemingly deep in thought, not really focused on each other at all. "But perhaps it's all turned out for the best. I wouldn't wish to be married to a lady who resented it. I had no idea her parents were pushing her so hard."

"They would, of course, have seen you as a most advantageous connection for the family."

"But not so necessary that they ought to be willing to

sacrifice their daughter's happiness." The two stopped walking and stared across the river. "The whole messy business gave me some sympathy for what Natalie went through last year with the Duke of Cortland. At the time, I thought I would strangle her for jilting him but..."

"She was right to do as she did," Penelope finished for him. Natalie had made more than just herself happy when she'd broken off the betrothal her father had arranged for her with the Duke. She'd left the path clear for Lilly and Cortland. And then she and Lord Hawthorne had fallen in love.

"I suppose, well, yes. She was."

"She was," Penelope insisted.

"That's what I said, is it not?" She'd argued with Rome in the past. He seemed pensive today. "I am considering growing barley."

Ah, he'd learned of the plans she had initiated on Hugh's estate. "You'll need a brew master." Penelope found herself on firm ground for the first time all day.

Dearest Miss Crone,

Forgive the brevity of this message but I must leave for Land's End immediately. Mother had this cough when I was there last, but she assured me it was nothing. I should have not have listened to her dismissal of it... I never should have left her. Margaret says it's consumption. I don't know when I'll return to London. I am not defaulting on our agreement, but it will be a matter of several weeks, at the least, before I am able to discuss the matter with your father. At this time, I am overwhelmed with the condition of my mother's health and cannot address our situation.

Yours sincerely,
Hugh Chesterton, Danbury

Post Script
Please take care! No more fainting!

Hugh had left for Land's End, literally the very edge of the country, four days ago.

And he did not plan upon returning for several weeks.

Penelope did not have several weeks to wait!

Two, perhaps three. Four at the very most! Her midsection had continued to thicken, and time was running out.

Rose read through the letter herself, not quite believing the words Penelope had read out loud. "Such romantic prose as this I've never read. He expresses no affection. He doesn't even beg you to wait for him. What kind of a gentlemen is he?"

Penelope stared out her window onto the street below. It had rained again this evening, the temporary fair weather of the afternoon already a thing of the past. The lack of amorous declarations in the letter were of no concern. She'd waited too long to inform Hugh of her condition, and now, the realities of her situation were suddenly much harsher than they'd seemed before. With Hugh residing not even a mile away, she'd felt she had all the time in the world. But now, in this very moment, the only person in the world who could protect her child from a life of bastardy was riding hell bent for leather across the country. He was riding away from her and away from his child.

And he was riding toward a mysterious and deadly disease.

"I've no choice," she said finally. "We must go to Land's End."

CHAPTER FIFTEEN

THROUGHOUT MOST OF his travel, Hugh found himself hoping this was just another scare, another miscommunication as it had been in February. His mother had not had scarlet fever; she'd meant to write dratted, or darned fever. Wasn't that what she'd said?

But deep within his heart, he knew there would be no mistake. Margaret was not one to exaggerate, not even a little. What frightened him was that she was more likely to gloss things over for him.

Would his mother still be alive when he arrived?

He chastised himself for not paying closer attention to her health when he'd been there. She'd been a little pale. And she'd had that cough.

Damn me! He ought to have insisted upon bringing in a physician. She must have known even then! Consumption didn't sneak up upon a person.

The thought of his mother coughing up blood terrified him.

She'd often harangued him; she'd thrown one debutante after another at him ever since his father's death. But if she'd done so, it had always been for his own good. Losing a husband at such a young age would have given her reason to fear for the security of the Danbury title.

She'd protected him. She'd not allowed the solicitors to appoint him a full-time tutor. His mother had thought it better for him to continue attending Eton, and then even Oxford, with his friends.

She'd known how much it had hurt him to lose his

father.

His happiness had always mattered more to her than her own had.

He'd been riding for five days. He'd wanted to remain on the road longer each day but there were not always replacement mounts, and it would not be fair to push a horse cruelly for his own convenience. And at last he was nearly there.

As he rode through the iron gates guarding Augusta Heights, Hugh signaled to his mount to break into a run. He did not know what he was going to find but the uncertainty was about to drive him mad. When he arrived in front of the house, a familiar footman rushed out greet him and take over the horse's care.

He had to ask, "How is she, William?"

The footman looked grim but before the man could answer, Margaret came rushing out of the large door. "Hugh!" She threw herself into his arms and proceeded to practically strangle him in her emotion.

She was weeping, which caused his heart to plummet to somewhere near the vicinity of his riding boots. "Is she...?" He could not bring himself to speak the word aloud.

"This morning." Margaret's voice was muffled by his jacket. "I so hoped you could arrive before. She kept asking for you, but she was not in her right mind. When she asked if you'd married Louisa Radcliffe, I assured her that you had. I told her she was going to be a grandmother. She was happy in the end, Hugh, even though I knew she was in a great deal of pain."

That was when he noticed the black armband worn by William.

Hugh closed his eyes and did his best to comfort his sister. Margaret hadn't had an easy time of it over the last few years. She'd lost her husband, delivered a stillborn child, and now lost her mother.

Their mother.

Good God, no wonder she'd not arrived in London when the season commenced! She'd been here, caring for their dying mother. And he'd been off gallivanting amongst the *ton*.

When the large front doors opened again, he glanced up, expecting to see her.

But it was not Mother. It was the housekeeper. The truth hit him like a fist to the gut. She was gone.

He swallowed hard and led Margaret inside. Ah, yes, he ought to have noticed. Crepe on the door, the windows covered with dark heavy drapes. He ought to have realized immediately, by Margaret's mode of dress.

She leaned upon him heavily. "Dearest," he said, "have you had any rest?"

"I could not sleep. I was hoping you would arrive to-day." The tears still fell, although she was no longer weeping.

Hugh sat his sister down on the sofa and rang the bell for some tea.

There would be so many details to attend to. He would need to make arrangements for the funeral, send out notices, suffer condolence visits.

He'd been the viscount for his entire adult life, but for the first time, he felt the full mantle of responsibility fall upon him.

The staff had already begun to prepare the house. He must send word to his other residences. He would have them observe the mourning period as well.

"I cannot bear it, Hugh!" His sister was completely done in. She buried her face in her hands as her body shook. "I wasn't ready for this." For the millionth time, he chastised himself for his absence at such a tragic time.

"Where is she?" Hugh had to ask.

Margaret knew exactly what he was asking. "She's laid out in the morning parlor. I figured since it was her favorite room... She just had it redecorated after the holidays." Another low moan.

All he could do was pat her hand and then pour her a cup of tea after the servant brought it in. He coaxed her into a drinking a little and then sent her upstairs to get some sleep. "I'm here, now, Margaret. You needn't worry about anything. I will meet with the vicar." He would also be called upon to meet with solicitors, acquaintances, and all of those neighbors who would feel it was their duty to visit after the funeral.

He wished Penelope were here.

Not that he wished to hand these details off to her, rather so that he could discuss them with her. He'd never planned a funeral. When a death occurred, such details had always fallen upon others.

Margaret was in no frame of mind to cope with all of this. She'd buried her fair share of loved ones already.

He retired to his study and, sitting atop the desk, discovered the most recent of his mother's journals. The sight of his mother's nearly illegible scrawl was bittersweet. Wishing for any sort of connection with her, he touched the paper with the tip of one finger.

On February 23rd, she'd written about an order she'd placed for new drapes. March 3rd, she wrote, *Hugh promised to meet with Miss Radcliffe and Mrs. Merriman in England. This is the one for him, I can feel it!* On March 28th the writing was even more impossible to read. *Blood on my handkerchief this morning. It is as I'd feared.*

April 4th, *I have barely reached my sixtieth year. I had not anticipated such an early demise for myself. If only Hugh had married and found happiness, it would be far easier to say farewell to this world.* April 22nd – *It is becoming difficult to write, even. Perhaps this shall be my goodbye to this world. To my darling children, I love you more than life itself. You have made this world a place of peace and joy for me. Be happy, loves...*

And that was the last entry. That had been two weeks ago.

A knock sounded on the door as the estate's ever pre-sent butler looked in. He, too, looked older and tired. "The vicar is here to see you, my lord."

And so, it began.

*I*T HAD BEEN Penelope's plan to embark upon the journey to Land's End as quickly as possible, but matters could not be dealt with so easily. Firstly, since she'd arrived in London a few weeks ago, her mother had once again begun to take an active interest in her only daughter's marital prospects.

If she only knew!

And unfortunately, Penelope had made commitments to attend several functions over the next few weeks. How could she convince her mother that leaving London had become most imperative? She'd tried explaining that Lilly needed her, but unfortunately, Lady Eleanor had been visiting and disputed such a statement emphatically.

"Glenda and Lord Spencer left for a visit just yester-day," Lady Eleanor helpfully provided. "You stay in town, dear. You're causing quite the stir!"

"Oh, yes. Finally, I no longer find myself apologizing for you." Penelope knew her mama meant no offense. Penelope had been something of an embarrassment to her parents by refusing to play the part of debutante. "More than one gentleman has gone out of the way to pay you his compliments, and the flowers... Eleanor, you'd never believe how many have been arriving on a daily basis!"

This was exasperating! For the briefest of moments, Penelope contemplated telling her mother the truth. *Mama, I need to track down Lord Danbury before the babe I'm carrying, his, mind you, begins to show any more than it already is! And, oh, by the way, he does not know the baby exists. He doesn't even know of its possibility. You see, Mama, I seduced the man after he'd had too much to drink and he remembers nothing of it. Now, may I be given leave to escape London or would you prefer I go for a ride in the park with one of the dandies who's been hanging about?*

But she could not. She was still hoping to get herself out of this situation with some semblance of dignity.

She'd never had difficulty going where she pleased before. It was just that her mother was *so pleased* with her recent transformation into something of a lady.

She needed to un-transform, somehow. She needed to be the embarrassment that she'd always been in the past. So, instead of the truth she said, "Mother, I believe I wish to open up our home in the evenings to host some progressive forums of discussion. We can discuss philosophy, history, science, and even the social sciences. Just last evening, I came across a piece of literature about a new method of thinking, which is in opposition to Unitarianism, called freethinking. Mother, it is earthshattering and involves rationalizing what we believe through logic and empiricism rather than tradition and religious dogma. I'm planning on sending invitations out to all of our acquaintances. If I cannot go to Lilly and discuss this, I'd like to begin discussing it with our peers, right here, now, in London."

When Penelope began speaking, her mother looked intrigued. That expression changed to exasperation, which changed to outrage, which then turned into resignation.

The baroness had been through all of this with her daughter before.

"Best go to Summer's Park then, darling. Perhaps you can host your salon next year, when your papa and I are in Bath."

Thank you, God.

"If you are certain, Mother? I've been planning it already."

"Tell me you have not sent any invitations out," her mother demanded.

"I have not. But, Mama, I—"

"Very well, you may take the carriage and visit with the Duke and Duchess." There was some consolation for her mother in that Penelope had ironically made connections with the *crème de la crème* of society. "I shall make my apologies for you." But her face looked as though all was lost.

Penelope wished she could tell her mother that she was not to be so disappointed after all.

If she could ever bring Hugh to ground, that was.

The thought pulled her up short. It was not even noon and if she and Rose took to the road today, they could be well out of Town by nightfall.

Not wishing to waste any time making excuses to her mother's visitors, Penelope discreetly sidled around to the other side of the room and slipped through the entryway with nobody any the wiser.

And after she located Rose in the kitchen, the two women began preparations for their departure. They notified Peter and Mokey to ready themselves and the carriage, packed up as many of Penelope's new dresses as was practical, and then changed into traveling clothes. It was to be a long and onerous journey. Penelope had only traveled to the Danburys' main country estate once, about six or seven years ago, to attend a house party with her parents and several other members of society who found themselves seeking entertainments at the end of a season. In good weather, without mechanical problems or mishap, the trip had taken over two weeks! Of course, they'd traveled at something of a snail's pace, and her mother insisted upon numerous and lengthy stops. Could Penelope be so hopeful as to believe they could get to Land's End in just over one week?

*S*HE COULD BE hopeful, but that did not mean it would happen.

The first afternoon, there was a great deal of traffic. Riots had broken out at Newgate, and a group of convicts had escaped, causing a long wait at the city gates while authorities searched vehicles heading out of town. The delay cost them nearly three hours. Not an auspicious beginning.

And as soon as they were finally free of the traffic congestions, rain began to fall.

They were forced to stop at an inn just outside of the city. It was crowded and not well kept, but they were lucky to find a vacancy. After eating the watered-down stew and wine they had delivered to their room, Rose and Penelope climbed into the bed and lay listening to the storm. Penelope did not ever force Rose to sleep on the small beds set aside for servants when she herself had a huge comfy mattress.

Neither of them was really very sleepy.

"Oh, Pen, I do hope the rain lets up tomorrow!"

"It needs to stop tonight. The roads are probably already a mess."

Rose was silent for a few minutes. "You mustn't worry about things you have no control over. We need to rely upon the fact that he *did* betroth himself to you, and he is a true gentleman when all is said and done. Viscount Danbury would not withdraw from the agreement."

"I know, Rose, it's just that once he discovers all that I've done, he's going to hate me. And for good reason! *I* would be livid with a person who has done what I have. I'm an evil woman, Rose. Hugh Danbury has betrothed himself to an evil, horrible, conniving woman."

"You're not entirely evil, Pen," Rose chuckled. "You did whip Augusta Heights into shape for him."

Penelope moaned and rolled over. "And manipulative. I am evil, horrible, conniving, and manipulative."

This self-pity was new for Penelope. She'd always been so very certain of herself. This wave of uncertainties crashing inside of her was quite foreign indeed.

"Well, you always said that if you were ever to marry, the gentleman in question would have to be an enlightened one. And if Hugh is able to look past your evil, horrible, conniving, and manipulative ways, he will have to be more than a little enlightened." And then Rose rubbed Penelope's back. "Go to sleep, Pen, you'll feel better in the light of day."

Penelope sniffed. She hoped Rose was right. She couldn't feel much worse.

*O*R SO SHE'D thought. She'd yet to add the cumulative effects of three days of motion sickness to the discomfort she had already been experiencing due to pregnancy. By the fourth night, Penelope fell into the bed they'd taken for the night before Rose could even change the bedding.

It was clean enough. She just needed to lie down on something that was not moving.

Rose did not appear right away with supper, nor to help her change into her nightgown but Penelope did not really care. She'd spilled the contents of her stomach so many times over the last seventy-two hours that the last thing she wanted was food. She just wanted to sleep and sleep and sleep.

Penelope did not know how long she'd dozed off when she heard voices whispering inside of the room. "She's not seen a doctor for it, and I'm concerned for both her and the babe," Rose was saying.

"And you say she has been carrying now for how long? Just over three months?"

"Yes, ma'am."

Who was Rose talking to? Penelope moaned and opened her eyes.

Rose bent down beside her quickly. "Pen, I've brought a midwife here to examine you. I can't deliver you to your husband in this condition, now can I?" Just as Penelope thought to chastise her maid, she realized that Rose was leading the midwife to believe Penelope was married.

"Now, Mrs. Chesterton, your maid says you haven't been feeling well. If you are amenable, I'd like to examine you to make certain all is going well for both you and your baby. Can you roll over onto your back for me?"

Penelope was so miserable she did exactly as the woman's calming voice asked. "It's all right, Pen, Mrs. Robey is a well-respected midwife. The innkeeper's wife said she assisted all of her daughters with their births and didn't lose a single one of them."

The woman pulled the covers down to Penelope's knees and then placed her hands upon her belly. Neither Rose nor the midwife spoke for several minutes as the exam took place. Penelope opened her eyes, however, and watched Mrs. Robey's expression as her hands palpitated and pressed almost uncomfortably into Penelope's abdomen. She frowned a few times before sitting back and pulling the blanket upward again.

"You are certain you did not come to be with child any earlier?"

Penelope nodded emphatically and then grimaced at the pain the movement brought her.

"I think there is more than one baby. In my experience, a lady carrying more than one infant begins showing sooner and also often suffers from the maladies of breeding more so than most women carrying only one child."

"What?" Rose said.

"What?" Penelope tried sitting up. "That cannot be! Two?"

The woman nodded grimly. "Or more. But your womb is larger than it would be if you carried only one child and what with the symptoms your maid has described to me..." She then shrugged. "I must advise you against any more travel. Your condition would be considered dangerous by many."

"But I have to get there. I don't have a choice." Penelope and Rose's eyes met for a moment, both in shock at what the midwife was saying.

Rose then turned back to Mrs. Robey. "My mistress is very far from home. She has no choice but to complete her journey. Is there nothing you can give to her so that she is more comfortable? Is there anything we can do to ensure her travel can be accomplished safely?"

The midwife pinched her lips but then nodded. "I have a few herbal teas I can send with you for the upset stomach. Peppermint, mostly. And your driver needs to proceed slowly. It is the bumping and the jarring that are worrisome. Too much of that sort of thing can cause the babies to come too early."

Babies. Bay BEES, Bay BEEEES. More than one.

No wonder she already looked like a cow!

"This cannot be happening." Penelope rolled back over onto her side and moaned again.

The midwife merely chuckled and patted her arm gently. "I want you to rest up a bit first before traveling any further. Stay here for two to three days."

She turned to Rose. "She needs to drink plenty of fluids and try to keep some food down. The wee little things need nourishment!" Rising to her feet, she looked around for her bag and then added, "I'll return in two days to see how she is doing. If all is well, no birthing pains, then you ought to be able to get back on the road. But, mind you, you may need to take the journey in stages. If your mistress grows weak again, you will have to take another rest."

"Of course," Rose said obediently. Why did she never speak so submissively when addressing her, Penelope wondered?

More than one?

What have I done?

CHAPTER SIXTEEN

WHEN HUGH WAS done speaking with the vicar, he walked the man out to the foyer and mentally braced himself to view his mother's body. The funeral would be held tomorrow. It was practically June, and the weather was already warm. The body could not be kept above-ground for even a day longer.

When he stepped into the room, a combined aroma of perfumes and death nearly overwhelmed him. He pulled a handkerchief from his pocket and raised it to his nose and mouth.

A small rose embroidered on the corner reminded him that it was not one of his own monogrammed ones. It was the one Penelope had handed him after she'd nearly broken his nose. It had been washed and pressed and instead of returning it to her, he'd oddly found himself carrying it around.

Remembering the sheer fury in her expression after he'd spouted that nonsense about her becoming his estate manager gave him some comfort in the light of his present task.

He stepped closer to the coffin and looked down at the face that had been so very dear to him for the entirety of his life. "Ah, Mama," he whispered. "Why didn't you wait for me?"

She did not answer. Of course. He had not expected her to. The body spread out before him wore his mother's clothing and had his mother's hair, but it was not his mother.

There was no life inside of her. No animation to brighten her eyes or raise the corners of her mouth.

There was no longer a soul present.

Hugh swallowed around the lump that had formed in his throat and then lowered himself to the chair somebody had placed next to her. Margaret, perhaps. She would not have wanted to leave Mama alone.

Hugh knew he'd disappointed his mother by not settling down sooner in life. He'd known it had been her greatest wish, to see him married, to know some grandchildren.

He'd always assumed there would be enough time.

He'd been an ass; a selfish, thoughtless ass.

"I'm sorry, Mama," he whispered. He tentatively placed his hand upon hers but did not leave it there. Her skin felt dry and cold. Dead.

"Would you believe I am an engaged man? Oh, not to Miss Radcliffe, as Margaret told you, you know this by now. I assume you know all." Hugh leaned forward and rested his forearms upon his knees. He stared at his hands, calloused and dry from the long journey he'd just completed. Looking at her had been unfulfilling. He'd felt closer to her when he'd read the words written in her journal.

"To Penelope Crone, of all people. Would you believe it?" he chuckled to himself. "I wouldn't have. And I've had several days riding to doubt myself but, the crazy thing is, it feels right." He unfolded the handkerchief and spread it out over one knee. He wished he'd had the opportunity to tie things up with her father before leaving Town. He'd scribbled out a brief note but could barely remember what he'd written.

She was not flighty. She never had been. He had no reason to believe she'd do anything but sit tight in London until his returned.

He hoped so, anyhow. This was Penelope he was talking about.

It would be a year before they could marry, what with the required mourning period and all. Could he wait a full year?

He would have to. What with his dead mother in the room, he could hardly give himself permission to satisfy his needs with one of the local barmaids while in mourning.

What *would* Penelope think of that?

Would she be jealous?

They'd never said anything about love, romantic or otherwise. He'd kissed her and found himself wanting more. More than he'd ever wanted from any other lady, gently bred or not, for that matter.

But she'd not said anything of her feelings. She'd seemed to participate in their lovemaking as much as he had but she'd not said much about it.

Why had Penelope suddenly abandoned her convictions regarding marriage? Had it been seeing the familial bliss at Summer's Park this past winter? Or was there something else?

She'd never told him why she'd fainted twice, nor why she'd shown up so unexpectedly at Augusta Heights.

What was she running from? *Who* was she running from?

A soft tap heralded the butler's presence. "I'm sorry to disturb you, my lord. There is a gentleman here to see you. I told him the family was in mourning, and that you were not receiving anyone today, but he says it is of the utmost urgency."

Hugh lifted his gaze from his hands. "Who does this gentleman claim to be?" A long lost relative, perhaps? A solicitor already eager to discuss the transfer of his mother's holdings?

"He says his name is Periwinkle, sir. And he says he'd like to sue you for breach of promise."

"**S**O, YOU SAY she sacked you without references. You say she did not allow you any severance pay." Hugh was strangely relieved to be dealing with this scoundrel. He'd not found any comfort in seeing his mother. And he was even less enthusiastic to be contemplating the oddities of his newly betrothed. "But she did not send the magistrate after you since she'd already discovered and reclaimed the money you were attempting to embezzle. Do you not think that was rather benevolent of her?"

Periwinkle was not to be cowed, however, "You are the master of Augusta Heights, and we had an agreement. I've given my life for that estate and then some baron's daughter takes it upon herself to have me physically removed? I'll not have it, my lord." He stuck out his chest and lifted his chin. "I am Matthew Periwinkle, and I'll not have my good reputation as a steward slandered by Miss Penelope Crone or anyone else."

"I'm afraid, my good sir," Hugh said, suddenly tired from the day's events and eager to send the steward off, "that you were the person to ruin your reputation, not myself and most definitely *not* Miss Crone."

And then the man's faced took on a deviousness Hugh hadn't seen before. "Ah, my lord, but Miss Crone has been equally as careless with her own reputation, would you not agree?"

Although lounging in the deep leather chair upon which he sat, Hugh suddenly came to be completely alert. He did not respond with questions as the man surely expected. He merely waited for Periwinkle to explain himself. People like him never failed in this regard.

"A lady." The man would have spat on the floor, Hugh was quite certain, if he'd been in the room with anyone but himself. "What would all of those nabobs have to say if they'd come to know that the lady stayed in residence with a single gentleman overnight, with no companion or nothing."

"She had a chaperone," Hugh stated casually. Thank Heavens she'd had Rose with her. "Nothing inappropriate about her visit."

"Maybe not that particular visit, perhaps." The little man drew out his silence for as long as he possibly could, in utter hopes of putting Hugh on edge even further, before at last revealing his hand. "Call me old fashioned, perhaps, but ain't it somewhat frowned upon for an unmarried lady of the *ton* to get herself into such an interesting condition?"

An interesting condition... what?

And then it all began to make sense. The fainting, the dizzy spells, the fullness of her...

Her sudden, inexplicable desire to marry him.

It could not be. But...

Why him?

What had happened to the man who'd fathered her child?

Rage replaced the sorrow and tiredness within him.

God damn that woman! She'd been going to use him! She'd been planning on going so far as to actually pass another man's child off as his heir! As these thoughts coiled around inside of him, he realized that the foiled steward was watching him for a reaction.

"Don't know where you got such an outlandish idea." Hugh had always been excellent at cards in that nobody could ever read him. And as angry as he was with Penelope, he'd like to strangle Mr. Periwinkle for his impudence. He sat impassively, waiting to hear more of what the damned man had to say.

"From her own mouth and her maid's. Awfully informal with her betters, that one." Hugh had known Rose for almost as long as he'd known Penelope. Periwinkle's opinion on the matter gave his earlier claim even further credibility.

Damn you, Penelope!

"Sitting, talking, they was, in the kitchen. Talking about how the babe was already showing, making the lady sick and all. But I'll tell you one thing, and it's from my mouth to God's ears. They was talking about how to get you to marry the lady. Her needing a husband and all that."

It took all Hugh's self-control not to slam his fists down upon the desk. She'd meant to use him. Did she not think he knew how biology worked? Did she think he would not notice when a child was born just a few months after the wedding? Did she, in fact, think he was a complete and utter fool?

Apparently so.

"Now, I can't help but be thinking to myself that this type of information is worth something to you. And to the soon-to-be mother, as well. I can't help but think she wouldn't wish this information to be shared with all those hoity-toities up in London. Would you, my lord?"

So, Periwinkle had presented himself to Hugh, at his mother's home on the day of her death so that he could blackmail him.

"It's not worth one pence." Hugh was wise enough to know that if one gave into a blackmailer once, the thief would never truly go away.

Perhaps that's why Penelope had been so afraid. Had

Periwinkle gone to her already?

Should Hugh care?

But he would deal with these questions later. For now, he needed to keep Periwinkle quiet. He did have some leverage after all.

"You have come to my home. Demanded my audience. On the day of my mother's death. You have stolen from me, stolen from others in my name, and are now threatening to blackmail me." Hugh spoke softly as he rose from his chair and casually moved around the desk. The look on Periwinkle's face had altered from smug arrogance to barely suppressed fear.

"The new steward at Augusta Heights, your replacement, mind you," Hugh continued, "has brought certain accounting irregularities to my attention; irregularities that are considered to be illegal. Do you really believe that my peers, mine and Miss Crone's, would believe words coming out of the mouth of a known criminal?"

The steward laughed shakily in one final attempt at bravado. "Maybe not my words but what are they to think when the little lady turns into a whale?"

That did it.

The ever-cheerful, easygoing, and mild-mannered Viscount Danbury lost his temper. And in doing so, Matthew Periwinkle was on the receiving end of one of the most debilitating blows ever thrown. The sound of his fist exploding off Periwinkle's face was a combination of a loud pop followed by gravelling crunching and then a gurgle or two.

Hugh's conscience suffered not one bit as he stood over the man who'd had the temerity to enter his own home and threaten both him and his fiancée.

With the assistance of a longstanding manservant, Hugh piled the man onto an old horse cart and headed into town. Of course, the captain of the Seven Mermaids was more than willing to take on an additional deckhand, for a small fee, that was.

Danbury handed a bag of coins over to the haggard-looking seaman, feeling satisfied indeed.

Matthew Periwinkle would not find many who would care to listen to what he had to say in the wilds of America. If he made it that far, that was. Life at sea was not made for the faint of heart, and Hugh suspected that Periwinkle was just that.

Whistling, Hugh jumped back up onto the pony cart and rode back to the estate in the dark.

But what should he do about Penelope? If only she could be so easily dealt with.

B Y THE END of their journey, Penelope and Rose would be on a first name basis with nearly every innkeeper and his wife in England. Penelope's condition had forced them to stop *that* many times.

After Penelope had rested for two whole days, the midwife finally gave them her blessing to continue on their journey. The woman was not enthusiastic about it though. And she was very adamant, however, that should Penelope experience any unusual pains or stretching, or if she was unable to keep food down for more than a day, she must stop and rest again.

Rose promised her mistress would follow those instructions.

And so, the longest journey ever made commenced once again.

At first, Penelope thought nothing of it. Yes, she was a

bit queasy and dizzy, but she'd felt that way for weeks now. Surely, she was not so delicately formed that she could not travel, in a plush and well-sprung carriage, mind you, for a week or so. But it was the pains, which at first she didn't even notice, that changed her outlook.

She was carrying two, possibly more, tiny little squalling infants inside of her, and they depended upon her to take good care of them. What good would there be in finding Hugh if she killed her babies in the process? The thought was a horrifying one. Penelope would rather live at the ends of the earth, alone, away from all society, with her healthy and well-formed children than harm a hair on their unborn little heads.

They traveled one or two hours in the morning, stopped for nuncheon and a nap, or even a brief nature walk, and then traveled for two or three hours in the afternoon. If Penelope had any doubts about her and the babies' health, she and her entourage skipped traveling in the afternoon and she laid about the closest inn, instead.

And she found herself knitting.

She'd never really been all that enthusiastic of a knitter, but with the image of her babies becoming more real every day, she suddenly found herself with a keen desire to create blankets, booties, and sweaters of the most miniature sizes imaginable.

And she met some interesting people as she traveled. She could not use her real name, of course, as it seemed her condition, for some reason she could only guess about, was apparent to many of the women she met up with. The innkeepers took particular care to make sure she was always given a comfortable and peaceful chamber and the maids doted on her anxiously.

Penelope assumed Rose was at the root of the extra consideration she received. She'd known Rose had been frightened for her when they'd had to stop that first time.

For all of Rose's candid lack of submissiveness and bluster, Penelope knew that her childhood friend was caring and sensitive at heart. She was frightened for Penelope's condition.

And so, they stopped.

And stopped.

And stopped.

But nobody complained. Not Coachman John, not Peter, nor Mokey, and most definitely not Rose.

For they all seemed to realize that there was greater importance to this journey than just a simple holiday. It was as though Penelope's personal crusade to locate Hugh Chesterton had become all of theirs, as well.

She supposed they all knew the truth.

Well, not the entire truth, but the truth of her condition. And that, surprisingly, was oddly comforting.

It was as though her babies already had protectors.

The journey took nearly twice the time it had when she'd travelled with her mother. It took twenty-four days, to be precise.

By the time they neared Danbury's estate at the very farthest southwestern part of England, Penelope was feeling rather as though control of matters was slipping away from her.

If Hugh was not here, if he'd bolted again for some other nether regions of this godforsaken kingdom, she would merely have to rent a cottage somewhere and figure out how to make a new life for herself.

She was exhausted. She didn't have the energy to go gallivanting any longer. And she'd never felt a greater relief than when, as the carriage drew to a halt outside of the majestic home, Hugh himself appeared at the top of the steps.

He looked grim, indeed.

CHAPTER SEVENTEEN

*H*UGH HAD FIRST thought the approaching carriage was another of his mother's sisters arriving to pay their respects. There had been four others in the two weeks before. But even from a great distance, he'd known. He'd seen that carriage before. It was not one of his aunts this time.

He could hardly believe that Penelope had the temerity to come all this way, uninvited, in what he was certain was an attempt to solidify their engagement.

Guilt warred with the outrage inside of him. He had, as of yet, not decided whether he was going to honor his proposal. For it had been given under false pretenses.

He'd proposed under the assumption that she had feelings for him. He'd proposed under the assumption that she would come to him not only chaste but free of any encumbrances that would prevent him from making a family with her—making a family that would be his, that was.

He was surprised, that in addition to feeling angry and betrayed, he was sad.

Sad to realize that what he had hoped was going to be a satisfying union might not be a union at all.

He'd promised to give her his name. With his name came protection. Was it even an option for him to cry off? Certainly, nobody else knew of their engagement, and even if they did, there was not a single person who would hold him to it. Her lack of virtue alone was just cause. Hell, he'd be considered a fool to follow through with it.

And then for some reason, his mother came to mind.

She would have been delighted at the prospect of a grandchild so soon. Only if it were his child, though. Surely, she would not have welcomed another man's bastard as his heir.

And suddenly Penelope was here, climbing out of the carriage, a footman assisting her.

She looked so drawn and tired that he very nearly let go of his anger for a moment.

He realized that she was staring at the house, at the black crepe on the door and the drawn curtains. Hugh wore the requisite black armband over his coat.

"Oh, Hugh, I'm so sorry!" She stepped toward him with her hands outstretched to take his, but he did not remove his own from behind his back. Rather awkwardly, she dropped her own and stood before him. Although her hair was confined to its normal harsh knot in the back, a few soft bangs had escaped to soften her look. The sun brought out golden strands he'd not noticed before. And the blue specks in her eyes burned even brighter as they seemed to plead with him for something.

"I know that I have not been invited," she stated baldly and then looked around at her anxiously hovering servants and the butler, who now stood holding the door wide for their entry. "Please, Hugh, could we have a word in private?"

Ah, so she was looking for reassurances from him— reassurances he was not, as of yet, certain he would give.

"I have an appointment, I'm afraid, and cannot make myself available until later this evening." He glanced behind him at his butler and nodded slightly. "I will have rooms readied for you and your maid. You are welcome to stay and rest from your journey." And without waiting for her response, Hugh marched down the steps and around to the stables.

He did not have an appointment, but he was going to make her wait. Damn that woman! He wished he'd never met her!

WHEN HE RETURNED to the house, he learned that the lady and her maid were indeed, locked up in their room and resting. They'd been served biscuits and sandwiches at tea time.

"Please tell Miss Crone that I will meet with her promptly in the drawing room."

"Yes, my lord." The housemaid curtsied before disappearing.

He did not have long to wait before Penelope appeared. And if he was not mistaken, she did seem to have thickened slightly about the waist. She entered the room tentatively but did not curtsey.

He did not stand.

He did, however, gesture to the chair across from his own. "By all means." He knew his voice was unwelcoming. Seeing her made him angry all over again. It bothered him even more that whereas his head quite clearly hated her for what she was doing, his body was still attuned to her. And his heart jumped, just a little, to be in her presence once again.

What fools men were.

She sat down carefully, a little awkwardly even, and then looked up at him.

"I am so sorry, Hugh, for the loss of your mother. I know how much you cherished her. I've always admired her. She was one of the most likeable ladies of the *ton*."

Hugh nodded, appreciative of the sentiments. If only he were hearing them under different circumstances. What if he had not been told of her condition? What if Periwinkle had lied and theirs was a simple engagement, after all.

He would have been pleased to see her. He would have chastised her for coming without her mother, but he would have taken her into his arms. He would have wanted to hold her and receive comfort from doing so.

He would have also scolded her for traveling so far, with only a few outriders for protection. Highwaymen were a very real threat, especially to single coaches.

She'd been lucky, indeed, to travel so very far without any such mishap.

And for that reason, he decided to pretend not to know. He would wait and see how far she was willing to deceive him.

He walked around his desk and sat down on the front of it, directly facing her, his feet practically touching hers. "I thank you." And then she rose, suddenly, practically knocking him backward in the process.

He reached out and grasped her elbows in order to stabilize them both. She did not release his arms where she'd grabbed as well. "I have so much to discuss with you. I wanted to speak with you about something when you proposed but I could not. And then you were gone." She looked up into his eyes and smiled in an attempt at self-mockery. "And..." She tilted her head to the side. "I missed you."

Forgetting his anger for the moment, he leaned his head down and found her lips. He'd missed her, too. God help him, but he had.

He released her elbows, wrapping his arms around her, and pulled her closer. He would enjoy this for just a moment. Her lips moved tentatively under his, opening eagerly when his tongue sought entry.

She tasted of lemons and pastries. She felt precious and soft.

And then he felt it.

A part of her that was not soft. A part that was not like anything he'd ever felt before.

He broke the kiss as if he'd been burned.

Turning from her he walked over toward the ceiling-high bookshelves and placed his hands along the shelf above his head. Closing his eyes, he leaned his forehead into the books lined up in front of him.

"That's what I needed to speak with you about, Hugh."

*S*HE KNEW THE second his body made contact with it, with *them*, that he'd realized her condition. She watched as he turned away from her, rigid with anger? Looking defeated? Hating her?

Most likely, all of the above.

Touching her belly, she massaged it softly. She'd come to love soothing the little bulge. She'd been feeling them now for two days—at least she presumed she was—tiny butterflies, fluttering their wings inside of her womb.

Suddenly, the words which had been so difficult to utter before came rushing up inside of her. "I know you'll think me crazy, insane even! What I've done was unconscionable. But I cannot undo things."

He didn't move or speak.

"And I won't blame you for hating me for it." Her voice cracked a little as she swallowed a sob. She was determined to get through this without breaking down into tears. He deserved that much. "It's just that you were the only one there. I wasn't thinking straight, and I was so overwhelmed by the birth of the little marquess."

Hugh turned around slowly and regarded her through narrowed eyes. "What are you talking about? Good God! Not Cortland!"

She was confused for a moment. "Oh, no! No! What must you think of me? Of course, I would never! He is my very dear friend's husband!"

"A servant then? Penelope? Was it a nearby tenant? Where is this man and why will he not take care of his responsibility? My best guess at this question is that he is already married. For if there were such a man within the *ton* who was unmarried, who put you in this condition and has refused to do what's right, I would have held the shotgun to his head for you myself, Penelope. I would have assisted you, as your friend. But why did you have to take this depraved course?"

Oh, she had not yet told him the very worst part. "Hugh, will you please sit down? Will you give me a chance to explain?" When he met her eyes, she twisted her mouth ruefully. "It's all rather embarrassing, really."

He contemplated her for just a moment before acquiescing to her request. He returned to the chair behind his desk and waited.

Penelope exhaled. She could do this. She *must* do this.

"I took advantage of you at Summer's Park... when you were... inebriated."

Hugh raised his brows. "*You?*" he said somewhat sarcastically, "took advantage of *me?*"

She rushed onward. "I had just watched the duchess give birth, you see? To this new life. And I was so overwrought. I'd finally come to terms with the fact that Viscount Darlington, Rome, was never going to reciprocate my feelings. I'd finally decided in my heart that I would never marry, never be a mother, never have a child. And at the time, I was at peace with my decision. But then…"

"But then, what? Penelope? Don't stop there."

"I held little Edward. And when the nurse took him away from me, to clean him up so that Lilly might feed him, I had the emptiest feeling right here." She pressed her fist up to where her heart was. "I became terrified that it would never happen to me and that I had waited too long."

"So, you changed your mind and what?"

She looked down at the floor, ashamed of what came next. More ashamed in this moment than she'd ever been in her entire life.

"I found you. In the library. And you were well into your cups."

He tilted his chin back and stared at her warily. "You do not expect me to believe that I was so overcome with drink that I bedded you? That I took your maidenhead in my dearest friend's home? You expect me to believe that I did all of this with no memory of it whatsoever?"

She shrugged. What else could she do? Fall on her face and beg him to believe her? "It's the truth, Hugh."

And then he laughed. Not a pleasant laugh but a derisive, disgusted, unbelieving laugh. "Oh, that's good, Pen. You certainly have put your imagination to work coming up with that fairytale."

She shook her head. "I know it sounds implausible, impossible even! But imagine my dismay when you lost consciousness at the… Well, when it was over. And then you left the next day!"

"You forget, Penelope, that moments ago I felt the size of your belly. You, my dear, did not come to be with child from me in February. Another man, in December perhaps, even possibly in November? You must be getting very concerned indeed. You cannot have a very long time to wait before the baby comes."

"There is more than one."

He truly scowled at these words. "Are you so wanton, Penelope? That there is more than one man who could possibly be the father? I'd never have guessed in a million years."

"No, Hugh! Listen to me!"

"I'm afraid that I have been. God, Penelope, why did you have to bring me into all of this?"

"More than one baby! Hugh! And only one man! Only one time. Ever!"

He was scaring her. She was certain he had to have remembered something? Surely? Oh, God. If he didn't remember, would he ever believe her?

Hugh glanced up sharply at the fervor of her statement.

"I swear to you! I would not lie about this. You must believe me!"

He simply stared at her, hoping he could read her mind perhaps? She wished he could so that he would know that she wasn't lying to him.

"You say you rutted with me at Summer's Park, got with child—twins, you say? And now wish for me to marry you? *Need* for me to marry you?"

Well, that was, baldly put, the truth of it. It sounded so very sordid. "I do," she answered solemnly.

A coldness came over him. A coldness like she had never experienced from him before.

He did not believe her.

"Very well." Glancing at her stomach, he spoke in flat tones. "In light of the dire consequence of waiting any longer, and in light of the fact that I did offer for you, I'll marry you, Penelope. I will obtain a special license, and we'll do so within the week." And then he pulled something out of his desk and went to work on it.

She remembered the last time he'd worked on some business in her presence, at Augusta Heights, when they'd worked together. After a moment, he looked up at her again. "Was there anything else you wished to discuss?"

Ah, so, he was tired of looking at her. "Er, no, I suppose not." She rose from her seat slowly. Now would be a very bad time to exhibit any weakness caused by her condition. She did not want to be such a burden for him. She'd never intended... She'd never thought...

"I know you must hate me right now, but thank you, Hugh. Thank you for being the man I knew you would be."

"My lord," he said.

She tilted her head. "My lord?"

"I'd prefer we dispense with the intimacies of an engaged couple. I have no affection for you and do not wish for any from you. So, if you will, please address me formally."

"Very well." Her own pride warred with her guilt. "Thank you, my lord." She hoped in time he could come to like her again. One day perhaps. Most likely very far into the future. Perhaps when they were presented with grandchildren, or great-grandchildren.

She found Rose and informed her that the deed was done. Hugh knew everything and had said he would still marry her.

It was not anything to celebrate but at least her babies were going to have a father. And they were safe now. She had Rose unpack her trunks so that they could settle in. Most likely, she would not leave here for a very long time. Hugh would probably be happy to consign her to the country for the rest of their lives and go about his life as though he had no wife.

Oh, that sounded horrible!

PENELOPE DID NOT seek Hugh out the next day. She assumed he'd had to travel to Plymouth, perhaps, in order to obtain a special license. She hoped the time away would give him pause to reconsider her claims.

It would be so sad for all of them if he persisted in his martyrdom, refusing to believe that he'd had any part in it all.

For he had, yes, he very well had, and lurking beneath Penelope's guilt was a growing anger at her reluctant fiancé. But as quickly as she acknowledged it, she pushed it back down. She was the villain in it all. All she could do for now was wait, and hope.

CHAPTER EIGHTEEN

PENELOPE'S WEDDING DAY was not exactly as she'd imagined it would be. Not that, as a girl, she'd ever fantasized about dressing up and what flowers she would carry and how the church would be decorated.

She'd had a different dream altogether. She'd thought she would only marry if she found a man with which she could create a perfect union. She'd always thought her wedding day would be a happy one. She'd not in a million years imagined she'd feel as though she might as well be carrying a shotgun down the aisle, forcing an unwilling man to say, "I do."

But that was how she felt.

And because there was not only herself to consider, not only herself and even Hugh, but at least two other lives, she proceeded accordingly.

Hugh was dressed somberly and still wore the armband for his mother. Penelope, too, wore all black. On top of everything else, she could not bring herself to wear colors, even a subdued lavender, so soon after his mother's death.

Rose had tried pressing some flowers into her hand before they entered the small chapel, which had been on Hugh's estate for centuries, but Penelope refused them.

She believed that any indication of celebration would only anger her fiancé further. And she did not feel celebratory. She'd won a father for her children but not a husband for herself, really. He'd already told her he did not wish for any affection.

No, there was no need to celebrate.

Which left her pledging herself to him with a grim, solemn determination.

The church was dark and cool, set in a thickly forested area. She presumed the sun rarely struck it full on. Hugh informed her earlier that the vicar would meet them at ten in the morning. Rose and his valet would be witness to the event. Hugh's sister, Lady Margaret, was to be the only guest.

They came into the vestibule and then followed the vicar up to the altar. Rose sat behind her, in the front pew, Margaret across the aisle, behind the groom, and Hugh's valet stood off to the side, a few feet from Hugh.

The vicar was perfect for the occasion—cold, formal, and humorless. Did he know? Ah, yes, she thought as he looked upon her with what felt like contempt. Her condition was virtually impossible to hide. From the front, a person could not really tell, but when viewed from the side, she was all too aware of what they saw. Her abdomen protruded just slightly more so than her bodice. How could one *not* know?

"Dearly beloved," the vicar began, "we are gathered here in the sight of God and in the face of these witnesses, to join together this man and this woman in Holy Matrimony: which is an honorable estate, instituted by God himself." At these words, Penelope glanced over at Hugh. Well, perhaps this marriage was not instituted by God, per se…

The vicar continued, "Therefore, it is not by any to be enterprised, nor taken in hand, unadvisedly, lightly or wantonly; but reverently, discreetly, soberly, and in the fear of God." These words felt like a sword piercing her heart. This marriage was commencing on the least happy of circumstances! She could not stop the tear that escaped. She forced her eyes to focus upon the vicar's Bible as he read.

"I require and charge you both, as ye will answer at the dreadful day of judgment when the secrets of all hearts shall be disclosed, that if either of you know any impediment, why ye may not be lawfully joined together in matrimony, ye do now confess it." Penelope was half afraid that Hugh might speak up at this point. Dreadful day of judgement indeed!

But a hollow silence echoed about the chapel instead. No one would stop this marriage.

The vicar turned pointedly to Hugh. "My lord, Hugh Chesterton, Viscount Danbury, wilt thou have this woman to thy wedded wife, to live together according to God's law in the holy estate of matrimony? Wilt thou love her, comfort her, honor and keep her, in sickness and in health? And, forsaking all others, keep thee only unto her, so long as ye both shall live?"

Without looking over at his bride, Hugh answered firmly, "I will."

"And Miss Penelope Beatrice Crone, wilt thou..." His words were lost, and the gravity of the occasion momentarily forgotten when one of the goldfish in her belly fluttered around, feeling more like a trout. She could not help it; a secret smile touched her lips.

"Ma'am?" the vicar prompted.

"Oh, yes, yes. I will."

Hugh watched her curiously. The vicar instructed them to face one another as he blessed the rings. He then prompted Hugh to repeat after him, "With this ring, I thee wed; with my body, I thee honor; and all my worldly goods with thee I share: In the name of the Father, and the Son, and the Holy Ghost. Amen."

Penelope had removed her glove before taking his hand and so he was able to slip the ring easily onto her third finger. It was the first time he'd touched her since that kiss on the day she'd arrived.

Both of them were then instructed to kneel before the altar as the priest read a blessing.

When it was over, they rose to their feet somberly. It was done.

Hugh turned away from her as the priest guided them all to the vestibule where they'd entered earlier. It was to become legal now. She signed her name Penelope Crone for the last time.

She'd yet to inform either her mother or father. It seemed not to matter so much in the face of what she'd done. Her little trout flipped about again. More than one…

*H*UGH HAD ALMOST given in to the intimacy of the occasion. When he and Penelope were declared man and wife, a part of him had wanted to take her in his arms and kiss her. He'd wanted to erase the worry from her brow.

His wrath toward her had cooled to an ever-present bitterness.

It bothered him, those occasions when it slipped, when he had a desire to make her smile or to seek out her opinion on some matter or other concerning one of his estates.

He ought not to feel any kindness or affection toward her. She was a selfish, conniving, and ruthless human being.

Margaret had been astonished when he'd broken the news to her. He did not tell her the entire truth, that the baby—babies—she carried were another man's. Margaret would have no tolerance for his wife, ever, if she were to even suspect such a thing.

Having been sequestered in her private chambers for the past few weeks, lost in grief, she had not seen Penelope yet. As he had been doing every day since his arrival, however, Hugh joined his sister in her private sitting room in order to take tea with her. He'd been determined to find some time to be with her, to comfort her every day.

It had been soothing. Although they had several aunts and uncles and cousins, Margaret and he were all that was left of their parents.

On the evening of Penelope's arrival, Hugh'd broken the news to his sister.

"I'm going to be away for most of tomorrow, possibly overnight."

"But aren't there guests in the house?" Ah, so she had been watching many of the comings and goings of the past few weeks. "Was that Penelope Crone who arrived today? I had not realized her connection with mother was close enough to merit a visit from her so soon after the funeral."

"Mama's cousin Matilda left this morning; Uncle Walter won't be arriving until next week sometime." But how to explain Penelope and the purpose of his journey. "And yes, it was Penelope who arrived this afternoon."

"How very odd," she said in the emotionless voice he'd grown used to since his return.

He did not wish for his sister to hate his future wife. As much as he hated Penelope right now, he would not want for there to be division within his home. "Not so very odd. We are betrothed," he explained.

Margaret looked more interested in this statement than anything else he'd said since his return to Land's End. "Surely, you jest. She is a bluestocking! Not that I don't enjoy her company on occasion but really, Hugh, she is most definitely not your type. And a future viscountess? Tell me you are joking."

Not his type? Did he have a type? He'd not ever really thought about it. He'd simply enjoyed women, all kinds of women, for most of his adult life. There was that thing he had about red hair, however...

"I am traveling to obtain a special license for us. We will marry before the week's end."

"You cannot marry for a full year, Hugh. You cannot have forgotten the mourning period."

"I have not, Margaret." His voice had been firm. "The lady's condition demands a speedy ceremony."

That quickly silenced her protests. "She is...?"

Hugh nodded firmly.

"Oh, Hugh." She'd reached for the fan on a small table near bye and begun waving it in front of herself a bit frantically. "Well."

"Yes."

She cleared her throat and then glanced around the room. He realized that her eyes had teared up.

"A baby?" she asked softly.

Another man's baby. "Babies." He'd best come to terms with this.

His sister smiled for the first time since he'd returned. "I am not surprised, you know. What with there being twins on both mother and father's side. And have you forgotten, Hugh, that I am a twin?"

He vaguely remembered hearing something to that effect. The other child had not survived for even a week. There was a small marker in the family plot.

If he were the father, it would all make perfect since. Because he was not, Margaret's statement meant very little to him.

That had been just two days ago. He'd not encountered any difficulties in obtaining the special license. He'd considered a quick ceremony in the drawing room, or in his study even, but changed his mind when it was time to tell Penelope.

The chapel on the edge of his property would lend itself to privacy and expediency.

And, he admitted to himself, a bit of sentiment. It was to be his damn wedding, after all.

Penelope had agreed with no argument or opinion. And now he stood beside her, pledging his life, his worldly belongings and his fidelity to a woman who had trapped him with his own conscience.

She was dressed all in black, not a good color for her, and there was no triumph or gloating in her manner whatsoever.

Smart girl, had she exhibited either, he was not sure he could go through with this.

He'd seen her refuse the flowers Rose had presented her with. It angered him to feel guilty that the ceremony was so austere. She angered him period.

How had this happened? Why him? He'd managed to escape some of the most manipulative marriage-minded mamas in all of England for that past decade, but he'd not been able to escape Penelope Crone.

It was still very difficult to imagine her doing anything so foolish as to give herself up to a man who could never offer his protection. Who had the man been? Did he know the man? If he was a member of the *ton*, most likely Hugh had played cards with him, or perhaps participated in the same hunt.

And if the man was not a member of the *ton*, who then?

He wished she would simply tell him the truth. He'd at least want to know who the man was so that... So that what? So that he would never come into contact with him? So that he could beat the bounder to a pulp?

The ceremony passed without incident and Hugh boldly signed the license. It was done.

Ignoring his new bride, Hugh stepped out of the church and into the smattering of sunlight that managed to penetrate the thick forest covering. Penelope had been driven over in an open barouche. Hugh suspected that he was expected to drive her back to the house in his curricle. Frederick, Rose, and Margaret climbed into the barouche and were promptly whisked away. Everybody seemed to understand that this was no typical wedding.

He stood silently and watched as the horses and vehicle disappeared down the road through the woods. When even the sound of the crunching wheels could no longer be heard, he became aware that his wife now stood beside him.

"Hugh?" She placed one hand upon his arm tentatively.

"I ought to have known you would not heed my wishes," he said in a cold, clipped manner. "You've not cared to heed my opinion where anything else in my life is concerned."

"You still wish for me to address you as my lord?" She did not sound sarcastic, only curious… and hurt.

He let out a long slow breath. He suddenly felt exhausted from being angry. He was not typically a foulnatured creature. "Hell, Penelope, does it matter?" If she began crying, he swore to himself he would leave her to drive herself back to the house alone.

"Does it matter how I address you? Or does it matter if I respect your wishes? Yes, I think, to both. Contrary to what you believe of me, I do not wish to cause you any more… inconvenience than I already have." She spoke rationally, as though contemplating a mathematical problem.

"Inconvenience! Ha! That's a delicate word for it."

"Hugh, I've told you the truth. I would never lie to you about something like this."

He looked over at her in astonishment. "You forget, dearest wife, that I would have had to be an active participant. You are merely making matters worse by persisting in your assertion that I am your babies' father."

She didn't say anything for all of a minute. "If I relent, if I admit to you that my story is untrue, then you would feel better about all of this?"

Hugh nodded slowly. "Yes."

She raised her hand to her belly, seemingly unaware that she had done so. "Very well then, if that is what you wish. You are not the father. I have never lain with you." Her voice sounded as flat as Margaret's had lately.

"Well, then." It made no sense at all that her words left him feeling so hollow. "Are you willing to tell me who the father is, then?" He somehow did not feel any better about this marriage. But he had told her he would. It was a rather large concession on her part, he would make one on his.

She seemed oblivious of him, in that moment, staring off into the woods, her hand splayed upon her abdomen. "You probably have no wish to hear of this, but I can feel them moving around now. They feel like crowded fish, swimming inside of me."

His gaze dropped to her hand. "Is the man married, is that it?"

She paused and then nodded slowly. "Yes, he is."

At last, they were getting somewhere. "Do I know him?"

"Yes." Her voice was a mere whisper.

"Does he know you are carrying? Will he know that my heir is his child?"

Penelope looked over at him somewhat wistfully. "He knows, but he does not believe it is his."

Ah, so she truly had been pinned into a corner.

Feeling mollified, albeit slightly, Hugh reached out and assisted her onto his curricle. Not the most auspicious beginning of a marriage, but at least he did not feel like strangling her. He picked up the reins and signaled to the horses. As the curricle jerked into motion, he felt a small hand on his arm.

She grasped onto him for safety.

It reminded him that he was no longer responsible for himself only.

No, he had a wife.

And other... obligations on the way.

CHAPTER NINETEEN

$\mathcal{M}$ARGARET HAD INSISTED upon leaving to stay the night with a neighbor, rather than remain in the manor with the newlyweds on the first night of their married life. As much as Penelope had tried to convince the prim and quiet woman that such a courtesy was not necessary, she would not relent.

Hugh returned her to the house but then said he was going for a drive.

She would spend the evening of her wedding with Rose.

"Carson is spending the evening away, at a card party," Rose said pointedly. Carson was Hugh's valet. Did that mean Hugh did not plan on returning tonight or did it mean that he did? "Most of the staff has been told to make themselves scarce."

"By whom?" Penelope said. She and Rose were furiously knitting. It had become something of a passion for the both of them.

"Lady Margaret."

"Ah." Although everyone, it seemed, knew of Penelope's condition, it was becoming apparent that he had not shared the entirety of what he believed with his sister or anybody else. Penelope pulled at the yarn she was using so that she would have a bit more slack.

It was very quiet in the house—too quiet.

"I still cannot believe that you would tell him he was not the father."

Penelope stilled her hands and dropped them into her lap. "He has been so cold and angry, Rose. There has been no tenderness from him, as there had been in London. It's as though I am no longer even his friend anymore. I had to do something, say something. It seemed the right thing at the time. And it seemed as though some of his anger left him after that. Perhaps one day, somehow, he will believe the truth."

Rose clucked her tongue in disapproval. "When will you tell your parents? What will you tell them?"

"I need to speak with Danbury about that. I thought to send out announcements, but I am uncertain as to what his reaction will be if I do." She picked up the stitch where she'd left off. "I wrote to Abigail last night. I told her everything. I know that she, at least, will not hate me for what I've done."

Abigail was her cousin and dearest friend from as long as Penelope could remember. Abigail had been ostracized from the *ton* the year of her debut after a reprobate of the worst kind took advantage of her and then told tales of it. Though no fault of her own, she'd found herself unmarried and increasing. That had been almost a decade ago.

Abigail now was married to the Duke of Monfort. Theirs was a love match but it had not begun that way. The duke had compromised her and then most honorably offered her his protection in the form of marriage.

Penelope missed her cousin. Abigail had a gentleness of spirit about her; she'd always managed to find the silver linings in the thunderstorms.

Penelope could use a silver lining or two.

"Her grace would never hate anyone," Rose stated matter-of-factly. "I've never known a more optimistic person."

Penelope laughed at the truth of those words. What would Abigail do if she were in Penelope's shoes?

Abigail would not be angry with Hugh at all.

Penelope knew that she'd made a horrible decision when she'd walked into Cortland's library that evening, but she could not help being hurt by the fact that he did not believe her. Did he not know himself? Did he not know what he was capable of while so far into his cups? What other things had he done when he'd had too much to drink? Things that he might not even remember?

"And your mother?"

Ah, yes, she was going to have to tell her parents eventually. Her mother would be in raptures over the fact that her only daughter had finally wed. She was not going to be quite as thrilled with the circumstances of the wedding, nor with the early arrival of her grandchildren.

It was odd. The babies would not be born for months still, and yet Penelope already felt like a mother to them, to her little fishes.

"I thought to speak with Hugh first about that, too. I've made so many of the decisions regarding his life, his future, that I feel it only fair to defer to him at this point— as inconsequential as these matters are."

This was so very unlike her. The old Penelope most likely would have already sent an announcement to the papers and all of her relatives. The old Penelope would... She dropped the knitting once again and smiled. "I've a nursery to prepare. And the estate books to look over. I need to meet with the housekeeper and discuss the poor quality of the meals we've been presented with since our arrival." There were things she could do without Hugh's opinion. Things that would improve the quality of his life here at Land's End. She would stop wallowing as of this moment.

Yes, it was her wedding night, and no, her bridegroom was nowhere to be found, but there was not a thing in the world she could do about that. She'd told him she was sorry. She'd tried to convince him of the truth. And today she'd even gone so far as to give him the story he'd wanted to hear.

Hugh was quite simply going to have to come to terms with a few things on his own.

AFTER LEAVING PENELOPE, Hugh drove around the countryside for a while and eventually found himself at a local tavern in the nearby village. He'd removed his jacket and cravat, but his clothing still reeked of quality.

He did not care.

He found a seat in the corner and ordered a pint from the curvaceous bar wench who waited on him. Conversation lulled slightly when he'd entered, but once they all realized there was nothing interesting about him, the volume of the room gradually increased again.

The beer was warm but strong.

As the sun set, the room filled. Eventually, he was forced to share his table and the bench where he'd been resting his boots. A few of them seemed slightly familiar to him; he wondered if any were tenants of his. Nobody addressed him, however, and nobody seemed to realize just exactly who he was. The conversation he overheard proved just that.

"Lord Danbury married today!" a voice rang out above the din. "What with the viscountess toes up for not even month, one wonders at the timing."

Laughter followed.

"Oy, that's the right of it," a different voice pitched in. "Word is the new lady up there is well on her way to delivering the heir. The viscount's tomfoolery has apparently caught up with him."

Hugh knew he had a reputation for some wildness in the past. He should not be surprised to hear such an opinion of himself.

"About time's all I can say. Someone needs to settle that pup down."

"The poor lad, for all his raking and carousing, one thing's for certain, that boy loved his mama."

A few mugs rose in a very casual toast. Everybody in the room seemed to know one another.

"Do you think he'll stay put for a while?"

"That one? Nah, he'll probably leave the ball and chain here and go back on up to London. Doubt he'll keep to one woman for long!" Lots of laughter followed this statement.

Hugh had been staring at the foam on his beer throughout all of this. He was only slightly surprised when the pretty barmaid fell into his lap.

"What's your story, mister?" She wiggled her bum against his lap. He'd been paying her well each time she brought him a drink. He supposed she was looking to see what other services she could provide for him.

She smelled of strong perfume and spirits. Her bodice was pulled so low that nothing of her shape was left to the imagination. She was pretty, but tiredness lined her eyes.

The memory of pulling Penelope into his lap just over a month ago—had it really been just a month?—jarred him. So much had changed. His entire life, turned over.

Holding Penelope that night had been sweet. Holding this woman now, this barmaid, felt slightly sordid. Penelope's actions, what she'd done to him, had been sordid. She'd been conniving to trap him, hadn't she?

She'd also been utterly desperate. He understood that now. Hugh gently pushed the woman back onto her feet. "I'll take another ale, ma'am, and then I'll be on my way."

She pouted for a moment but then quickly shrugged and flounced back to the bar. Women were never happy to be dismissed. Hugh pulled out his fob watch.

It was nearly nine o'clock. Was Penelope sleeping already? He'd left her at home nearly ten hours ago.

When the woman returned with his drink, Hugh paid her handsomely and left. He'd realized that he hadn't the stomach for dalliance outside of the vows he'd made today. Perhaps someday but not today. And he guessed he would not likely feel comfortable with it for a long time.

He knew his father had kept mistresses on the side while he'd been alive, and he also knew of the pain it had caused his mother. Was he made up of the same cloth?

Not today.

ROSE HAD GONE to bed hours earlier, but Penelope could not sleep. So, she pulled out the most recent household books, reluctantly handed over to her by the housekeeper, and began perusing through the expenses and allowance entries in order to develop an understanding of the goings on here at Land's End.

Several candles sat burning on her desk, and her reading spectacles perched upon her nose somewhat crookedly when a sharp knock sounded at her door.

The servants had moved all of her belongings into the mistress' suite. Lady Danbury had not utilized the room for years, but it had been cleaned and aired out nicely.

Penelope knew that it adjoined Hugh's.

"Come in," she answered automatically. She wore her night rail and nothing else, but the billowing gown covered her from neck to wrists to ankles.

The door opened to reveal a more disheveled Hugh than he'd been when she last saw him.

He was dressed in only his shirt, waistcoat, and fitted breeches. He appeared unshaven, and his hair was windblown. She could smell the yeasty hint of ale upon him.

She dearly hoped he was not drunk.

As he entered, he didn't sway or stagger. He appeared to have all of his senses about him. He walked in and sat down on one of the brocaded chairs near her bed. She noticed he'd removed his shoes.

"I should have known you'd not be frittering your time away sleeping." He watched her with a curious light in his eyes. He wasn't glaring at her, though, and that was a welcome change.

Penelope glanced at the books and shrugged. Setting her pencil down, she turned to give him her full attention. "Did you travel far today?" She wasn't quite certain what to say to him in his present mood. He looked tired, though. He looked as though he'd journeyed a hundred miles.

He shook his head, "Not far." And then Penelope realized why he was here. Had he, in fact changed his mind about... intimacy?

He met her eyes, and she recognized the intensity there. She wasn't sure what to call it. Was it desire? Was it lust? She knew it was not love.

But it wasn't that cold hatred she'd been on the receiving end of all week long.

"Is it safe? For the babies?" His question confirmed her realization.

Penelope swallowed hard. "The midwife said as long as I'm not feeling uncomfortable." At the time, she'd scoffed at the midwife's instructions regarding such matters, but now she was glad to be informed.

"Are you?"

"Uncomfortable?"

"Yes."

"Not presently. But I don't know about during..." She knew one thing for sure. She had been craving this. That was another thing the midwife had told her about. The increased sexual desire that a woman in her condition might experience.

Hugh's eyes watched her. "Are you willing...?" He let his voice trail off.

Suddenly, Penelope's mouth felt dry, and she was certain he could hear her heart beating from across the room. "Yes." Her voice was barely a whisper. "Yes," she said more firmly. She wanted to add that she was his wife, and it was her duty, but that would be hypocritical of her. This had nothing to do with duty. This had nothing to do with obligation.

Hugh reached up and began unbuttoning his shirt. He'd not disrobed that night in Cortland's study.

She pushed memories of their first time out of her mind. For now, she'd dare to hope that this time could be a new beginning for them.

He peeled his shirt off and she watched, fascinated, as the muscles on his arms and torso moved and rippled. Chestnut hair led a trail down past his belly, into his breeches.

Unsure of what he'd expect from her, she simply waited. Her palms were suddenly damp as heat poured through her. Hugh stepped forward and pulled her to her feet. She knew her night rail was tent-like.

Because she needed a tent!

And then he took hold of the long braid that fell across her shoulder. "Like a silken rope." The words left his mouth almost of their own volition. He untied the ribbon and slowly unraveled it, combing his fingers through the long strands.

"It's not so very red," she apologized.

Hugh raised his gaze from her hair back to her face. "It's golden-red."

Penelope reached out one hand and touched the skin that stretched over his muscles between his shoulder and his elbow. It was smooth, slick almost. She remembered how they had strained, before, when he'd held himself above her.

And then Hugh was distracted from her hair by the tie at the neck of her gown. He meant to unclothe her. "The candles," she said. Her reluctance to appear naked before him did not stem from modesty but from fear that if he saw her swollen belly his desire would flee. She didn't want him to be reminded...

Hugh stopped and turned to extinguish the lights she'd set up for her work.

Now there was only the moonlight slicing across the counterpane. Penelope, feeling ignorant and tentative, nonetheless scampered onto the large bed and under the covers. If he removed her gown now, at least he would not see the bulge that had once been her abdomen. Hugh stepped in front of the window and became a looming shadow beside the bed. She could tell, though, that he was unbuttoning the falls of his breeches and then peeling them off.

He was naked when he pulled back the covers and climbed in beside her.

His aroma was musky, masculine and earthy. She only detected a hint of the cologne he normally wore. She swallowed hard. It shouldn't hurt this time. He wasn't drunk and she wanted this.

"Penelope," He pulled himself up beside her. "Stop

thinking so hard." One of his fingers smoothed the furrow she must have made on her brow. And then his hand was in her hair, behind her neck. She could barely make out his features as he lowered his mouth to her throat.

That warmth that had flooded through her before was suddenly a burning heat rushing to her thighs, her gut, her womb. She wrapped her hands around his head and held onto him as he trailed his mouth down to her breasts.

His hands had gathered her gown up to her waist. Without warning, he pulled it over her head. The rush of chilly air did nothing to cool her sudden ardor. "Please." The word escaped on a whimper. She craved this. She craved him.

His hands explored her breasts, her side, down to her waist and thighs. He moved over her and allowed his weight to settle upon her. It would not have been unpleasant, normally, she assumed, but... "Hugh," she managed. "I don't think..."

He'd felt it. He'd felt the hard mound between them. She did not want him to stop! But his weight exerted too much pressure.

He raised himself up, for only a moment. But then before she had time to realize his intentions, he rolled them both over so that she lay on top of him.

All she was aware of now was the hardness that was Hugh. Straddling him now, she lifted herself upward and then lowered back onto him.

"Ah. Oh, oh, yes." She could not stop the gasps as his member slid inside of her. It felt so very, very—she searched her mind for the proper adjective—so very...

He removed himself slightly and pulled back before pressing upward and penetrating her completely. It was as though he knew exactly what she needed.

So very...

He thrust again, holding her by the waist now.

So very...

Good.

She stopped thinking and surrendered to simply feeling.

Sitting upright, she arched her back and shifted herself in an attempt to take him deeper. The moonlight reflected in his gaze as it flicked from her eyes, to her lips, and then her breasts, and then her eyes again. His parted lips glistened and a bead of sweat appeared on his brow. When he reached up and cupped her breast, she experienced a hint of pain, but something else, a burning need. She raised one of her hands and pressed it over his.

A squeeze and then another profound thrust drew a moan from her.

His breathing hitched as they moved together, each creating and then satisfying the other's need.

He taught her how to ride him, urging her upward, forward, and backward. And he placed his hand down there, too, creating even more need, making her dizzy with sensation, almost hysterical in her motions.

Finally, Hugh grasped her thighs tightly with both hands, increased their rhythm, seemed to search for her very center, and then pinned her tightly against him. His seed poured into her at the same time she dissolved into a million pieces.

When he stilled, she collapsed into a boneless heap of woman. She could do nothing but lie there and attempt to catch her breath.

His hands caressed her backside, rubbing and massaging her buttocks before eventually pulling the covers up and over them both. When she finally could summon the strength to slide off of him and curl up to his side, she was startled at what she saw.

One tear drop had escaped from Hugh's closed eyes.

A tear?

He would not want for her to ask him about it. He would most likely be mortified.

She inched higher onto the pillow and wrapped her arms around his head. Ah, she felt another drop of moisture fall upon her breast. But he was silent. He did not move or say a word.

They slept. Made love again. Slept and then made love a third time.

CHAPTER TWENTY

*H*UGH AWOKE TO the gentle sound of snoring. Peaceful, rhythmic, and soothing. It reminded him of when, as a child, he slept with an old hound.

Soft hair tickled his nostril and a smooth leg nestled under one of his thighs.

He'd married yesterday.

Penelope Crone.

Penelope Chesterton, now. His wife. And not in name only.

He slid his arm out from beneath her head and untangled himself from the rest of her body and the covers. He did not want to talk with her this morning.

He wasn't sure how he felt about anything anymore.

Gathering his clothing from the floor, he tiptoed across the room. Once inside his own chamber, he let out a deep breath and closed the door behind him.

His muscles ached, which was ironic, since Penelope had done much of the work... if one could call it that. She'd been on top of him for all but that little while, when he'd used his mouth...

He did not really wish to admit it to himself, but Penelope Crone's sexual appetite was nearly as ravenous as his own. Good God! No wonder she'd found herself with child!

Her passion had nearly overwhelmed him, if that's how he wished to describe those mortifying moments when he'd felt like weeping. He'd not expected the torrent of emotion that engulfed him when they'd climaxed together.

It had not been because of the sex.

It had simply seemed like he'd found a release, at last, for the pent-up grief he'd felt since his mother's death. And for the fact that the children his wife would bear were from the seed of another man. It had all... caught up to him.

And she'd noticed.

She'd held him.

He tugged at the bell pull three times before he remembered he'd given his valet the night off. The entire house was quiet for that matter. He pulled on breeches and managed to wrestle his feet into his boots before realizing that he was no longer alone.

Penelope, with her hair falling wildly around her face, stood peeking through the doorway, once again dressed in that tent of a nightgown she'd worn last night. He'd never seen her so terribly disheveled. Her lips were plump and swollen and her eyes had a sleepy look to them still. He grew hard almost instantly.

"Your housekeeper informed me that the neighbors were hosting a breakfast for all of the servants this morning. I understand it is a tradition to abandon a new bride and bridegroom to their own devices the morning after..." She looked anywhere but at him. "There was a tray of food left outside my door, however. I believe it is so that the two of us can break our fast." And then she bit her lip.

As long as he'd known her, she'd always been confident and managing. It was... satisfying to see her a little off balance.

He *was* hungry.

He'd not eaten anything last night. And he'd exercised plenty to build up an appetite.

At his hesitation, Penelope opened the door wider. "Do you want to share it with me, or...?" She gestured for him to come back into her room. "Or would you prefer to find something alone?"

He nodded, slipped his shirt over his head, and then followed her back into her chamber. She'd set the tray on a conveniently placed table and poured him some tea. Her hair fell over her face as she did so, making her look more like a lost waif than the bittersweet lover she'd become.

Careful not to spill, she added a spoonful of sugar and then handed him the cup. She did know him rather well, for all the turmoil they'd been through. Her hand shook slightly but he did not comment.

She did not pour herself a cup but tore off a piece of bread and nibbled at it.

"Are you sick in the mornings?" He didn't want to know about these babies and what they were doing to her body, to her life, *to his life*; but some part of him was strangely curious.

"I was at first, but I've learned if I eat something right away, it isn't as bad." She flushed slightly. This was the woman he'd had moaning and writhing last night?

As though she could read his mind, she looked up at him from beneath her lashes. Her tongue peeked out to catch a wayward flake of bread crust and then dipped back behind her lips.

Had she done that on purpose?

Did it matter?

"Are you ill now?" he asked.

She shook her head. A long lock of hair fell forward as she did so.

He wanted her again. He hated a part of her, he admired a part of her, he pitied a part of her but mostly, he just wanted her. He reached out and took hold of the collar of her nightgown in one fist. It must be a favorite of hers. The material was well worn.

With a sudden jerk, he tore it down the front of her body. She jumped as though scalded and then covered herself with the torn material and her hands. Her eyes were wide with uncertainty, but she did not chastise him as he'd suspected she might. And she did not push him away nor order him to leave.

And so, Hugh reached up and pushed the material off of her shoulder. As it dropped into the crook of her arms, he used his thumb to massage the pulse near her neck. It raced. By God, she was as aroused as he was.

This time would be quick. This time, she had nowhere to hide. Would he be repulsed by the sight of another man's babies growing inside of her womb?

He jerked the gown off her arms, out of her hands, and tossed it to the floor.

She was round all over. If anything, he grew even harder.

Deliberately, he turned her so that they both looked into the mirror. There, she met his eyes fearlessly. He stood clothed, while she was completely nude. His eyes swept over her form, taking in her pale white skin and the red thatch of hair between her thighs. The curve of her stomach was firm, but the babies within caused the skin to stretch and her navel to appear somewhat flattened.

Her breasts were full, and his eyes were drawn to the rosy tips, resting, it seemed, upon the mounds of flesh and pointed upward. A ferociousness grew inside of him. He would take her as he pleased. Hugh covered her breast with one hand, flicked the tip with his thumb, pinched, and then slid his hand down and over her stomach.

Sunlight poured through the window, casting her female form in light. She arched her back and pressed her head into his chest. So responsive, she wanted this.

Nudging her feet wide with his still dusty boots, he

spread her legs apart. He then hastily unbuttoned his falls and pushed her forward so that she braced herself on the vanity table. Impatiently, he located her opening and slid into her heat with one forceful shove.

A few glass jars and tiny brushes crashed to the floor with his first thrust. Less so, with his second, but he barely noticed. Her eyes met his in the mirror, half closed in a haze of lust. As he grasped her by the waist, he didn't pretend this was affection. It was a storm that needed to exert itself before the sun could come out again.

He did not spend himself quickly. Although his thighs began to burn and his heart raced, he buried himself inside of her again and again. Her bottom was flushed red from where his groin slapped and ground against her.

Was he punishing her?

Was that what this was?

He felt her climax first and, as a flush crept over her body, he quickened his own movements. It did not take long thereafter for him to find his own completion.

Penelope slumped forward onto the dressing table and Hugh rested against her back, still inside of her, both of their breathing labored.

He was afraid to move. Afraid of what he'd done.

She was his wife, for God's sake.

The skin above her hips remained red where his fingers had dug into her. He'd treated her ruthlessly. It was possible she'd have bruises from his touch.

He reached around with one arm and held her in a protective embrace.

She'd been raised a lady. She'd made a ghastly mistake, one which could have ruined her life and the lives of her children. He'd just treated her like a common whore.

For all the wrongs she'd done to him, she did not deserve his depravity.

"Have I hurt you, Pen? God, I'm a brute." The words tore from him.

She did not answer. This was not the marriage he had wanted. This was not anything he'd ever planned for in his life.

He slid out of her, did up his falls, and located her dressing gown on the end of the bed. Her hands remained on the dressing table, her face turned away in... shame?

Feeling an overwhelming combination of tenderness and self-loathing, Hugh draped the gown around her and lifted her into his arms. When he did so, she buried her head against his shoulder until he settled her on the bed.

As he pulled the coverlet up and over her, she finally met his eyes.

He could not see the blue flecks at all. They were a deep forest-like green. It dawned on him that the blue lights in her eyes appeared brighter when she was animated.

"You think me a whore," she said finally. "Because I find pleasure in this; because you believe I have done so indiscriminately."

Hugh's heart skipped a beat. He had a choice to make. One that might set the tone for the rest of his marriage.

He could continue hating her, blaming her. Or he could forgive.

"It was a mistake. You should not have to pay for it forever."

"But you did not make the mistake and I've made it so that you, also, will pay. You have already paid. You have lost your freedom. I had thought after last night that you might come to forgive me someday. I thought that perhaps you already had." As she spoke, a few of those blue flecks began to appear. "You are still very angry with me. And that is not all. You have just recently lost your mother and are suddenly being pressed at from all sides with responsibilities you have put off for a very long time. You are angry with yourself."

Leave it to Penelope.

But there was no anger inside of him right now. His body, mind, and spirit were engulfed in a tidal wave of weariness.

And then Penelope did something completely unexpected.

She pulled back the cover and patted the mattress beside her. "Come back to bed, Hugh. There is no work to be done today and neither of us slept a great deal last night."

He dropped into a chair and tugged off his boots. Not bothering to remove any of his other clothing, he climbed into the bed. Penelope scooted over so that he had plenty of room. It was she who pulled up the covers this time.

*P*ENELOPE LAY QUIETLY on her side and watched Hugh. His breathing was steady, and his chest rose and fell evenly. She noticed tiny wrinkles around the corners of his eyes. He'd laughed a great deal in his life but not lately.

He was changing.

He'd always been considered the easygoing one, the fun one, the bachelor who would never be captured. She'd known this because, being Penelope Crone, the men her age had at times welcomed her into their discussions regarding business and politics. They'd allowed her on more than one occasion to enter into the inner sanctum that was usually reserved only for gentlemen. She'd come to know many of them in ways that their wives, daughters, and mothers never would.

But Hugh was not merely the rake, the playboy. He'd

been a dedicated son and older brother. He'd honored his responsibilities in Parliament and been loyal to the people who were lucky enough to count themselves among his friends.

Had she merely chosen him because he'd been in the right place at the right time? Or, the wrong place at the wrong time, depending upon how one wished to look at it? She did not think she would have done what she did with any other man.

Except for, perhaps, Rome. But Rome would never have allowed himself to drink to such an excess. Rome, it was known, could be something of a killjoy.

Even in her tiredness, as she'd contemplated that she'd nearly waited too long to marry and have children, she'd known that Hugh would act honorably.

If only he'd remembered! Or if she had waited until he'd awakened! That had most definitely not been a part of her ridiculously impulsive plan.

He did look terribly handsome, even sleeping and disheveled. She wanted to reach out and touch his hair but was afraid to wake him.

He was a bit of an injured tiger these days.

Glancing over at the dressing table, she shivered at the way he'd taken her earlier. Initially, she'd been frightened, when he tore her gown. But she had done nothing to stop him. A part of her had known that Hugh needed something more from her. He'd needed a forfeit, of sorts.

And so, as his eyes had burned over her, she'd braced herself for his demands. When he'd turned them both to look into the mirror, she'd surprised herself in that she, too, wanted whatever was going to happen, desperately.

Pain and pleasure collided. She'd throbbed inside as she'd felt him use her. What was wrong with her? No lady would ever admit as much to herself.

Everyone she'd even known had considered her unfeminine, lacking in sensuality and carnal needs. If they only knew! At the tender age of fifteen, she remembered, she had begun to realize the pleasure one could give to herself.

Perhaps that was why she hadn't cried and wept afterwards... even that first time.

But, Heaven help her, when he'd bent her over the table, she'd wanted all of it! The release she'd found with him had robbed her of even the ability to stand. She'd nearly collapsed to the floor afterward.

Both of them, though, had been left feeling guilty.

Surely, he believed her to be a woman of loose morals. She'd given him no reason to think otherwise.

Penelope could not imagine any of the ladies she knew accepting such treatment from their husbands. Would they?

The Earl of Hawthorne was all solicitousness and manners with Natalie—in public. Was there more to marriage than met the eye?

Lilly and Cortland, too, always treated each other with the utmost of respect and affection. She supposed one never really knew what transpired between a husband and a wife. The glaring difference between her marriage and the wedded bliss of her dearest friends, though, was that they all loved each other. None of them had forced their spouses into doing something they absolutely abhorred—like taking on the paternity of a child they did not believe to be their own.

Hugh rolled onto his side, his back toward her now. She could see that even in sleep, his muscles, beneath the linen of his shirt, were honed and well defined. His hair was long, falling over the collar by an inch or two. She'd not realized how much he'd let it grow. It had been more fashionably styled when they'd been in London.

She was tempted to curl up behind him and take solace

in some of his strength. But he would probably not appreciate that. So, instead, she slipped out of bed and went into the dressing room to clean herself.

When she did so, there was more than a little stickiness between her legs.

She was bleeding.

CHAPTER TWENTY-ONE

*R*OSE. SHE NEEDED Rose. She could not get Hugh to help her. He would believe it was all his own fault. He would think he'd caused it.

None of that really mattered. What mattered was that her little fish were in trouble. *Where is Rose?*

Penelope took the washcloth and wiped herself clean to see if the bleeding continued. The first swipe was startling, in how much there was, some congealing together in slimy strands. The second swipe showed some whitish material. Was that Hugh's seed? When she dabbed a third time, with a new cloth, there were just a few spots.

What to do? What should she do?

She folded another cloth and placed it between her legs. The midwife had stressed the importance of bedrest. Strict bedrest if there were any pains, she'd said. Strict bedrest if there was any spotting, she'd said. She'd advised Penelope to be cautious in allowing a physician to examine her. Sometimes, she'd warned, they could do more harm than good.

Penelope slipped back into the bedroom and oh, so carefully climbed onto the bed. She then placed a pillow beneath her knees and laid back, staring at the brocaded canopy above her. She would not allow herself to become upset. These babies needed her breathing deeply and not upsetting them any more than she already had.

Please stop bleeding, please stop bleeding. She placed her hand on her stomach and rubbed it gently. *It's okay, babies. It's going to be just fine. I love you! You must be okay! You have to be okay! You're all that I have now!*

"Are they moving?"

Hugh was awake and watching her. But wait, *were* they moving?

"They are." That sensation was not cramping. It was her little fish, flipping around, she was certain of it. They would not be flipping around if they were in distress, would they?

And then he reached out and covered her hand with his own. "Can you feel them from the outside?"

Penelope looked at him and raised her brows. "I don't know. I'm not sure I would notice if you could. I am so very aware of what they feel like inside of me."

Hugh nudged her hand away and cupped the small mound with his own hand. He closed his eyes as though concentrating very hard.

When he finally opened his eyes again, he smiled ruefully.

"No?" she asked.

"Not yet."

She could not believe they were having this conversation. She'd thought he hated these babies. Oh, how she wished he could believe they were his own!

"They are most certainly very tiny still."

"Even if you are not," he said. But she could see he was teasing her.

And then her stomach chose that moment to grumble. She'd not eaten hardly at all the previous day and had only had a few bites of toast before Hugh had *ravished* her.

Hugh patted her tummy and laughed. "Now, that, I know, is not your babies. We need to get some food in you, else they'll think they are cocooned within a thunderstorm."

With that, he swung his legs off the bed and fetched a

few plates off the tray from earlier. Penelope did not want to move. She wanted to be sure the bleeding was stopped first.

She also did not wish for Hugh to know what had happened.

He handed her the plate and some tea, and she lifted herself to somewhat of a sitting position. This was not an easy feat to do without spilling anything. But she knew the tea would be good for the babies. The midwife had also told her to drink plenty of fluids. She gulped the tepid tea and then reached to set it on the side table, but Hugh took it from her first.

"You are tired," he said. He still had that sheepish look, but it was far better than how he'd been before.

Sighing, and thankful for the excuse to stay in bed, she nodded. "I am." But she smiled back at him. She took a bite of a strawberry on her plate and then handed that over to him as well. By now, he was looking at her curiously.

He looked like he wanted to say more, but then changed his mind.

Uncertain as to what to do all of a sudden, he bowed slightly toward her and took a step backward. "Very well, then. I will leave you to rest." Again, looking as though he had more to say, he turned and left her alone.

Oh, where was Rose?

PENELOPE WAS NOT alone for long. Rose had merely been waiting for the viscount to exit her chamber before barging back in, a discretion for which Penelope was eternally grateful. Imagine if Rose had come in when he was ravishing her!

"Why are all of these perfumes strewn about the floor, Pen?" With a teasing twinkle in her eye, she glanced over at Penelope and gave her a sly look. "Has he remembered? Does he believe the babies are his now?"

Penelope shook her head. "He still labors under the misconception that they are another man's but..." She did not wish to get Rose all stirred up, but needed her maid's assistance. She needed to make sure her little fish were still thriving. "I started, well, bleeding—afterward, that is." At Rose's frightened look, she rushed to add, "I can feel them moving, and I think the bleeding has stopped but I did not wish to take any chances, and so I think I ought to remain horizontal for the rest of the day. It's just that..."

"It is the day after your wedding."

"Yes, and I don't want for Hugh to feel, well, guilty. I think we've managed to come to some sort of a truce, but he's likely to be set off again by any additional, er, complications."

Rose was not a very submissive maid, but she did usually seem to know exactly what Penelope needed. When it really mattered, that was. She deftly wet a cloth in the basin and brought it over to the bedside. Reaching out her other hand, she said, "Let's see how much blood there is now. If there is more than a drop or two, I think we need to call on the local midwife. You ought to meet with her anyhow. You *are* a married lady now."

Both of them sighed in relief to see that the bleeding had most likely stopped, but Penelope agreed that she probably ought to do as Rose suggested. "Do you think you could have her come without making a fuss over it? I could tell Hugh, if he asks, that is, that it is... precautionary."

"Do you think he's going to want to do it again? Tonight?" Rose wrinkled up her nose in disgust. This was a pertinent question, however. She did not think she ought to participate in any more sexual activity, for now anyhow, possibly not until after her fishes were born.

Which would not bode well for a happy marriage. She had heard about men and their *needs*. And, after partaking of a night of satisfaction, herself, she felt a little regretful to put it off for so long.

She'd also liked the intimacy. She'd liked it when he let her simply hold him. It had comforted *her* to comfort him.

Their night together had been oddly enlightening. She'd read of the scientific theory that men and women were complementary to each other, rather than equal, and always considered it to be erroneous. She did think that perhaps men and women ought to be considered equal to each other *because* they could be complementary to each other. It was a thought she stored at the back of her brain for later consideration.

In the present moment, she had more personal concerns to contemplate.

If Penelope were to withhold herself from him, *might* Hugh seek gratification outside of their marriage? She'd not even considered this aspect until now. She'd been so very concerned with the fact that he hated her, it had been the least of her worries.

Except that now it worried her.

"Do you, Pen?" Rose persisted.

"I don't know," Penelope answered honestly. Perhaps he still felt guilty, as she had, for their uncivilized bout of lovemaking—if one could even call it that. Perhaps he would leave her alone for a few nights, thinking a new bride needed a break, so to speak. "But I don't think that I should." And then, making a decision, she turned to Rose. "Please, will you send for the midwife? There are a few things I think I ought to have a better understanding of with all of this marriage business."

"You and me both," Rose said. "I'll send for her immediately."

MRS. MARY HUBER was a strong-looking woman. She was not timid or foolishly feminine in any way, and yet she was gentle when she examined Penelope and seemed to not judge anything about Penelope's recent marriage and premature condition.

Penelope liked her and felt confident speaking with her regarding such personal matters.

"It ought not have caused you to bleed, but I don't see anything of concern at the moment. You are certain you did not experience any stretching pains, or pains in your back?"

"I did not," Penelope answered after confirming her answer in her own mind. "But there was enough blood to frighten me—some of it thick-like."

The woman's hands were feeling around on Penelope's stomach, firmly but not uncomfortably so. "I'm relatively certain you are carrying twins. You will most likely deliver earlier than a normal term."

"You can feel them?" Rose asked.

The midwife, unsmiling until that moment, nodded. She took one of Penelope's hands in hers and held it over the babies. Penelope felt a lump.

"I think that's one," the midwife said. And then, moving her fingers around a little, she placed Penelope's hand along the side. Another lump. "And that's the other one."

Penelope was in awe. Rose looked about to burst. Penelope reached out for Rose's hand and placed it where the midwife had just showed her. "You have to push in a little, Rose, it's okay."

The midwife nodded.

"What should I do now? Can I get up? Can I walk about the estate? Ride a horse?"

Rose had removed her hands and so the midwife drew Penelope's gown downward and the sheet up. "To be safe, I recommend you keep to your bed for at least two days. And after that, lots of rest. I don't want for you to take on any strenuous activity. No lifting, no long carriage rides, and most definitely no horseback riding." She looked over to Rose and wagged her finger. "Be certain your mistress drinks plenty of liquids. Tea is good and perhaps some watered-down wine or a bit of ale. She also needs to eat regularly. The wee ones she carries get all of their nutrition from the mother. If the mother doesn't eat, the babies don't either."

"Should she enter confinement?" Rose asked.

"It would not hurt. Soon, perhaps."

"What about marital relations?" Penelope asked, not wanting to let the midwife escape without having some very pertinent answers. "Does it hurt them?"

The midwife pursed her lips. "It does not hurt them, per se. But your womb, your body, is vulnerable right now. My belief is that the womb responds to signals it receives concerning the woman's health. If your health is compromised, in any way, the womb will go into early labor. It's better that way. If the womb doesn't receive such signals than the woman's health can be in peril. These babies are tiny. Your female body needs all of its strength in order to protect and grow them. So, relations with your husband are fine, but they must be tender. And the husband must be willing to halt if the woman feels anything troubling." The woman frowned. "Carrying more than one child most definitely poses more danger to both you and the babies. They are born smaller than single births. They cannot always breathe enough to survive. I don't wish to scare you, but you are a plain-speaking lady and I have no wish to wax things over for you."

Penelope considered the woman's words and nodded thoughtfully. She and Hugh had not been tender with each other this morning. She was lucky, indeed, that things hadn't ended up badly.

Her little fish were doing well, and she would not jeopardize them for anything.

If Hugh decided to visit her bed again, they were going to have to have a discussion. This was not the time for squeamishness!

Things between the two of them had become so… complicated. Surely, not all relationships were this way! The Duke and Duchess of Cortland had met and courted before he had become the duke. They'd been engaged, even, from what Lilly had told her. And then they'd had a great misunderstanding, which had kept them apart for nearly a decade! They'd serendipitously found each other again, but the duke had been engaged to Lady Natalie, now the Countess of Hawthorne.

When Natalie and Lord Hawthorne had courted, he'd been something of a pariah. That had not been a simple courtship, she was certain of that. But when the respective couples had married, they'd been in love. It had seemed as though everything had been settled.

Abigail and the Duke of Monfort had not married for love. But something had happened after their wedding, and they were now a most loving couple.

Perhaps all relationships required more effort than was apparent. Perhaps the calm and warm behavior she saw between the couples now was merely a result of working through the maze of male/female differences.

As long as both members of the couple were willing to do so.

Was Hugh willing?

He'd returned last night. Although he still believed she had betrayed him, lied to him, and trapped him in order to father another man's child, he'd made an effort at beginning their marriage with some aspect of intimacy.

Was that all about sex?

He'd needed some comfort.

And this morning, he'd held his hand upon her abdomen and expressed curiosity about the babies.

She wished he could trust her. She wished he had believed her. Oh, how different things might have been between the two of them if only he could be certain that these babies were his.

Would further discussion bring them closer together or wedge them further apart?

There was only one way to know.

Until then, she must lie abed. It was late in the afternoon already, but the sun remained high in the sky. The urge to move about, to seek out her new husband even, was strong indeed. It was going to take a great deal of self-discipline to curtail her activity, but she would follow the midwife's instruction. She would listen to what her body told her.

Rose escorted the woman out and was just now returning with a tray loaded up with tea and sandwiches. Apparently, she took instructions from the midwife much better than she did from Penelope.

She assisted Penelope to a reclining position and handed her a cup of hot tea. "Drink up, Pen." She placed a tiny sandwich on the saucer as well and watched her closely. "And eat. I'll not take the blame if anything happens to your little ones. We've come too far to finish this race empty-handed."

Penelope raised her brows. This was, in fact, something of a race. A race of endurance and strategy. Taking a bite of the sandwich, she nodded. "We won't, Rose."

Rose bit her lip and looked down at her apron. "And what of Danbury?"

Penelope considered the question thoughtfully. "It's high time he jumped into this race with us, Rose. And not as an opponent. We need him to become a member of this team."

Rose nodded in agreement.

How she would accomplish such a feat? She did not know for sure. But it was time for some plain speaking between them. When he returned, that was.

If he returned.

He'd made a bad habit of disappearing in the most inconvenient times lately.

CHAPTER TWENTY-TWO

*H*UGH KNEW HE'D ill-used Penelope this morning.

Except that... she'd found completion as well. And she'd not been angry with him at all. As he contemplated the events of the past twenty-four hours, he had to admit to himself that he was not so filled with anger as he'd been before the wedding.

During the ceremony, he'd felt hostile resentment. Standing beside her, solemnly swearing to keep her and honor her for the rest of his life had left him feeling dead inside—cuckolded before he even signed the license.

It had been his *wedding*.

It had felt more like his sentencing.

And yet, when he'd returned on his wedding night, he'd found a profound satisfaction with her. It had been different than any other lovemaking he'd experienced. He'd been tempted by the barmaid, earlier that day, aroused even when she'd sat in his lap, but it was as though his body knew he was no longer an unmarried man. He'd felt compelled to return to his home—to his wife, by God!

And Penelope had not been shy with him. At first, perhaps, but as the night progressed, she'd been adventurous and uninhibited.

He did not allow himself to dwell on those moments when he'd lost control of his emotions. Even though the emotional release had untied the knot he'd carried around for the past week.

He'd cried.

God, the last time he'd cried had been his first year at

school, when he'd been homesick, lonely, and a little bullied. He'd lived over half his life without giving in to such a bout.

He felt the loss of his mother deeply. These rooms, these hallways, had always been filled with her presence. And now, on his wedding day, his mother had not been alive to see it.

Was that partly why he'd felt such bitterness in the chapel? Ah, the ironies of life. Three weeks after his mother's passing, he became a married man. He'd dodged and maneuvered out of numerous bachelor traps only to be caught by, of all people, Penelope Crone.

Penelope Chesterton.

He'd imagined announcing the birth of a son one day, making his mother happy at last. He'd thought he had an endless surplus of time. What a fool he was!

Yes, his life had, indeed, turned into a comedy of errors. And he had mostly only himself to blame.

He *had* proposed to Penelope.

In London, he'd decided he wanted a wife who could assist him with his estates, with his finances, but also one who aroused him physically. He'd decided she would suit.

If he'd not been so blinded by his own wants, his own needs, would he have realized her circumstances before proposing?

She'd fainted while at Augusta Heights!

She'd sickened at the ball. He'd watched her turn slightly green while dancing with Pinkerton.

He was a fool!

And now, he was a married fool.

He had a wife, who this very moment awaited him in her bedchamber.

She'd not emerged for supper, or at all, for that matter. Did she await his presence or was she merely avoiding the animal appetites of her husband? He could not help but wince at the memory of the jars and cosmetics falling to the floor as he'd taken his satisfaction with her. He also could not help the surge of blood that flowed to his groin at the memory.

Without making a conscious decision, he found himself heading toward the master suites. He would not learn anything new by sitting alone contemplating matters. He tapped three times upon the door separating their chambers and stepped in confidently.

Except that she was not alone.

Penelope's maid, Rose, sat on the chair beside the bed and looked at him accusingly. Penelope was in virtually the same position she'd been in when he'd left her. She was lying down on the bed, her knees slightly elevated.

Her hair had been braided, though, and she wore a different gown. This gown was less tent-like, he could tell, even with the covers pulled up to her bodice. This gown had crocheted flowers about the neckline and appeared to be made of a less durable material.

Except the other had not been so very durable after all.

Penelope appeared healthy enough, but had something happened? Was there a problem with...? "Are you well?" He paused in the doorway, suddenly feeling less confident than he had a mere moment before. At her nod, he turned to leave, but her voice halted him.

"Hugh," she said. And he realized he liked the way she said his name. It made her sound breathless and less managing. "Please stay." And then she looked purposefully at the maid.

He didn't enter any farther until Rose passed by him and closed the door with one last meaningful look. Damned impertinent chit.

"Please," Penelope said, "Come in." She gestured for

him to sit in the chair her maid had vacated. This was not at all what he'd had in mind when he'd come.

But he acquiesced. And as he did so, a horrible thought hit him like a punch to the gut. He'd been rough with her this morning. And now she was bedridden, it seemed. "Oh, God, Pen. Is everything...? Are you...? The babies?"

"The babies are fine. I am fine." She turned her head on the pillow to look at him.

When he sat down, he took her hand and pressed a kiss to the back of it. "I'm a brute. I'm worse than a brute." But his words only made her smile; a secret, sensual smile.

"You are!" She sounded breathless again, without even saying his name. "Husband."

He stared into her eyes. "I am." He kept hold of her hand. He was surprised at how fragile it seemed. Penelope was always so capable. He was learning she'd hidden an astounding level of sensuality behind her starchiness. "But? You are abed. And I think you have been abed all day."

"I have been. And I've had the midwife come in to attend to me." She had grown serious, but her hand squeezed his reassuringly. "I wanted to seek you out but... I am to rest for a few days." She seemed hesitant now.

"What did she say?"

"I want to speak plainly with you." She bit her lip. Her other hand rested atop her belly, protectively, almost lovingly. "But I do not wish to anger you again."

"I would not have you anger me again, either, Pen." He released her hand. This would always be a barrier between the two of them. Was it not best that for now, anyhow, they avoid it? He'd rather she not throw down the gauntlet again.

"I want to be your wife, not only in the eyes of the church, but with a meeting of minds... and of bodies. We are friends, too, are we not?"

Had he considered her a friend? He supposed he had. But now? He looked into her eyes. Seeing the intelligence there, intelligence he'd recognized the first time he'd met her, he nodded. He respected Penelope. And yes, he would have her as a friend.

"You will be the father to these babies when they are born. You are their father now."

She could not let it rest. He was her husband and any children borne of her body would be considered his own. If one of the babies was a boy, he would one day become viscount.

"I am," he conceded but felt his irritation returning.

"The midwife says we may have relations." She held up a hand. "Not for a few days. She said it is best to be certain things have... settled down a bit first."

His own guilt from this morning returned swiftly. "I *did* hurt you."

"*We*, Hugh, *we, together*, hurt me. I was a full participant. Do not insult me as to insinuate I had no will in the matter. I... well... I..." She stumbled around for her words before blurting out, "I liked it, Hugh. I mean, I really liked it. It opens all possibilities up in my mind as to the type of satisfaction our joining can bring."

He sat up straight at her words. Would she ever cease to surprise him? Damn if all his blood wasn't rushing to his cock. His breath hitched and he couldn't help but notice the flush spreading up her neck and into her cheeks.

Sexual tension suddenly filled the room. Oh, yes, he desired his wife. His proposal had been as driven by this as anything else and her condition had not diminished it at all.

"Afterward," she persisted, "there was blood. It stopped rather quickly but was of some concern to me. That was why I had Rose summon the midwife."

Her words cooled his sudden ardor significantly.

These babies were to come between them, then. They would always come between them.

"She said that for after a few days anyhow, and for just a few months most probably, marital relations would be safe."

He was beginning to understand the gist of this conversation. "But not, I presume," he finally understood, "against the dressing room table."

Penelope smiled, obviously relieved to have gotten her point through his thick skull. "And, Hugh, she said that if I feel discomfort, or pain, my husband must be willing and able to desist, no matter how advanced matters have proceeded."

He nodded slowly. So, he was not to be banned after all. "Do you trust me in this?" She had no reason to.

"I trust you, Hugh. You've no idea how much I trust you." She suddenly looked vulnerable, a little lost in such a large bed, and a little alone.

Hugh bent down and removed his boots. If he returned to his room for his valet to assist him, this moment would be lost. For the second night in a row, he would disrobe in his wife's chamber. "In that case, I will settle for a good night's sleep." When she went to move over, he stayed her with his hand. If she needed to be abed, he would not have her exerting herself on his behalf for any reason. He walked across the room, extinguished the candles, and then climbed onto the opposite side of the bed.

It was a comfortable mattress, softer than his own. The scent of the sheets was Penelope's and Penelope's alone. Clean, floral, with a hint of citrus. He burrowed into the covers and plumped the pillow under his head. There was no moonlight to come into the room, no, the maid must have drawn the curtains earlier.

He knew by her breathing that she was nowhere near

sleeping. "Are you scared?" he asked into the darkness.

She would know what he referred to. "At night, Hugh, when it's dark. The midwife says that the birth of twins can be more complicated than a regular one. She said it's quite possible that both will not survive."

She *was* afraid.

For all logical intents and purposes, the thought of her children not surviving ought to give him some hope. They could have *his* child at a later date—a child born of his seed, not some other anonymous bastard. But the thought brought him no satisfaction. In fact, it made him slightly ill.

He moved closer to her and tucked her in beside him. "Don't be afraid." It was the only thing he could think to say. There were no reassurances where such matters were concerned. He'd watched Cortland near sick with worry as Lilly had labored. And Margaret had been a twin. The other child had been stillborn. He did not know the details but remembered hearing something to the effect that it had not ever really developed properly.

Penelope turned on her side and put one hand upon his chest. "I wish..." She sighed. He knew what she wished. He wished the same. He would always wish for the same, most likely until his dying day.

He wished that the babies were his.

"Hush," he said, and then he sighed. He realized then she had grown tired after all. For the Penelope he'd always known would not be hushed so easily. He rubbed his cheek against the top of her head and closed his eyes.

Marriage was proving to be a complicated business, indeed.

*I*N THE WEEK that followed, there was something of a truce between them. Penelope completed the requisite two days in her chambers and then began venturing out in gradually increasingly long bouts of activity. Nothing strenuous physically, but more than most ladies of quality did under normal circumstances. After learning the details involved in the running of Land's End's domestic endeavors, she turned her inquisitive mind to that of the more interesting aspects of the estate, such as details regarding livestock, tenants, farming, and other investments. These were when she was most stimulated.

While perusing some reports from ancient times—for how could one understand an estate in its current condition, truly, when one does not know what has prospered and failed in the past—Penelope sat tucked on a comfortable chair in the study, while Hugh labored over some accounting books sent down from the new steward of Augusta Heights.

She was not really learning anything she would not already have guessed and so her mind wandered a bit. She knew that Hugh was concentrating intently. His brows were furrowed, and he'd loosened his cravat.

In his unguarded moments, she could find herself nearly overwhelmed by his good looks.

"I suppose I ought to write to my mother," Penelope said, breaking into the silence. "My parents probably ought to be informed of our marriage."

Hugh glanced up. He'd been so absorbed it took him a moment or two to comprehend what she'd said. "I hadn't considered them." He grimaced. "Does she know about the other...?"

"Oh, Heavens, no." Penelope closed her book and tucked it under her chin. "I can only imagine her reaction." There would be fainting, the smelling salts, the moaning and berating of her only daughter... and then? The realization that her daughter was married. The realization that she would become a grandmamma. Never mind the little matter of such a thing as a five, four, or would it be a three-month long pregnancy?

"Before you arrived, I was up to my ears in correspondence regarding mother's passing." That shadow flitted across his features but only for a moment. She assumed one never adjusted completely to the loss of one's parents. Poor Hugh. "I suppose I ought to send a notice to the papers in London."

The season would be winding down now. Families would be packing up in preparation of returning to their country estates. It was a wonder how much her life would be different than it had been before. For years now, she'd flitted from country house parties to more intimate visits with friends during the off-season, her most pressing concerns being growing her library and tolerating the inevitable insipids in attendance.

"All the debs shall go into mourning. I'll be the most hated woman in all of England." She smiled at him. He had been considered a most fortunate catch. He'd never been netted, however. Until...

Hugh smiled weakly. Unsettled matters remained between them. It was difficult to be with him, in moments such as this, and not feel the urge to convince him he was her children's father.

They had not been intimate again, either.

Perhaps it was time she took matters into her own hands. He most likely was still fearful. She hoped he'd not been repelled by her condition. He had not seemed repelled before. Not at all. Hopefully he had simply been waiting for a sign from her.

The summer sun burned warm and the doors and windows had been thrown wide open. Over the past several days, they'd developed a comfortable understanding by avoiding any discussions of their relationship. They'd covered politics, crops, estate matters, even stories from both of their youths, but never addressed the tension, the unnamed emotions simmering between them. Their stale mate called for a change of scenery.

"It's a beautiful afternoon. Would you be opposed to taking tea outside? As a picnic?" He'd spent several hours outdoors, riding, visiting tenants, working with the very capable steward here but Penelope had kept close to the manor.

He shrugged but then nodded. "Are you certain?"

Rising to her feet, Penelope waved away his concerns. "You can show me some of the grounds. It will be good for me." She pulled the bell cord and instructed the servant to have Cook prepare a small basket. "Give me a moment to collect my bonnet." She wrinkled up her nose. "An unfortunate side effect of my red hair is the intolerance of my complexion for direct sunlight."

Hugh's eyes went to her hair. They then settled back on her face. "Then I would have you collect a large and floppy one, for I've a fondness for both your hair and your complexion."

Warmed by the compliment, she held his gaze steadily before dropping her lashes with a nod. She would flirt with her husband, pregnant or not.

CHAPTER TWENTY-THREE

*H*UGH DID NOT have to wait long for Penelope to reappear, and just as she returned, a footman delivered a basket with picnic rations. The only change she'd made to her appearance was to don a straw hat with a large floppy brim.

"That is not a bonnet," he said jokingly. At first, he'd been a bit annoyed by her suggestion, but the thought of an outdoor excursion *was* appealing. And ironically enough, he was eager to show her more of the estate, the grounds where he'd spent most of his boyhood.

She laughed at his comment. "The sun is so high and bright today that I decided I needed all the shade I could get."

He picked up the basket and held out his arm. "Where would you like to go?"

She leaned into him. "Take me somewhere secret, Hugh. Someplace where you played as a child when you could escape all of the adults."

Her request surprised him. At first, he drew a blank, but then a long tucked away memory surfaced. There *was* such a place. He'd not been allowed to go down to the cove without an adult, but he and Margaret had found a most excellent substitute. And it was not too far for Penelope, he did not think.

As they stepped outdoors, a very slight breeze was the only indication that they were near the sea. It was unique to Land's End, salty and yet fresh at the same time.

But the day was warm.

He led her across the park and into the woods. The shade was a relief.

"Margaret and I spent many a day playing in these woods," he broke into their companionable silence.

Penelope released his arm and skipped ahead of him. He was growing familiar with the notion that he knew her intimately now. How very strange it was, to go from friend to lover after so long of an acquaintance.

She was a different type of beautiful; he acknowledged the appreciation he had for her person, in that he knew her outer surface hid such a unique individual.

"When we were at Augusta Heights, before I departed. I said something that angered you."

She turned her head back toward him, a little startled at his comment. Did she remember? Yes, yes, she remembered. What exactly had he said? Oh, yes. *I never did understand you. So set against marriage, determined to emasculate every man you've ever met. Don't you ever wish you didn't have to be so... different?*

That was when she'd pushed him off of her. He'd been contemplating kissing her even back then. "You have always been different, Penelope. I think that marriage to you will not always be easy, but it shall never be boring either."

Penelope halted and stared down at the ground to contemplate what he'd said. "I could not be confined to a 'typical' lady's existence." He could tell that she was searching for her words carefully. Perhaps this was a difficult subject for her. "Reading gives a person a sort of freedom; to travel, to learn, to think and explore. In case you haven't noticed, I read voraciously."

He nodded.

"But then all of these ideas are always swirling around in my mind. Sometimes, they involve science, sometimes philosophy or government, sometimes all of them together. And I have a need to discuss them. To me, anyhow, this need is almost physical, Hugh. If I cannot exchange what is going on inside my head from time to time with other like-minded, intelligent individuals, I might be fit for Bedlam."

"I understand."

"If I were to appear frivolous, feminine, and silly, as many ladies do, I don't think I could ever be taken seriously. I would find myself barred from the occasional male dominated discourse. I would be..."

"Left out?"

She shrugged. "Exactly."

Memories of Penelope joining a few select gentlemen, on subdued occasions, reminded him that she'd been accepted somewhat into the masculine domain. He could not imagine any other lady ever doing so. "And so, you felt the need to set yourself apart."

"Yes. I am still a woman, though. I am very much a woman, Hugh."

But, he considered, he did not think she had always been so very certain of this fact.

"What of your cousin, Abigail? The Duchess of Monfort? I know you have always spent a great deal of time with her. I only met her a few times, but she does not seem to me to be as interested in learning as you are."

Penelope turned and began following the path once again, in front of him. "Abigail has always been different as well. We needed each other. For although I could not converse with her on as many of the topics as I'd like, she did not rebuke me for my pursuits. She has always accepted me exactly as I am."

"And did she ever make you feel less than a woman?" He surprisingly discovered that he was truly interested in Penelope's answers. In this moment, he could not believe that there was another woman in all of England with as many different facets as his wife.

"Abigail is not that way." They were nearing the edge of the woods. He could see the sunlight and blue sky at a distance. The trail sloped downward somewhat. "Abigail was not seeking a husband when she met Monfort. She had decided that marriage was not going to be in her future. And so, she did not fuss and giggle and make me feel any lack of femininity."

He thought that perhaps he understood what she was saying. But he was not certain. The female mind, no, *Penelope's mind*, was like a deep unchartered ocean. Most women relied upon their looks and their coquettishness in order to garner masculine attention. He knew this because it was often very effective. It was also one of the reasons he'd resisted marriage for as long as he had. How long could one find flattery and simpering attractive? He'd have been bored to tears before the first year was out.

He watched Penelope's back as she strode ahead of him. She was rounded from behind, he could see. Her arms swung at her sides freely.

"Oh, Hugh, it feels so wonderful to be outside again!" She twirled around a few times with her face to the sky. "I do not always need to be in nature, but I require it from time to time."

They had reached the open meadow once again. The trail went just a little ways forward before the land met the cliffs. The sound of the ocean was everywhere now, even though the waves crashed far below. He caught up to her and grasped her hand, pulling her off of the trail and around the trees. He had noted she wore her half boots. Slippers would not have sufficed.

She raised her face to his and smiled questioningly.

"You did say you wanted to go somewhere secret," he

laughed. "Margaret is the only other person I've ever come here with. Though I imagine others know of its existence."

And then they were there. His "secret" place hid behind a small copse of trees and was really not a place for children to play at all. For the cliffs jutted inward here, and there was not a great deal of level land before the edge.

It had been exciting to be here as a child. One could look down and see the waves crashing into the sharp rocks below. At low tide a miniscule sandy beach beckoned dangerously. He would have to be certain his own children never ventured to this place alone.

Penelope walked right up to the edge and looked down. He held tightly to her hand and pulled her backward. "I always hated it when Margaret did that."

Penelope looked over her shoulder at him with questioning eyes but didn't resist him. "I don't want your sister to feel uncomfortable living with us, Hugh. I think she left because she feels she would be an intrusion. I don't feel that way about her at all. This is her home!"

Hugh pulled Penelope against him, wrapping his arms around her waist. He rested his hands upon her protruding abdomen. "Margaret did not leave because she felt she was intruding," he explained reluctantly. "She told me that she cannot bear to be here when you grow large with child. She cannot bear to be here when you finally give birth."

"Does she hate me so much?" Penelope sounded confused and hurt. "Is she so offended by…?"

He shook his head. "She delivered a stillborn just after her husband's death. She told me she cannot bear to be reminded. It is too soon."

Penelope sighed and rested against him. "I didn't know."

"Not many did."

"She has not had an easy time of it over the past few

years, has she?"

"No." They stood in silence together. All that was in front of them was ocean. Endless, ocean. They were, quite literally, at England's edge.

The mood had become melancholy rather quickly. But Penelope shook it off for the both of them.

"I'm starving, Hugh! Let's see what Cook has prepared."

The next few minutes were spent opening the basket and spreading a blanket over the untamed grass that grew there. Penelope took out a few dishes and napkins and began piling various delicacies onto two plates. Cook had provided a bottle of wine but no glasses. They took turns drinking directly from it, in between bites of cucumber sandwiches, pastries, and fresh strawberries. Hugh regaled her with some of the adventures he'd had here. Penelope would interrupt to ask him for more details or explanation. She was a very good listener. Eventually, he persuaded her to speak about herself. She shared a few stories of the foibles she'd managed to get herself into with her cousin over the past several years.

Abigail had been a very important person in her life for a long time. He knew the lady had married last summer. He wondered if her cousin's absence had left Penelope feeling lonely. He'd felt a bit of that himself, he reluctantly admitted, when Cortland had wed. He and Penelope were two of the last single people left from a handful of friends who'd experienced that first season together in London after Waterloo. That had been nearly a decade ago.

Feeling content and full, Hugh stood up and stretched. While he did so, Penelope returned the leftovers and dishes to the basket. When she was finished, she leaned back on the blanket and propped herself up with her elbow. A suspicious gleam lit her eyes.

"Hugh?"

He chuckled. "Yes?"

"I've been thinking about something and wondering." He watched as she bit her bottom lip. A shot of heat surged to his loins.

Men were such simple beings.

He crouched down and then lay beside her. "What have you been thinking?" He raised one hand and ran his index finger from the edge of her sleeve down to her wrist. She shivered.

"The night of our wedding, you, well, you did things with your mouth." She did not meet his eyes. She plucked at the blanket, instead, and watched her fingers as she did so.

"I did." Hugh's own voice sounded husky.

"It was, well, really, rather extraordinary." And then she met his eyes. The blue lights danced. "And, well, I have seen renderings... in this one particular book."

Hugh raised his brows. "My dear Penelope," he teased lightly. "What are you trying to tell me?"

"Well..." She plucked at the blanket again. "I'm asking, really, if you might enjoy having, um your, well, my mouth..."

Hugh nearly choked. And without warning, the hand that had been playing with the blanket reached out and touched him over his breeches.

"There was this one picture..." she continued.

Hugh would not interrupt her for the world. Good God, his wife was well read indeed! Her fingers stroked him rhythmically, almost absentmindedly as she seemed to be gathering the courage to continue.

"A picture?" he prompted her.

"It was, well, backward. Or more accurately, flip-flopped, I would say. Both the woman and the man were giving pleasure, and both receiving it, as well." He couldn't take it any longer. Was she suggesting what he thought she was?

Hugh lunged forward and pressed his mouth against hers. He could hardly contain himself. She'd aroused him, utterly and completely, merely by uttering a few words and while barely touching him on the outside of his clothes.

He pushed her off of her elbow and used his body to cause her to lie back on the blanket. He kissed her thoroughly and relished every corner and crevasse inside of her mouth. He would do likewise with other parts of her person. For now, though, he felt an overpowering need to simply adore her.

And then he pulled away and stared into her eyes. They held an unimaginable question. And then she said, "May we try it?"

Oh, good incredible almighty God in heaven!

In answer, he reached down and grasped the material of her skirt. He was going to choreograph this very carefully. He wanted her to enjoy this as much as he was most assuredly going to. He thought through various scenarios quickly. They could lay on their sides with him propping one of her legs up with his hand. Or she could remain how she was, lying on her back looking up at the sky.

But, considering other matters, he expected this might work best if Penelope was on top of him. He pulled her skirt up to her knees and spun himself around. Her ankles were still very slim, her legs a delightful creamy white, and her thighs soft and supple. "Climb on top of me, love," he said.

Unabashed, she raised herself to all fours and then lifted her leg across and straddled his chest. He was suddenly enshrouded in the material of her dress. He inhaled that clean fresh scent he'd grown fond of, as well as the subtle perfume of her arousal. The sunlight penetrated the material, and he had an incredibly appetizing view of her derriere. He took hold of her hips and pulled. She seemed to know what he wanted and scooted backward at his urging.

Just as he was about to reach down to unfasten his falls, he felt petite hands begin undoing them on their own. He was most certain there was nothing in his life he'd ever done to deserve a wife so bold and so willing.

Not willing to wait and hoping she did not change her mind, he parted her folds and leaned his head forward. At the same time, fresh air hit his cock and then the warmth and moist paradise of her mouth. He could tell already that she was as stimulated as he. He enjoyed watching what he was doing and only closed his eyes a few times, when he needed to summon other thoughts in order to keep himself from spending too soon. He used his fingers, his thumb, his lips, and his tongue on her. She used her lips, her hands, her tongue and, good God, the depths of her throat on him. Occasionally, he would feel the edge of a tooth, but she was careful. And there was something about the knowledge that pain was so near that only enhanced his excitement.

And then she began to jerk and shudder. Her juices had found their way all around his mouth and chin. He was going to spend. He could not help it any longer.

"Pen, you might want to, I'm going to—" Surely, he could not spend in her mouth.

But she grasped him tightly. He was trapped. He pumped once, twice, a third time even deeper into her mouth and then allowed his release to come.

She held him there until his member stilled. The only indication either of them yet lived was the pulse he could feel of her heartbeat, and he knew she could feel the throbbing pulse of his. She collapsed atop him and he slid out of her mouth. He was still shrouded in her skirts with the sunlight filtering through. As his heart slowed down, he once again heard the waves crashing below. A sea gull let out a squall.

Both lay exhausted for several minutes before Hugh could summon the energy to speak. "Hell, Penelope. I'm going to have to take a look at *your* library."

Her hand began caressing the lower half of his stomach and her fingers combed the hair on his belly. It was a pleasant sensation, soothing. "You may, Hugh," she said matter-of-factly, "But I've always found that the scientific method is the best way to learn."

CHAPTER TWENTY-FOUR

PENELOPE BEGAN TO realize, as the long summer days passed, that there were many different layers to a marriage.

There was the practical side, the business and administrative matters. Yes, she'd finally sent word to her mother. Yes, he'd sent an announcement to the newspapers in London, and yes, they were going to need to find a new cook soon. She had grown quite elderly and seemed to be struggling with her duties. And in spite of their wedding and marriage, in spite of Penelope's interesting condition, the house was in mourning. A black wreath hung on the doorway, and Penelope had had some gowns made up locally of bombazine and crepe. They were not very comfortable, but nothing seemed very comfortable lately. Hugh persisted in wearing the black armband but also a black cravat. She knew he still felt the loss of his mother deeply, even though he didn't discuss it with her very often.

There was the public aspect of their marriage. Hugh had told her it would not be necessary for her to meet with the tenants, yet, due to her condition, but while she still felt energetic, she wanted to know more about the estate.

And so, he'd taken her about, to the tiny cottages interspersed amongst the holdings and introduced her formally. She always brought with her a basket filled with staples and preserves from the manor's own inventory. If Hugh told her there would be children, she'd pilfer a toy or two from a collection of Margaret and Hugh's in the attic. Nothing of sentimental value, however; she always checked with Hugh first. She wanted their children to have access to some of the same playthings their father had entertained himself with as a boy.

They also attended church together weekly, sitting in the front pew. Initially, Penelope felt self-conscious. The surrounding gentry were very forgiving of their precipitous marriage. Hugh was a viscount and she a viscountess. That was what mattered most. And Hugh had always been extremely popular. There were a few younger ladies who eyed her with distaste and envy, but Penelope would not be bothered.

For there was also the physical side of marriage, which the two of them were working out very nicely. Penelope had discovered, after the day of their picnic, that she truly was not squeamish when it came to sensual pleasures. Hugh was not at all either.

It was not unusual for either of them to approach the other with a new idea they had from a picture or book. They'd devised many scenarios that allowed them to satisfy each other without putting pressure on the babies, nor undo stress, it seemed.

Penelope had not counted on experiencing such physical pleasure when entering marriage. She'd been all too intent on everything else. But now that she had discovered it, she deliberately kept scenarios in mind that could be used for when Hugh and she did not wish to procreate anymore. Ways that involved other things than merely the male withdrawing his member before spending. Because she was more aware, now, than she ever had been before, of the dangers that came along with childbirth.

And in the early hours of the morning, when Hugh slept softly beside her, she worried.

There was more than one baby to be concerned for.

Two hearts, two heads, two brains, twenty fingers and

twenty toes. Not only did she worry for their lives but for the quality of their health should they both live. She'd heard of early babies being compromised for life with debilitating ailments. She told herself, rationally, that these apprehensions were unproductive for both her and the babies, but she was unable to dismiss them.

And there was another aspect to marriage—one that presented she and Hugh with the greatest challenge—emotional intimacy.

As husband and wife, Hugh and Penelope trusted each other implicitly with their bodies, their possessions, and the day to day decisions about the estate, but there was a wall of sorts between them when it came to trusting each other outright.

This kept them from sharing their dreams, their thoughts, their fears.

Hugh had decided that there was no possible way that the babies were of his own seed and was not ever willing to discuss it. If she even began to bring up the subject, he either cut her off, changing the subject, or removed himself physically. That dark and distant mood settled in him and would not leave for a day or two. She did not think he did it intentionally, but she still felt as though he would punish her for every attempt.

A resentment grew in Penelope's heart and she was unable to dismiss it. She was hurt by his continued refusal to even consider her claim. Did he care for her? Did he respect her? It was obvious he did not trust her.

He loved her with his body, but never spoke of other feelings he might have for her. And what frightened her most was that she had fallen in love with him. One could not share so much with a person, a person they liked and respected, and not come to love him, could one?

Yes, she loved him.

She loved the way he constantly pushed away the lock of hair that was always falling into his eyes. She loved the earnestness he exhibited in finally taking on his full responsibility as viscount. She loved the tenderness he had in his voice whenever he mentioned some memory of his mother, or his concern for his sister.

Yes, she loved him.

But she was growing increasingly angry with him.

This was the state of affairs within their marriage when a great catastrophe fell upon the entire household.

Penelope and Hugh were just returning from church that morning when an ancient carriage, one Penelope recognized instantly, rambled up behind them. They'd just alighted from an open barouche themselves, and Hugh looked at her questioningly.

She gave him a pained look and conceded the inevitable. "It's my mother."

"OH, MY DEARS! Would you just look at her, my lord? Look at you, Penelope! You are absolutely huge!" And then, turning toward Hugh, the baroness wagged her finger at him, apparently deciding it was necessary to take him to task. "I always knew you were a scoundrel, Danbury. Swearing you would never marry! Avoiding the ladies of the *ton* at every turn. Your poor, dear, departed mama! I'll bet you regret that you did not do your duty to Penelope before she passed. I told the baron he needed to take you to task for your actions, but at least you did the gentlemanly thing and have taken responsibility at last."

Penelope winced as she watched Hugh's face. "Mother, you must be exhausted! I wish you would have let me known you were coming. Come inside with us, out of the sun, and I will have a chamber prepared for you."

Although the calendar showed September, summer had yet to retreat and Penelope had been looking forward to a glass of lemonade since the second hymn ended. Besides that, her back hurt after sitting in the wooden pew and her halfboots suddenly felt a size too small.

"Well of course, why haven't you invited me in before now? This sunlight will ruin your complexion." The baroness took Hugh's arm and allowed him to assist her up the steps to the door.

Penelope arched her back and then followed the two of them. A footman rushed over to assist her.

Once inside, settled in the drawing room, Penelope ordered tea and a light nuncheon to be brought in to them. Her mother had sent the maid who'd always been her companion up to unpack her belongings and proceeded to berate the couple for breaking both God's laws as well as society's. Penelope was uncertain as to which mattered the most to her mother.

At first, Hugh had looked uncomfortable, but as her mother went on and on, he'd taken on that distant and cold look.

His mother blamed him for trying to run away from Penelope in London. Her mother blamed him for not marrying her much sooner. Her mother blamed him for taking advantage of her daughter. And if the baron were here, he would have taken some skin off of both of them.

Penelope's father, she knew, had already corresponded with Hugh, and they'd signed the contracts of her dowry without dispute. Her father was a rather passive man.

Several times during the reprimand, Penelope did her best to steer the conversation toward a less disagreeable subject, but her mother could not have been any more tenacious. It was Hugh, excusing himself, which finally brought about an end to the tirade.

"I've an appointment this afternoon, my lady," he said as he bowed, "and I'm afraid I shall have to leave you to Penelope's care."

"An appointment on a Sunday? And while you are in mourning? What is the world coming to?"

Hugh bowed again. "If you'll excuse me." He met Penelope's gaze only briefly and she sent him an apologetic smile. He'd already withdrawn, however to that dark and distant place. Despair filled her at the cold look in his eyes.

In the ensuing silence, she turned to her mother and burst out, "Mother, how could you?"

Her mother merely waved a gloved hand in the air. "It was his due, dear. Why, look at you. He made you wait months before owning up to his immoral behavior."

"No, Mother! You do not know what you are speaking of! He did *not* know! It was I who delayed in telling him! The late date of our marriage was *my* fault!"

But then her mother teared up. "I had never thought that a daughter of mine would do what you have done. I've always been tolerant of your radical ideas, but this time you've gone beyond the pale. Why, I could barely hold my head up in London after I'd received your letter. My dearest friends and acquaintances all congratulated me on your marriage, but also got their digs in. 'Why such haste?' They all speculated that you would marry so shortly after Lady Danbury's death. Why would they marry and not invite the bride's mother? Do you realize what you've done to me?"

Penelope sighed in exhaustion. Rubbing her hands over her face, she groaned. "Mama, I am very sorry. I am so very sorry, for bringing any shame upon you. I can only tell you that I did not intend for any of this to happen. I'm doing my best. But I cannot discuss this with you today any further."

She stood up and rang the bell. When the manservant appeared almost immediately, she asked him to please show the baroness to her chambers. Her mother bristled, but it was obvious that she, too, had grown weary.

Before leaving, though, she turned to Penelope. "I will speak with both of you again at supper."

Penelope merely nodded.

She felt tired, angry, and hurt. She could only imagine what damage her mother could do before her visit was over.

She gave her mother plenty of time to get settled into her chamber before climbing the stairs to her own. Her back hurt, and her feet ached. When she came into the room, though, Rose was ready for her. Rose had known her mother for nearly as long as Penelope had. She labored under no misapprehension as to what the afternoon had been like for Penelope.

Penelope collapsed on a chair, and Rose immediately assisted her in removing her boots. This pregnancy had brought out a nurturing side in Rose that Penelope had not realized was there. Kneeling down, Rose began massaging Penelope's feet, ankles, and calves.

"Was is so very bad?"

Penelope gave her a look.

"Forget I asked. Of course, it was."

But Penelope felt near tears. "She was horrible to him." Rose's thumbs slid along the arch of Penelope's aching foot. "She berated him for compromising me and then avoiding the repercussions. He got that look, you know, the one I always tell you about. Only this time, it was Mama, and not me, and she just kept going and going and going..."

"You need some rest," Rose announced. She pulled Penelope to her feet and assisted her out of her dress and into a night rail. "There is plenty of time for a nap before dinner. And if necessary, we shall have your meal brought up here."

"I can't do that, Rose, that would leave Hugh alone with my mother."

"He's a grown man. He can handle it."

Penelope climbed into the bed and Rose pulled up the covers. "I'll be fine afterward. Wake me when the dinner gong sounds if I'm not already up. I cannot leave Hugh to deal with Mama alone."

Rose pursed her lips but nodded. She closed the drapes and then poured a tumbler of water to sit beside the bed.

"Thank you, Rose," Penelope mumbled.

Rose smiled weakly. "Not to worry, Pen." She then backed out of the room and pulled the door closed, leaving Penelope alone with her thoughts.

Penelope wondered if Hugh thought she was very much like her mother. Oh, she hoped not. Besides, Hugh was not like her father, really, was he? Of course not. Hugh would not be run over by a managing woman as her father had been for most of his life. He'd not let her manage him, not really. Had he? And on that thought, she drifted off.

*H*UGH WAS TEMPTED to stay away for the evening. It would have been the height of rudeness. He was his mother's son, however, and on such small matters as this, he would not let Penelope down.

But that woman!

After about a quarter of an hour in her company, he'd

had to mentally focus on anything else in the room but the words spewing from her mouth. No wonder Penelope had spent so much time gallivanting about England away from her parents.

Being berated for something he'd taken no part in had galled in the extreme. For the first part, he had not compromised Penelope into such a predicament and for the second part, he was making atonement for something another man had done! He was the victim in all of this.

Perhaps victim was a stronger word than necessary, but he most certainly was not the villain that the baroness had decided to paint him.

He would not absent himself from the evening meal.

When he returned to the house, for the most part, things were quiet. He knew the staff was preparing a formal meal, but Penelope was nowhere to be found. She must be in her room resting.

He hoped that was where she was, anyhow.

A pang of guilt niggled at him when he remembered how he'd left her in the salon earlier. He'd known she'd been tired when they returned from church. He'd seen it in her eyes as she'd thanked the vicar and then been trapped by a few of the local meddling elderly ladies. He'd rescued her then, steering her away with some vague excuse.

And when they'd climbed into the barouche, he noticed that she was rubbing her back again. She did more and more of that lately. Surely, she did not have a long wait before the babies would be born.

And again, the frustration arose inside of him, for these children would be born just a few months after he'd first lain with his wife.

As always, he tried to subdue his anger over this. He tried to reconcile the reality of the situation within himself, but the irritations arose again and again.

As he ascended the stairs to his chamber, the dinner gong rang out.

He and Penelope had not used it very often, choosing instead to dine informally together. The deep solemn chime reminded him of his mother. What would she have said to the baroness this afternoon? Would Hugh have told his mother the truth of his and Penelope's marriage?

Most likely not.

Most likely, she would have chided him much the same, only in a more loving and less shrill manner.

In fact, upon consideration, he remembered that his mother and the baroness had been more than acquaintances. But, of course, both were titled members of the *ton*, of similar age. He wondered if the baroness mourned his mother. She'd arrived quite flamboyantly, dressed in vibrant reds and oranges. She'd most likely slept in a nearby inn the previous night so as not to arrive at Morrow Point wrinkled from a long day of travel.

Rose was just entering Penelope's suite. She grimaced when she saw him.

"Rose," he said. "Is she all right? Her mother was... not very agreeable when she arrived."

The maid seemed to contemplate her answer carefully. "My lady was more worried for you. She knows the subject is a sore one."

Surely, Rose knew the truth of all of it. Would the maid tell him more than Penelope had?

As soon as the thought registered in his mind, he dismissed it. It would be unfair to seek answers from the person Penelope most likely trusted more than anyone else in the world.

He wished it would ever be like that between the two of them but did not have much hope. "Her health is what matters most right now. Is she well enough for dinner?"

"I suggested having dinner brought up to her this evening, but she is determined to protect you from her mother."

Hugh smiled. "I will dine with her mother. If she is sleeping, do not awaken her."

"She won't be happy with me."

There were times when he simply must be master. "As it may be." He turned on his heel and entered his own chamber quietly. Damnation and bollocks, he realized, he was to dine with the baroness alone.

CHAPTER TWENTY-FIVE

$\mathcal{F}$OR MOST OF their marriage, Hugh had slept through the night in his wife's bed. On the first night of her mother's arrival, however, he did not come. And Rose, drat that girl, had not awakened her so that she could go down for dinner. It was nearly midnight before Penelope opened her eyes, confused at the darkness, and realized what she'd missed.

Angry as she was, she grudgingly admitted to herself that the sleep had been well needed. Unfortunately, now that she was well rested, everyone else was already abed. But it felt wrong. It felt wrong not knowing where her husband was.

He'd joined her, many a night, after she'd already taken to bed, and awakened her to make love. He would lay behind her and skim his hands along her body until she was ready for him to...

But where was he now? She'd not ventured into his room before. She'd never had the need. Ought she to? Had he merely refrained from coming to her because he was concerned for her wellbeing?

Penelope chewed her bottom lip, contemplating what to do. He was irritated with her. Her mother had unearthed their buried issues and thrown them into Hugh's face. Penelope paced about her room for several minutes before coming to a decision.

Without knocking, she pushed open the adjoining door between their two chambers. It squeaked loudly as she did so. How had Hugh entered her room those nights before without awakening her?

Emboldened by the quiet, she tiptoed over to his bed and...

He was not there.

Where had he gone? He must be in his study. She returned to her room, donned a dressing gown and then padded barefoot downstairs ever so quietly. Good Heavens, she had no wish to awaken her mother.

A hint of light peeked through the door, and sure enough, Hugh sat in the large winged-back chair cradling a glass of scotch.

Ah, the irony.

"Hugh," she spoke softly. "I'm sorry I missed supper."

He glanced up but didn't smile. He did not look to be fuming over an evening spent with her mother, though. He looked rather pensive, instead. He shrugged away her apology. "I told Rose not to wake you. It's important you don't overtire."

She tiptoed toward him. If he were in a different mood, she would feel comfortable perching herself upon his lap. It was an intimate setting and they most certainly would not be interrupted at this hour. Instead, she opted for the settee. She pulled her feet up off of the floor and tucked them under her gown. "You did not kill her, did you?"

He raised his brows. "I refrained."

"What did you talk about?" Sometimes, he could be so open with her, but others, as in now, he kept his emotions shuttered.

He took in a deep breath and then expelled it slowly. "Oh, hell, Penelope, what do you think we talked about? Surely, not the weather?"

"There is no need to be sarcastic with me. If you are angry with her than be angry with her. If you are angry with me, be angry with me." Although her words were a rebuke, she kept her voice even.

Hugh leaned forward and rested his forearms along his thighs. "That's the devil of it, Pen. Her complaints would be well deserved by me if there was any truth, any truth at all in them. But there is not. The fact remains that I am your husband. You are going to give birth to another man's children, and I shall be forced to claim them as my own. As my heir, even, if one is a boy." He set his glass down on the table beside him and looked at her intently. "I have tried so very hard to move beyond this, to find some reconciliation within myself. You are my wife, for God's sake! I have never found such pleasure, nor enjoyment with any other woman. But, God damnit, Penelope, there is a part of me that is sickened by it. I see your body grow large with child, with children. I touch your body, I join my body with yours, and yet still, this pregnancy... At times, it mocks me. No matter how much I wish it away, the truth remains."

His words confirmed the worries that had been building up inside of her. But they *were* his children! Penelope held back a sob and raised her hand to rub her forehead. "Please, Hugh. Won't you please give some consideration to the possibility that what I told you in the beginning is the truth?"

"Delude myself, you mean?" His top lip curled in disgust. "I wish I could. God, I've tried. But I just cannot. It would be like trying to convince myself the sun is blue, or the ocean is dry. I just... can't. I simply cannot."

"I am a liar, then. Forever a liar? You surely can have no respect for me at all if you refuse to believe the remote possibility that you," a hysterical laugh emerged from her, "Hugh Chesterton, could not possibly have imbibed to the point that he had no memory whatsoever of swiving somebody—of laying with me." She took a deep, slow breath before continuing. "It was early in the evening.

Cortland had gone up to be with Lilly, and I had been awake for… too long… attending the birth. After watching Lilly give birth, I went outside for some air. I stood and watched the sun set and as I did so, I was overwhelmed by a physical urge, as likely to any hunger as you can imagine, to make my own baby."

At his look of scorn and disbelief, Penelope forced herself to forge ahead. "You had been with Cortland, drinking. *Good God*, you'd been drinking *for days*. I came to you with the intention of flirtation. I wished to see if I could lure you into a compromising situation so that you would offer for me. And yes, I am aware of how horrible that in itself would have been! But I did not intend for any of this!" She gestured toward her belly, toward the room about them. A sob broke from her. "As God is my witness, I only wanted, I only wished for…"

"Stop it! Enough!" He sprung to his feet and strode toward the hearth. His voice echoed through the room, sharply, commanding.

Penelope went to stand as well, only to be frustrated by her gown trapped beneath her. So, she rose to her knees instead and implored him. "I know it was wrong! It was manipulative and dishonest and immoral. I used you! God, Hugh, I am *so very* sorry. You cannot know how I regret the way I chose to go about all of this. But I cannot regret these children. I did not intend to get myself with child that morning. And, Lord help me, you are the only man I've ever lain with. I swear to you this is the truth. All I can do is ask you to forgive me. To believe me and forgive me. *Please* believe me."

She took a breath. She did not even realize she'd been holding it. All that could be heard in the room was her breathing now. "Please, Hugh, please believe me." Her last words were little more than a whisper.

Hugh remained staring down into the empty fireplace.

The words he spoke were not at all what she expected. "I am going away. I do not know when I will return. I've decided to leave you to your mother's care. I cannot be here, watch as you..."

His words struck her as no physical blow ever could. "But... what about...? Where will you go?"

He seemed to consider her answer. "I don't know. London, Summer's Park, perhaps, or maybe Augusta Heights."

Penelope felt a desolate loss. She'd failed. She'd done all she could to convince him and he was no closer to believing her than he had been on the day she arrived. She could not change his mind.

"I love you." She did not know why she said it now. For him? For herself? She knew it would not change his mind, but could her love change his heart?

He looked over at her and nodded. "I will be leaving at sun up. Tell your mother whatever you wish. Tell her there is trouble in Manchester, I don't care. I can't be here right now. Perhaps, afterward."

Penelope dropped back into the sofa. He would ruin their marriage over this? It seemed, perhaps, he might. For if he did not return in time for the birth of their children, she might be the one who could not forgive.

Hugh bowed in her direction and left the room.

"Damn you, Hugh! God damn you!" But it was only a whisper. And it was for her ears only.

Hugh was gone.

*P*ENELOPE DID NOT sleep much that night. As strong as the urge was to seek him out, to say more, anything else which would convince him not to leave right now, she had an even stronger conviction that it would prove futile.

She could not *make* him believe her.

He'd been adamant that he was not able to reconcile his feelings toward her and his feelings toward the babies she carried. Even after she'd told him that she loved him.

He'd probably believed that had been a ruse as well. He did not trust her. It was possible that he never would.

She was married, but alone, it seemed. She wept some, she slept fitfully, and she fumed. By the time she awoke the next morning, with the sure knowledge in her mind that he'd most certainly already left the estate, both her body and her mind were exhausted.

Rose knew something was wrong immediately. Penelope's eyes were bloodshot and swollen and the viscount had not joined her in the large bed. Only one side of the coverlet and blankets had been disturbed.

"Pen, Oh, Pen. What happened? I was going to awaken you, but he ordered me to let you have your rest. He assured me that he was more than capable of dining alone with your mother."

Penelope did not even glance at Rose. She just sat on the bed, staring out the window at the grounds of Hugh's home. "It doesn't matter. It wasn't your fault. It would have happened eventually." And then, turning to look over at her loyal companion, she grimaced. "He can't get over the babies. And he refuses to even consider the possibility that I have not lied to him regarding his part in their conception."

"Where is he?"

A lump formed in Penelope's throat, forcing her to stifle the urge to cry again. "He's gone away. He didn't know where, but he said he could not bear to be here for the remainder of my confinement, nor for the birth of the babies. What does he expect me to do after they are born? Send them away? Surely, they will be a constant reminder to him."

"And what, might I ask, will he think if they come out looking like a couple of miniature Danburys?"

Penelope had not even considered such a possibility. With her luck, they most likely would turn out to be the spitting image of herself. Poor little mites. She shrugged and shook her head. "Years of his mistrust, months even, will be enough to harden my heart against him. He doesn't trust me. He refuses to believe me. What kind of relationship can we have if there is to be no trust?"

Rose scratched the side of her head, thoughtfully. "I see your point. And I had thought things were going so well. You have gone about like a couple of happily married newlyweds."

At those words, Penelope's eyes welled up with tears again. She swiped at them angrily. "He is willing to throw it all away. That is what makes me so angry. He does not respect my word enough to trust me. I cannot do anything about it. I don't have the energy to persist with him regarding the truth. And I *will not* pretend there was another man before him. I am in the wrong for a great deal of things, but I never, never tried to pass another man's baby off as his. I would not do that. And if he wishes to believe that that is what I did, that that is who I am, then good riddance! To hell with him!"

Rose handed over the steaming chocolate she'd brought in. "Don't get worked up, Pen. It's not good for the babies."

Penelope nodded and dutifully took a sip. Rose was right. All that mattered right now were the babies. She would do what was best for them. They were her entire life right now.

And on that thought, a shrill, yet all too familiar voice called into the room, "Penelope dear! Are you dressed? Good Heavens, look at you! I was never so large with child as you are!" Perfumed and coiffured already, her mother found a seat and examined Penelope critically. "Tsk, tsk tsk, it is going to be difficult to regain your shape afterward. Perhaps you need to restrict you eating a wee bit. A husband such as Danbury is sure to lose interest in you, dear, if you don't take proper care of your looks."

Penelope restrained herself from tossing the leftover chocolate in her drink into her mother's face. And now, she would be obliged to explain Danbury's absence.

"My lady." Rose, the dear sweet girl, curtsied "If you don't mind my interference, your daughter has done exactly as has been recommended by the midwife."

"Mind your tongue, girl." The baroness turned to Penelope. "What does a country midwife know anyhow? I do so wish you were in London so that we could bring in a proper doctor. Much better for the baby!"

"*Babies*, Mama, remember, there are two?"

As though Penelope had not spoken, her mother continued, "Midwifery is practically witchcraft! I imagine, right now, a physician might even recommend a bit of blood-letting. You claim to be so knowledgeable of all things modern and yet you would leave the care of your husband's heir to a mere midwife! You *do* intend a physician be the attendant at the birth though, I hope."

"The midwife will do just fine." Penelope was of the opinion that there were more fatalities with male physicians than there were with midwives. A woman attending her birth seemed more natural to her though. What with a woman being, well, a *woman*.

"At least allow dear departed Lady Danbury's physician to examine you. For my own nerves, Penelope."

Penelope rolled her eyes and then nodded. She would concede this one point.

But she could not go on this way.

"If I do as you ask, will you leave, Mama? It is not that I do not love you, nor enjoy your company, but I am concerned that I cannot provide you with any entertainment whilst you are here." *In other words, you will most certainly drive me to Bedlam if you stay.*

"Well, I never!"

"Mother, Hugh left this morning. What did you say to him last night?"

"He left? Left where?"

"Mother, he left *me*!"

Her mother appeared not to be overly troubled by the announcement. "Most likely for the best. Not to worry, he'll be back. Men are squeamish where childbirth is concerned. You'll not want him underfoot when the baby comes."

Babies!

"What did you say to him?" She loved her parents dearly, but there were days... Penelope closed her eyes and forced herself to remain calm.

"I merely told him what he needed to hear. Why, what he did to you was criminal! I told him it was going to be necessary that he change his disreputable ways and become a proper husband. We had some plain speaking, if I do say so myself. I told him no more whoring about. Men get diseases from such sinful depravity! And then they put their genteel wives at risk. I'd not have that for my only daughter. That man has a horrible reputation, you know. You'll have to take him in hand when he returns."

It had been exactly as she'd feared.

"It was not what he needed to hear, Mama. It was exactly *the opposite* of what he needed to hear." But none of this mattered now. It most likely would have all come to this anyhow. She'd felt the tension building every time their conversation grew too intimate. She sighed heavily. "I love you, Mama, but I would rather not have you here right now."

Her mother was fine with plain speaking? Well, so be it.

"I've only just arrived!"

"I know."

Her mother stood up and examined herself in the looking glass. "Child birth is a rather messy affair." She sniffed. "I'd not intended upon staying very long anyhow. I only did it for you. I rather felt it was my duty to address the wrongs the two of you did, and, of course, to offer my felicitations."

"Of course."

Meeting Penelope's eyes in the mirror, her mother narrowed her own. "Give me your word you'll bring in the physician and I'll go. Promise me, now, Penelope." Her mother almost looked relieved to not have to stay so far away from London. It was the little season, after all.

"I promise."

Her mother paused just a few seconds before nodding. "Very well. Perhaps I'll make a visit to Lady Fredericks in Plymouth first." She then kissed Penelope dutifully upon the cheek, smoothed a non-existent wrinkle from her dress, and closed the door firmly behind her.

Rose was all astonishment. "If only you'd told her that yesterday."

Penelope surprised herself by chuckling softly. Ah, if only...

So now, she truly was alone but for Rose. If only Abigail were here. Perhaps, if Hugh did not return within a day or two, she could write to her cousin. Abigail had been through childbirth twice now and would know what to expect. Abigail had also given birth to twins.

She would not wait to write. Abigail had delivered an heir for her husband just three months ago. She'd written that all had gone perfectly and the baby was absolutely beautiful.

Would the duke object to his wife visiting her cousin so soon? It was hard to know. He'd always been such a cold man, although he had warmed considerably since his marriage.

Yes, Penelope would write to Abigail.

CHAPTER TWENTY-SIX

LEAVING MORROW POINT, no, leaving Penelope, was more difficult than he'd imagined it would be. As he'd ridden down the long drive away from his home, he had to fight the overwhelming urge to turn right back around and make amends with his wife.

But his original reason for leaving would still be there: A pregnant wife, large with two babies that were not his.

It frustrated him to no end that she'd persisted in maintaining his paternity. It would be convenient, if he could only convince himself and go forward believing such a blatant falsehood.

But he could not.

Could he even believe that there were two children instead of one? Was that claim another falsehood in an attempt to make up for the fact that she was already so very far along in her pregnancy? It would most certainly be convenient for the midwife to announce to him that one of the children was stillborn, and then conveniently dispose of the child's body, in an effort to cover up the lie.

Hugh had turned the horse onto the road heading east most purposefully.

And then she'd gone and told him that she loved him!

He'd nearly bought into that as well.

She'd looked so forlorn and desperate.

There had been moments, when they'd been making love, when he'd nearly declared the sentiment himself. But he'd always held back.

How could he allow himself to love a woman he did

not trust?

He rode onward firmly.

He'd told her the truth when he'd said he'd never found greater pleasure with any other woman. The irony!

If only he could find such satisfaction with her character as he did with her body and her mind. That, of course, was asking far too much from the great almighty.

By the time he was well into his third day of travel he convinced himself that he'd done the right thing. Perhaps, when he returned, when she no longer was the walking evidence of her treachery, he could reconcile himself to what she'd done, to who she was.

By the third day, he'd also determined a destination. He would make an inspection of Augusta Heights. He would visit with the new steward there and let the man know that he was not to be taken advantage of.

Once decided, the miles passed quickly. The weather was cooperative, as were the roads, the horses, and the inns. Less than a week had passed before he arrived.

And what he found there was quite disappointing.

He'd been looking forward to several arguments and reasons to walk about yelling and barking at the staff.

But it was not to be so.

In fact, the first thing he saw upon arrival was several masons replacing brick where there had been cracks on a manor which no longer seemed to be listing to the left. Damn Penelope. He swallowed hard around the sudden lump that had appeared in his throat.

And the grounds, he noted, were trimmed tidily, and in some places, cleared completely and replanted. The drive had been smoothed and even the front mahogany door now gleamed with a rich ebony shine.

As he approached, a footman appeared to take his horse and then that gleaming new front door was opened by a man who appeared to be a butler.

"My lord, it is an honor to serve you. I am Mr. Charles Bridge, your butler." He bowed formally before Hugh realized there were other servants lined up in the foyer. "When we heard you were staying at the Boar's Head last evening, we took the liberty to prepare for your arrival."

What a difference a few months made.

That and a particularly meddlesome little redheaded witch.

Hugh nodded and proceeded to be introduced to each of the new servants. At the end of the line stood a capable-looking man in business attire. The new steward, he presumed.

And he was right.

But of course! Penelope had in fact hired one of the finest stewards in all of England.

After less than a fortnight in residence, Hugh found himself superfluous. After addressing his responsibilities at Morrow Point, practically daily, the lack of tasks required here left him far too much time to think.

He had a fleeting thought of traveling to London but had no wish to encounter those who would congratulate or berate him for his summer nuptials. Most certainly the other bachelors with whom he'd spent many of his evenings with while in town would declare that he'd finally capitulated.

He would not be appreciative of such comments.

No, he would go to Summer's Park. A visit with Cortland most likely was exactly what he needed.

He'd always been able to discuss matters, both of a personal and business nature, with his longtime friend. Once decided, he allowed his mind to return once again to the pressing problem awaiting him at home. The last time he'd been to Summer's Park had been in February, where, he thought with a jolt, Penelope claimed this had all begun.

Twenty six days had passed since he'd left her. Had she'd given birth yet? He would know for certain, of that he was sure, upon arrival at Summer's Park. For Lilly would receive notification right away.

She would chastise him, no doubt, for leaving Penelope alone.

He would stay just a sennight, maybe not even that.

He missed her.

As he'd rambled about Augusta Heights, her influence and capabilities obvious everywhere, he'd begun to make a decision in his mind.

Perhaps he could forgive her.

He would never forget, no, that was impossible, but there was this empty feeling inside, as though a piece of himself was missing.

He would forgive her. They could begin anew.

Unfortunately, once he made this decision, a new worry assaulted him.

He'd been unusually cruel to her when he'd left.

He'd left her to give birth alone—with her mother—no less. Would *she* forgive *him*?

Their marriage was going to require more than a little compromise on both sides. As he was already so near Summer's Park, he decided he would stay the night and then ride, hounds for horses, and return to her. Several clouds had gathered on the horizon and the evening looked to be a stormy one. Yes, he would take shelter from the weather, rest for the night, and then return to his wife.

NEITHER CORTLAND NOR the duchess were pleased to see him. Penelope and the duchess corresponded regularly. He was certain Lilly would have sent him packing if it hadn't already begun raining.

Cortland knew him though. He knew that there must be more to Hugh's absence from his wife at such a time than met the eye. After a slightly uncomfortable dinner, Lilly excused herself so the men could take their port.

Cortland opened the touchy subject first. "Out with it, Hugh. What transpired between you and Miss Crone—pardon me, Lady Danbury?"

His wife. His countess.

Hugh ran a hand through his hair and took a long sip of the sweet aromatic liquid. He'd not really thought through exactly what he would tell his old friend. So, he decided to ask a question instead. "How did you come to trust Lilly again, after?"

Lilly had married another man, even though she had led Cortland to believe she would betroth herself to him. At one of the very worst times in Michael's life, she'd abandoned him.

It had been astonishing, really, because he'd just inherited a dukedom. But in order to do so, he'd lost both his father and older brother.

Cortland looked at him levelly before answering. "The question you ought to ask is how did she ever come to trust me again? It was I who inadvertently had failed her. There were circumstances I'd have never believed, if I'd been told at the time. All I knew was that she'd married another." He took a sip of his own port. "At the time, she believed the worst of me, as well. Both of us were wrong. Neither of us had enough faith in the other, in our new and immature love, in order to trust at the time.

"When we met again, it all came out. I only thank God

that she saw fit to nbelieve that I hadn't wantonly abandoned her. What happened, Hugh? What is it that you
believe Penelope has done? Or does she believe you've been
unfaithful in some way?"

Ah, how to answer that one. A footman moved about
the room quietly, gathering used dishes and silverware.

"Let's retire to the study, shall we? Lilly has informed
me that she is going to spend the rest of the evening with
little Edward."

Hugh nodded and the two of them proceeded out of the
dining room. This was most definitely *not* something he
would discuss with anyone in front of servants.

When they entered the study, the familiarity of it comforted him. He'd spent many an hour secluded in this room
with Cortland, discussing business, politics, and of course,
women. Michael Redmond, the Duke of Cortland, had not
lived such a dissolute life as Hugh, but there had been a few
long-term mistresses after things fell apart with Lilly that
first time. They'd had quite the evening the night of the
little marquess' birth. They had, indeed, put one on.

It was amazing Cortland had been able to rouse himself
in order to go to his wife and newborn son.

Upon further consideration, perhaps it had been Hugh,
more than Cortland, who had done most of the drinking.
He remembered now, that he'd been feeling the pressure of
his responsibilities more so at the time. He'd been preparing to tackle Augusta Heights.

He dropped into his favorite chair, and Michael handed
him a tumbler of scotch. A few ice cubes floated in the
glass.

"I've never tasted scotch before." Penelope's voice rang
around in his head.

He took a sip of the amber liquid and relished the fla-
vor as it warmed his throat, chest, and gut.

"We ought to celebrate, don't you think?"

Again, it was Penelope's voice. He remembered now, the dream he'd had, a faint memory. He'd dismissed it, of course, for the very thought had been preposterous at the time. But now...

He glanced over at the long leather settee.

"Touch me, Hugh."

"You're so wet, so ready for me."

The sensual imagery struck him like the shock of a nearby explosion.

He'd lain on top of her.

In all the times since their marriage, he had never made love to her in the traditional, missionary position. In his dream, he had.

His body went momentarily numb as his heart seemed to skip a beat. Good God, it hadn't been a dream!

Lightning flashed, and a loud crack of thunder followed within the blink of an eye. The storm was directly over them.

He glanced at Cortland in horror.

"What is it, Hugh?" Michael asked. "You look as though you've just seen your own ghost."

"I'm going to be a father!"

He burst to his feet. He needed to leave. He needed to get to Penelope now!

"I know, Hugh, sit down. You aren't going anywhere in this storm." Michael's voice was calm but more concerned now.

His hands were shaking. He'd not realized Cortland had crossed the room until he was there, crouched down before him. "What is it, man? Is the notion of fatherhood really so deplorable to you?" He took the glass out of his hand, stood up, and poured another splash into it.

Hugh had not intended to explain the entire situation

to his oldest friend. He'd not wished anybody else to think poorly of her for what she'd done. No, that had been his exclusive right.

But now, in light of his revelation, it all came pouring out. It was surprisingly simple, in a complicated sort of way.

He had taken her bait far too easily. He'd swived her and then gotten her with child. To uphold his honor, he'd married her. The rest of it ought not to matter. It only revealed more of his own weakness and wrongdoing.

But it did. It mattered greatly.

He'd left her! He'd abandoned her when she needed him most!

She'd told him she loved him.

"I need to go to her. Now." He ground out the words as he headed for the door.

But Cortland grasped him by the arm. "It's a downpour out there. Not safe for you or your mount. You're of no use to her injured or dead."

Hugh realized the truth of Cortland's words. Rain pelted against the windows in droves and the wind could be heard tearing through the trees.

He could do nothing for now.

He sat down and buried his head in his hands. All he could think, all he could imagine, were scenarios of her giving birth knowing he was gone. Of her pain, of her courage. "She'll never forgive me."

$\mathcal{I}$N SPITE OF Penelope's disgust with her husband, she could not help but hope to see him come riding up the lane, returning to beg her forgiveness. But after four weeks of his absence, she'd considerably hardened her heart.

And now, the time had come it seemed, and he was yet absent.

The stretching and pulling sensation awoke her just before dawn. Was it real? Was this it? She lay in bed on her side for several minutes before another one overtook her. It was tighter, and somewhat more painful even. When she got out of the bed and walked over to the window, Rose rushed in.

"Are you all right, Pen?" Rose wore only her own nightgown, and her hair was in a long braid behind her back.

Pen rubbed her back and winced. There must have been either pain or fear in her face, for Rose became more alert instantly. "I'll get the duchess."

Oh, yes, Abigail.

Both Abigail and the duke had come quickly after receiving her letter, along with two additional carriages, a nurse, a wet-nurse, and a virtual army of outriders.

Nonetheless, her cousin, as always, brought her peaceful and calming influence to the entire household. But even more importantly, she managed to strengthen Penelope's courage for the coming blessed event. She'd not uttered inane platitudes, nor promises that meant nothing. They both knew of the risks, but Abigail had delivered twins successfully years before. As an unwed mother, she'd been forced to give them up and had since discovered that both of them had died tragically as children.

And Abigail had endured it all.

Penelope could do this, circumstances notwithstanding.

Women had done this for years. They'd given birth to live children, and they'd given birth to stillborns. And some women died, but most of them lived.

Penelope was in excellent health and of a strong willful

mind. The babies were actively moving inside of her. In these final days of her confinement, it was most important that she focus on all of these things.

Abigail had been a godsend.

Even the duke, the most coldhearted man she'd ever met, had been reassuring to her.

He, too, had lost children, and yet he and Abigail could only be described as a warm and loving couple. Their lives were not shrouded by the tragedies of the past. They both found joy in the present and hope for the future. And in each other.

Abigail entered the room just then, as another pain crawled through Penelope's back and around her abdomen. This one, although sharper than the others, was endurable. Penelope grasped the bedpost and leaned into it. Abigail was there instantly and rubbed her back in a slow circular motion. When it appeared to be over, she finally spoke. "When did they start?"

"I think sometime in the middle of the night, but I had not realized what they were. About a half an hour ago, I think, I realized their purpose."

Abigail glanced over at Rose, who stood by nervously. "Some water and tea, I think, Rose dear. We need to keep her strength up. The work has just begun."

Rose nodded and left.

But Penelope's mind was elsewhere. "He isn't here, Abby. He's going to miss it."

Abigail, of course, knew exactly who "he" was. Penelope had told Abigail everything, from the very beginning through the agonizing end result.

"Do you think he was caught in the storm? Do you think his horse has gone lame? What if something happened to him, Abby? What if ...?" God, what if the unthinkable had happened? He could have been overtaken by highwaymen or thrown by his horse. He could be lying dead in a ditch somewhere.

"Shh... Don't think of that, Pen." Abigail helped Penelope lay back down on the bed, on her side, and placed a pillow between her knees. "He's most likely hale and healthy, sulking in some inn. He may be a dunderhead, but he isn't a fool. He'd not risk his own life unnecessarily."

"But what if something has happened?" Penelope moaned.

Abigail was silent for a moment. "Well," she said thoughtfully. "Would you feel better if I sent Monfort out to look for him with his driver and some manservants? Perhaps they can discover where your husband has gone off to. It's possible he's never even left the area. Would you like for me send them?"

Penelope did not wish for Abigail to be without her own husband but the idea of simply knowing that Hugh was well appealed immensely.

"Oh, Abby, would you mind?"

Abigail smiled and patted her hand. "Not at all. If it brings your focus back to the task at hand, it will be well worth it." She rose from the seat she'd taken on the bed. "Don't go anywhere," she joked. "I'll be right back."

Penelope laughed weakly. *Oh, please, please find him.* She did not hate him, really. Really, she did not.

Rose returned with a large tray. She set it on the table and met Penelope's eyes. She appeared much calmer now. Abigail must have had a word with her. Penelope would think of this as 'the Abigail effect.'

"What will it be, Pen, chocolate or tea? Or just water? I've also some lemonade."

Penelope laughed. She'd come well prepared. "Lemonade. But quickly, before another pain comes." She swung her feet to the side of the bed and drank heartily. She'd not realized how parched she was until that moment. She made it halfway through a piece of toast before another pain began creeping up on her.

It was Rose who rubbed her back this time. Really, she ought not to be so needy of her husband with such wonderful women as these here to assist her. This pain was very much like the other had been. Perhaps this wouldn't be so very difficult after all.

SEVERAL HOURS LATER, Penelope lay on the bed, gasping for breath, barely able to stand the torture that this labor had become. It took all of her will to breathe, to rest, to endure, and to breathe again. The doctor had arrived earlier that afternoon and examined her in a most embarrassing fashion only to announce that she was not even halfway there. He'd put his hand down there and poked harsh fingers inside of her. It had been painful and mortifying. She'd closed her eyes and buried her face in the pillow. A pain had gripped her at the same time but the physician, nonetheless, completed his task. The man had furrowed his brows and scowled. A large set of metal forceps lay on the table beside him.

"I'll return in a few hours." His voice was cold and impersonal.

Now, Penelope wished she'd not promised her mother that she would give care of herself and her babies over to the physician instead of Mrs. Huber. For the midwife had been somewhat offended. It would not do to call upon her at this late stage. Penelope wondered if she would come even.

Only Abigail's ever-present calm kept her going. Although Penelope had known she'd disapproved of the doctor, Abigail would never say anything. There had been a certain look in her eyes, though.

Another pain. Penelope gave up her attempts at stoicism and let a low moan escape. It helped. She moaned again. Abigail dabbed a wet cloth at her mouth. Penelope imagined some of the pain exiting her body through her cries.

As the pains progressed, the world around her was becoming something of a white haze.

The doctor returned.

He told her to turn and lay on her back and then put his cold hands upon her again. "Well, now, let's see if you have done your work, madam. Hmm," he said as he pushed her thighs open. "I suppose we ought to give this a go, then, shall we?"

This isn't tea, for God's sake.

She yelled out as something excruciating began happening.

"Push, madam, push hard. Your babies are ready to be born."

She pushed.

And pushed.

And cried.

And moaned and breathed and endured each pain. But nothing was happening. How long could this continue? Why were her babies not coming out? She was growing weary. She could hardly lift her head and her best efforts weren't nearly as enthusiastic as they'd been before.

Abigail held her and spoke steady encouraging words near her ears. Rose held her hand, helped her to change positions, and wiped her face with a cool rag.

The room was stifling. She couldn't seem to get enough air.

Penelope pushed and cried and then collapsed again.

"Position her on her back," the doctor ordered Abigail. And then both Rose and Abigail assisted her to lay back on the bed. This was so very uncomfortable. Breathing became even more difficult. When she resisted, masculine hands pushed her back. "Hold her still, ladies. If necessary, we will use restraints."

God help me!

Penelope moaned and turned her head from side to side. Abigail was there beside her, but there was a great concern in her voice now. "For the babies, love, for the babies," she whispered.

A cold metal instrument was inserted inside of her. Penelope screamed.

CHAPTER TWENTY-SEVEN

*H*UGH WAS FORCED to wait nearly thirty-six hours before the rain let up. And after that, the roads not washed out promised to be waterlogged and muddy. Entire bridges, they'd heard, had been taken out. But Hugh was growing frantic. He'd been away from home for nearly an entire month! When he announced to his hosts that he could wait no longer, Cortland nodded toward his duchess and ordered both of their horses to be readied.

Lilly stepped forward, one arm holding the child who had inspired Penelope to come to him in such a crazy, inspired, desperate move.

She was the perfect duchess for Cortland. Her platinum hair was pulled back into an elegant knot, her golden eyes glowed in encouragement. "Penelope will forgive you, Hugh. You must love her and love her and then love her some more. And then, she will be everything you ever wanted. Don't allow pride or sorrow to take away the joy you both deserve." Her Grace, Lilly Redmond, was not only a duchess. She was woman, mother, and friend. She kissed him lightly on the cheek. "Be safe and send my husband back to me soon."

She would not allow her husband to send his friend off alone.

A S WISDOM HAD predicted, the first few days of travel netted them barely enough miles for it to have been worth their troubles. Hugh kept waiting for Cortland to halt and announce his intent to return to Summer's Park, but his good friend determinedly marched alongside Hugh the entire time. For the first two days were spent on foot, pulling and tugging their mounts behind them.

Hugh would not have stopped at all, at night even, if it had not been for the sheer exhaustion that set in each evening.

Cortland remained at his side.

Finally, on the afternoon of the third day, the sun shone brightly, and the roads dried up enough so that they could ride for long periods of time without putting the horses and themselves at risk. It was tempting to push the animals harder than they ought to, but Hugh knew that would serve no good purpose in the end.

But he was a man possessed as he rode toward his wife and unborn children. Or would they already have been born? And if they had been, were they well? Did they live? Did Penelope yet live? A stabbing sensation pierced his heart at such a thought. A woman's lot was a dangerous one. And Penelope had two children to deliver into this world. What an ass he'd been! He was a bastard; a pigheaded, egotistical, arrogant fool. He chastised himself inwardly for most of the journey.

As they maneuvered through one particularly boggy area, Cortland spoke of the trials he and Lilly had gone through. It only comforted him in that he would realize that perhaps not only he, but all men, were inferior to women.

And then late on the fourth day, as they finally drew near to Land's End, two riders met them on the road. One of them had an air about him, cool, distant, noble. The other wore livery.

The Duke of Monfort and one of his servants. If the duke had been at Morrow Point, that meant Penelope was not alone with her mother. She was with her cousin, Abigail.

Hugh swallowed hard and met the man's eyes. He saw no judgment there, but a seriousness that could only mean one thing. "She began laboring yesterday morning," the duke said. "She has asked for you."

They were still maybe twenty miles away. Hugh nodded and took off at a breakneck pace. They'd only stopped to sleep for a few hours each night, at Cortland's insistence, but Hugh was wide awake.

Without hesitation, the other riders fell into place behind him. This was not the time to hold back his horse.

I'm coming, Penelope.

He did not even realize that he chanted her name in his head, over and over again. *I'm coming for you, love.*

She had asked for him.

The terrain was familiar now, the road, and then the drive, and then the large stately mansion that he'd always considered home. The cold, dark thought flitted through his mind that the last time he'd arrived here, he'd been greeted with the news of his mother's death.

As he rode up to the house and swung off the horse, a woman came running out the door. She wore an apron, covered in blood, her hair disheveled about her face. Monfort was off of his own mount in a flash, and Abigail threw herself into the duke's arms. "Alex! It's horrible," she cried. "The first one isn't breathing and the second one refuses to be delivered! The doctor has torn her up with the forceps and oh, God, my dear poor Penelope. I don't know what to do.!"

Not even stopping to consider what needed to be done,

Hugh rushed past the two of them and into the foyer. He ran up the stairs, two at a time, and down the corridor toward his wife's chamber. In that moment, a man emerged, closing the door behind him.

"You are the viscount?" he asked. The man, like Penelope's cousin, was covered in blood. At Hugh's nod, he spoke solemnly, "There is not much more for me to do. I was able to remove the first baby with forceps, stillborn, unfortunately. But I cannot get a hold of the second one. There is no telling if the remaining child lives. I will leave the choice to you."

"What choice?" Hugh demanded. Cortland stood behind him.

"I can cut the child out of your wife in an attempt to save the baby. If the child cannot be delivered, both will die. If I use a knife to take the child out, at least the baby stands a chance."

This was no choice. Hugh remembered this man, always rushing to his mother with various tonics and leaches, ready to utilize the modern techniques he'd read in some journal or other.

"Get out of my home." Hugh could barely contain himself from punching the man in the face. But this was not the time. Hugh was barely aware of Cortland leading the worthless physician away as he entered the birthing room.

He would have rather taken a punch to the gut.

A bullet even.

Heavy curtains covered the windows and a fire burned in the grate. Several candles flickered, creating eerie shadows on the walls. Rose sat in a chair, cradling a naked and bloody infant against her breast. She had a war-torn look in her eyes. The infant was still. As was Penelope.

His beautiful, courageous, wickedly intelligent wife lay on the bed, a bloodied sheet covering her.

"We tried to stop him, Hugh," the lady's maid said. Except he knew that Rose was so much more than a maid to Penelope. They were more like sisters. "She begged us to stop him, but he wouldn't stop." Tears flowed freely from her as she tucked the tiny head of matted hair beneath her chin. "He wouldn't stop."

All that mattered now was Penelope.

He would not allow her to die. His eyes focused on the situation.

Penelope's hand twitched ever so minutely, giving him the signal he needed to take action. A calm like no other took hold of him.

She yet lived.

Gently steering Rose away from the bed, Hugh came up beside his wife, wrapping his arms around her gently. "Penelope, love, it's me."

Her lashes fluttered but couldn't seem to open. "Hugh," she said.

"I'm here, darling, and you and I are going to deliver our child."

At his words, her eyes fluttered again. "You've come back. You've come back."

"I am here."

"I cannot, Hugh." Her voice was thin and weak, barely a whisper, "I'm so tired."

"I'm going to help you." He knew what he had to do. His experience from years ago, working with his father's farm animals, suddenly provided the answer.

He turned away and washed his hands in a nearby basin. They were covered in dust and animal sweat. Locating a clean sheet, he dried them and then returned to the bedside.

The forceps lying beside her sent an icy, controlled anger through him.

Taking slow, even breaths, he reached beneath the sheet and slid his hand along her thigh. It was slick with blood and other fluids. He massaged her leg tenderly, covering his hand in the slippery concoction. There would be need of lubrication if he were going to be able to do what was necessary.

"Try to relax, love, I'm going to try to do this quickly." He located her opening with the tips of his fingers. Her body was prepared for this. There was just barely enough room for his hand to slide inward.

At first, she jerked and cried out, but he had his other arm around her, and he pulled her up against him. "This one needs a little help, that's all, love."

As did he.

He closed his eyes and prayed.

There it was, he could feel the back of the infant. At least if felt like the infant's back. And, yes, the little bum. Hugh needed to turn the tiny body so that it could enter the birthing canal.

Penelope's head had fallen back. A tremor ran through her.

He nudged, with his fingers at first, and then attempted to pull downward on a shoulder. "Come on little one, a little more. There you go now, just like that." The baby was moving. The shoulders turned slightly and then he knew the head had turned also.

Hugh removed his hand. Penelope's body must do the rest now.

She lay perfectly still but for the almost imperceptible rise and fall of her chest. She needed revived of the lethargy she'd fallen into. "Don't leave me, love. Don't you dare leave me."

Hugh moved behind her then, wrapped his hands around her from behind, and lifted her to a sitting, almost squatting position. "Help me, love, I need you to help me, now. Our baby needs everything you've got."

He turned to Rose. "Pull back the curtains and open the window!"

She'd been looking on in a paralyzed sort of awe. At his command, still clasping the other child to her, she moved into action.

Penelope moaned, but he could feel her efforts now. "Hugh? I can't."

Penelope was covered in sweat, but her body was contracting again.

Using one hand, he whipped Penelope's gown over her head and allowed the cool air to hit her. "Now, Penelope, now is the time. *You must push.*"

The air did exactly as he wanted. Penelope was awake now. And she was pushing.

He supported her from behind, his muscles cramping in the awkward position. But he paid no heed to them as Penelope pushed until they could see the baby's head begin to appear between her legs.

Rose lay the other infant down and rushed to the bed. The child emerging was moving.

And then, Abigail came running in, took one look at Penelope, naked with Hugh behind her, a live child between her legs, and rushed to action.

The head was out.

And then the shoulders. And then, amazingly, a shrill cry broke into the room as this child announced his arrival loudly.

Penelope slumped back against him. She went completely limp with relief and utter exhaustion. But she was breathing. When her eyes fluttered open, he knew he would never forget this moment. His wife glowed. He'd never seen anything so beautiful in his life. And he'd never felt such joy.

Abigail had draped Penelope's lower half with one of the few clean sheets left in the room and was efficiently working with the afterbirth. Rose was attending the second baby. Hugh climbed off the bed so that they could attend to his dear wife. When he did so, his attention was caught by the other child.

His.

Theirs.

Lifeless.

Was it possible to feel intense happiness and yet the worst sort of sadness all within the space of a single moment?

It was.

He lifted the unmoving babe into his arms. His own shirt unbuttoned, he pressed the naked baby against his skin, over his heart. He rubbed the child. He kissed its head. He had not even looked to see if it was a boy or a girl, but it was his. The child was his own flesh and blood.

Still holding the child to his heart, he returned to Penelope.

She was not yet out of the woods. She'd lost so much blood, and there was always risk of childbed fever.

Rose was laughing in relief and cleaning the other squirming infant. He was most definitely a he, Hugh realized, as a stream of liquid went flying into Rose's face.

The maid was shocked at first, and then looked over at Hugh and laughed. She sobered, however, at the sight of the motionless child tucked against him.

And then they both looked over at Pen. Abigail had placed a cool rag on her forehead.

"She asked for you, the whole time," Rose said softly. It was not meant as a rebuke.

He nodded. "I know." He experienced a thousand

regrets for his stubborn-hearted refusal to believe her.

He'd left her.

The maid looked as though she would say more and then gave him a weary smile. "They are yours, you know."

Again, Hugh nodded. "I know."

Abigail had been efficiently cleaning Penelope, but at this point turned to Rose. "Lay the baby by Penelope, Rose, and fetch a few maids. We need to get things cleaned up in here. We must change the bedding, and she needs a fresh and dry night rail."

The mattress was most likely soaking wet.

"Prepare the bed in my chamber," Hugh decided. "We will move her there."

Abigail did not argue. Nodding in agreement, she continued tossing bloodied rags into a wastebasket. A sob escaped her. He had not realized until that moment that tears were flowing freely down the duchess' face.

"I failed her," she whispered.

He did not know what to say. Abigail had most assuredly done her very best to assist her cousin. "No one has failed her so much as I," he responded.

Abigail swiped at her eyes. "You..." She gulped. "You saved her! I do not know what you did. The doctor said it was hopeless. And when I heard the horses, I nearly fainted in my relief."

He'd forgotten that. Abigail had always been a fainter. "But you did not. You came to her in her time of need. You sent your husband to find me. If I had arrived even five minutes later, I fear..." He would not say the words. Penelope was unconscious. Her chest rose and fell weakly. She needed rest. She needed healing.

He would do whatever was necessary to help her regain her strength.

"Is she still bleeding?" His voice caught.

She'd lost so much blood. It was everywhere.

"A little. I've packed some towels against it."

And then he could help himself no longer. He went to the other side of the bed, climbed up, and crawled to where he could lie beside his wife. He was aware that Abigail then quietly exited. He tucked himself beside her, his heart, as she fought for her life.

"I love you, Penelope." His voice was barely more than a choked whisper. "I doubt you can ever forgive me, but I love you. And I believe you. And then I remembered. I remembered making love to you on Cortland's damn leather settee."

She didn't speak, but he felt her turn her head ever so slightly.

"I will love these children till the day I die." He swallowed hard. "The thing is, I want to love them with you by my side. I want to watch you teach our children to be little hellions, little monsters who will drive their governesses crazy. I want another chance, but I need you here with me. I need you to give me a second chance.

"You've always known what a fool I am. I want you to be here to call me a fool every morning. I want to read with you. I want to look at the stars with you. I want to make love to you, over and over again by the sea, until both of us are too old to get ourselves down to the cliffs. Stay with me, Penelope. Fight, my love, so that every day of my life you can tell me that you told me so." Tears streamed down his face, and he could barely swallow around the sob caught in his throat.

He reached his free hand around to touch the living baby's cheek. He'd stopped crying and seemed to be watching him intently. He had bright red hair. "Oh, my God, he's beautiful."

And then he lowered his chin to his chest so that he

could take in the sight of his other child. The one he would never have a chance to love properly.

His breath caught. Had God entered this room and performed a miracle? For the babe was sucking on its fist, furiously, completely unaware of the astonishment its father felt.

Penelope, too, must have sensed something, for she opened her eyes and turned her head.

"A miracle," she said.

CHAPTER TWENTY-EIGHT

*P*ENELOPE KNEW SHE was not dead. She was pretty certain of the fact, anyhow.

Most of the time, Hugh was there beside her, and if she could believe what she'd thought she'd seen, both of her babies lived.

She was in her husband's chamber, lying under the covers on his high, masculine bed.

Rose, Abigail, and Hugh attended her every need. They spoke to her cheerfully about the babies but couldn't keep the concern from their voices. She knew they feared childbed fever for her.

She feared it herself.

She was a mama. She wanted nothing more than to hold her babies, suckle them, coo at them, and count their tiny fingers and toes.

And she wanted to know that the words Hugh spoke to her had not been a dream.

She slept, was spoon fed broth, swallowed the water pressed against her lips, and then slept again. She did not know for how long she went on this way. Hours, days, weeks?

She gave into the sleep and the ministering hands but would not give into death. There was too much to do! She allowed the nourishment to fill her body and the sleep to restore her energy. Until she awoke and felt an urge to open her eyes and examine her surroundings.

The sun shone through the windows casting a golden light in the room. As though the sun were setting or just about to rise. Hugh reclined on a rocking chair beside her. A bundled baby rested against his chest, and his eyes were closed.

He was snoring softly.

She'd not dreamt that he'd returned. She was not dreaming now.

His hair was even longer than usual and was pulled back into a queue, but that single rogue lock had fallen across his forehead. He'd not been shaved recently. She liked the shadow of a beard covering his jaw and upper lip.

It must be evening.

"Can I hold him?" she tried to speak, but her voice came out a whisper, little more than a croak.

Hugh's eyes flew open and then a warm, slow smile spread across his face. "Her," he corrected. "Our little future viscount is currently being spoiled in the nursery."

After rising to his feet, he lay the baby in a nearby cradle before turning back to her. "Let me get you situated, and I will bring her to you."

He leaned forward, as though to plump her pillows and sit her up slightly, but then shuddered and with a gasp, buried his face against her neck. His arms wound around her tightly, almost fearfully.

Penelope reached her own arms around him and felt truly alive again. She rubbed her hands along the muscles of his back and soothed away the tension rolling through him.

So right. So perfect.

"I've missed you," she whispered against the side of his face.

Not meeting her gaze, he gathered himself and went about the business of helping her to sit. She could see that his eyes were unnaturally bright as he tugged at the pillows and pulled up the coverlet. Once she was sitting, he turned for the child.

How was such joy possible? Holding the precious bundle in her arms, Penelope felt a surge of warmth creep over her heart. And then the warmth became even more of a physical sensation, moving into her breasts.

"Everyone says she has more of the Chesterton look to her, but the boy has your hair, and I think, he will have your eyes." He was glowing with pride as he reached down to stroke the baby's cheek.

"Did you name them?" She really had no idea how long she'd been resting.

Hugh pulled the chair closer to the bed and sat down, unwilling, it seemed, to let either of them out of his sight. "We never discussed names—before—that is. I would not name them without you."

Penelope gazed down into this tiny creature's delicate features. "I had thought of naming a baby girl Luella, for your mother." She'd never known Lady Danbury by her Christian name but had discovered it as she'd gone through the workings of the estate. The woman had been a fine manager in her son's absence.

Hugh could not have looked any more pleased. "I know it is unorthodox, but would you mind so very much if we named her Luella Miracle? I've been calling her my little miracle for nearly a week now."

"I think Luella Miracle is perfect." She touched Luella's cheek. It was downy and soft. "So, she is the one? I remembered she'd awakened, but I still don't understand."

"The midwife says she has seen such an occurrence before." But he did not continue.

"What?"

Hugh swallowed. "She said it was perhaps because I held the baby against my skin, against my heart. The warmth and the rhythm, perhaps, but there is really no explanation. I only know she is our miracle."

"And the boy?" Penelope was very curious now. "How is he?" She had the greatest urge to hold her other baby, too. As though it was the most natural thing in the world.

"Hale and hearty, already charming his nursemaid."

"Is that so?"

Hugh placed his hand on her arm and squeezed it gently.

Without answering her question, he leaned forward and dropped his forehead on it, overcome, it seemed once again. "I know it is early. I know you have only just gone through a most overwhelming labor and birth, so I do not ask for it now. But when you are feeling more yourself, I beg your forgiveness." He lifted his face and looked into her eyes. His were bright with unshed tears again.

Love for him settled into every fiber of her being. She placed one hand along the cords of his neck. It was warm and strong. His pulse beat evenly. "Only if *you* will forgive *me*."

He smiled. "I will thank you. For your desire for a child and your decision to make me a part of your passion."

She laughed. "If you would thank me then I will forgive you." And then she grew serious again. "I do love you, Hugh."

He leaned forward and pressed his lips against hers in a chaste but tender kiss. "I love you Penelope."

She moved her hand into his hair and felt the warmth of his scalp. "It's about time."

EPILOGUE

"*I* CAN WALK, you know." Penelope hooked an arm around her husband's neck as he swung her up and into his arms. Hugh sent her a threatening glance. In all the time she'd known him, she never would have suspected he could be so bossy.

She'd endured it up until this point.

Since the day the twins had been born, he'd involved himself in both her recovery and the babies' care. Furthermore, he'd hired a wet nurse to take on half of the feedings, made certain Penelope ate properly and insisted she spend far too much time abed.

She rather enjoyed most of his attempts to spoil her, but enough was enough. "If I have to spend one more day indoors, I'll positively scream," she'd told Hugh that morning.

Whereby, he'd surprised her by relenting almost immediately. With a most annoying smirk and then a smug glance, he informed her that he already had a picnic planned for the two of them that afternoon.

The remainder of the morning had drawn out endlessly until just before noon when Rose assisted her into a day dress that she hadn't worn in ages. Her midsection hadn't returned to its normal size yet, but over the last week, she'd begun to see changes. She doubted, however, that her breasts would ever be the same.

"Nonetheless, it's just as easy for me to carry you. You lost a tremendous amount of blood—" He began his usual explanation.

"—and I need to regain my strength. Yes, darling, you're absolutely right. Whatever was I thinking?" Penelope clung tightly to him as he descended the staircase. Not that she thought he'd drop her but because she rather enjoyed being carried after all. She rested her head on his shoulder and placed her free hand on his chest.

Just this week, she'd begun to imagine making love with him again.

Not yet, but soon. They had a few other matters to address first.

Milton, the elderly butler, held the door wide and as Hugh stepped outside. For the first time in what felt like forever, Penelope felt the warmth of sun touching her skin. Across the lawn, a blanket was spread beneath a large oak tree, along with a basket and a few small pillows.

Penelope squinted her eyes to keep them from watering. She'd been indoors for far too long.

It was time.

Away from her chamber, away from the nursery, Penelope needed to have a serious talk with her husband. Although he didn't speak of it, she knew he blamed himself for all the difficulties of the twins' birth. How easily he'd forgotten that he'd also saved them all.

She needed to set matters straight, once and for all. Fall was well under way, and she'd rather enter this new season of their lives with nothing hanging over them.

When he lowered her to the ground, she patted the blanket beside her.

For the first few minutes, neither of them spoke. It wasn't an awkward silence, but it wasn't completely comfortable either.

After breathing in the fresh air and listening to the rustling of the leaves overhead for all of two minutes, Penelope opened her mouth. "I—"

"You forgave me far too easily." Hugh spoke before she could get two words out. He was shaking his head, looking off into the distance.

"Look at me," Penelope demanded.

When he turned his head, all the guilt that remained lurked in his gaze.

"I am alive."

"But—"

"*Our children* are alive." She took his hand and placed it on the fabric of her dress just above her left breast. "Do you feel that? My heart beating? It is strong. No?"

He paused for a moment before nodding slowly.

"Not once have I blamed you for anything. Did you know that?"

"But you should have." He swallowed hard but did not remove his gaze from hers. Oh, but she loved this man. Such warm, honest eyes. He'd never once pretended to be anyone other than who he was. With his mother's death, and then all that happened afterward, he seemed to have lost himself.

"Do you still blame me for seducing you? I did a horrible thing, you know, taking advantage of you in Cortland's study." She wrinkled her nose. "How did you remember? You never told me."

Hugh dropped his hand to her knee and drew imaginary circles with his finger there. "I saw the settee, Cortland's settee. And I remembered you beneath me." He looked up at her solemnly. "I've not taken you that way since we married."

Because of the babies...

Their gazes locked. They had been quite creative intimately ever since their wedding. The memory sent her heart racing.

"I didn't mean to actually lie with you that evening,

you know. You were deep in your cups. I should have known it was reckless, and thoughtless, and manipulative... It was the stupidest thing I've ever done... but now." Penelope bit her lip. "I wouldn't change any of it for the world. Because I have you. We have our little miracle, and we have Creighton."

"Creighton looks more like you every day." A grin flashed across her husband's face. "And Louella's resemblance to my mother is uncanny." He turned more serious. "I was returning to you anyhow. I'd decided I couldn't live without you and that I would love your children as my own."

Penelope simply nodded. He'd needed to say all this for a while now. So much had happened since his return, they'd not had a chance to simply 'be' with one another.

Hugh's brows furrowed while he shook his head. "I was a mess. I was so angry and yet I couldn't be without you. But I realized how much I loved you. My love for you was so much greater than any anger I felt. I want you to know that. Always." And then he scrubbed one hand down his face. "I about lost it when the memory of that evening hit me. God! What an ass I've been all this time! How is it that you do not hate me? I took your maidenhood on a settee, where we could have been interrupted at any moment. And I was so damn drunk I thought I'd imagined all of it. By the time you caught up with me, I forgot even that. You should have hated me. But you didn't. You gave me nothing but love—and the truth. I don't deserve you. I don't deserve Louella or Creighton. You labored while I gallivanted around England like a fool. And then there was that damn storm. Thank god for your cousin and her husband."

Abigail had been absolutely wonderful. As had been Rose.

As had been Hugh.

"We are lucky," she agreed. Again, their gazes locked. "I have missed you." This came out almost a whisper. "Please, come back to me. Let us be happy with the past, because without it, we would have nothing."

"I am here."

He didn't understand for a moment. But then a light seemed to glimmer in his eyes. With the utmost of tenderness, he pulled her closer and then down to the blanket. "I've missed you, too."

Penelope wrapped her arms around his neck, not once moving her gaze from his.

And then his lips found hers. Tentative at first but then eager, knowing, demanding. And as his kiss deepened, all the needs that had been stored away ignited.

Hugh had kissed her briefly on the lips numerous times since coming home. He'd lifted her, hugged her, patted her on the head even.

God, how she'd missed this.

"How long?" Hugh gasped into her neck. She didn't need him to explain what he was asking. Oh, but she wished she had a different answer.

"Three more weeks." She groaned, and then he groaned and then both of them were laughing. "I love you, Hugh."

He propped himself on his elbows above her, his weight pressing her into the soft grass beneath the blanket and studied her intently. "I love you, Pen." And then he smiled.

This was what she'd wanted. This smile. This Hugh. Dancing laughter barely tucked away.

"Was it good?" he asked.

"Was what good?" But in an instant, she knew what he was asking and couldn't help laughing out loud.

"This is serious, woman. I have to ask, you know,

because I was there but can't seem to recall most of the details."

Penelope suppressed a grin. However did she get so lucky?

And her mind drifted back to the Duke of Cortland's study, an evening that seemed a lifetime ago.

She remembered how Hugh's sleeves had been pushed up to his elbows, how his cravat had hung loosely around his neck, and his hair had stood on end. That night, after all the years they'd been acquainted, he'd looked at her as a woman for the first time. And then he'd kissed her, and she'd realized she loved the taste of scotch.

By god, but she'd loved the taste of him. And now they belonged to one another forever.

"Was it good?" She repeated his question and licked her lips. "Oh, my love. So much better than good."

He toggled his eyebrows. "How much?"

"Earth shattering."

The End

Dear Reader,

Thank you for reading *Lady at Last*! I loved Penelope and Hugh, and was so excited to finally take all of my readers on their journey. In addition to telling their tale, I was happy to show you all that Lilly and Cortland, Natalie and Hawthorne, and Abigail and Monfort are all still living their happy ever afters.

But oh, my! There is more to come! Remember Natalie's brothers? Rome, Stone and Peter... So many stories demanding to be told. Oh my and Rose! I don't think she can remain a ladies maid much longer. And Hugh's poor sister, Margaret, deserves a second chance at love....

If you would like to be the first to learn when the next book in this series arrives, *Lady be Good*, you can subscribe to my newsletter or follow me on BookBub!

Keep reading for a special preview from one of my other series, *Hell Hath No Fury*, Book 1 in my Devilish Debutantes series. Enjoy!

HELL HATH NO FURY

By
Annabelle Anders

CHAPTER ONE

*I*F IT'S THE last thing I do, I will free myself of that scoundrel. Sipping her third glass of champagne in an absentminded motion, Cecily Nottingham, the new Countess of Kensington, glared daggers across the crowded ballroom at the man she'd pledged to love, honor, and obey in a church of God, less than one month ago. *Even if I have to kill him.*

Tonight, her husband's hand caressed the delicate arch of another woman's back as he guided the lady across the parquet dance floor and outside to a romantically lit terrace.

Cecily wondered if anybody present did not know that that woman was his lover. For since their nuptials, Flavion had exhibited no discretion whatsoever. All too late, Cecily realized that she'd married a narcissistic, good-for-nothing, parasitical bastard.

Both Cecily and her father had been fleeced.

Swindled.

Duped.

The villain, Flavion Nottingham, the Earl of Kensington, stood at above-average height and was slim with blond hair and gloriously cobalt eyes. In addition to being inordinately handsome, he possessed an uncanny ability to charm any lady he so desired. One might call it a gift.

His lady love, Miss Daphne Cunnington, nearly equaled him in beauty. A twinkle caught Cecily's eye and curdled something ugly in her stomach. For Miss Cunnington's dark ringlets were being held in place by a heavily bejeweled barrette purchased with the money from Cecily's dowry.

Which now belonged to Flavion.

It was not the first gift he'd bestowed upon his lover since his windfall.

A fleeting urge gripped Cecily, to run across the ballroom, slip outside and rip the barrette off Miss Cunnington's head. Cecily would not be sorry if she pulled a few strands of hair out as well. In her mind, she could picture the scene—Miss Cunnington's high-pitched wails drowning out the sounds of the orchestra as she clutched at her ruined coiffure, her face pinched and red. The thought could almost make Cecily smile.

Almost.

Instead, she lowered her gaze from their retreating figures to watch the bubbles in her champagne glass. She would not give in to boorish behavior. Cecily was a lady now.

It was not Miss Cunnington, anyhow, who vexed her most; her degenerate louse of a husband deserved that honor.

And herself for being so gullible.

"I had no choice but to court you. I have responsibilities—quite noble of me, really," he had told her, with not even the tiniest trace of regret in his voice. "The earldom needed the blunt."

He had explained this to her approximately two minutes after consummating their vows.

That had been twenty-four days ago.

Every night since then, she'd locked the connecting door between their chambers and wrapped herself in a cocoon of icy anger. Based upon his persistent requests to enter, he still expected her to present him with an heir. His sense of entitlement knew no bounds. Cecily, however, would not allow him to touch her ever again.

During mealtimes and in passing, the bounder impudently assumed that she would be a cordial and biddable wife. He expected her to peaceably accept her circumstances as though she were any other lady of the ton. But she was not, never had been, and never would be. As the only daughter of the well-known, self-made millionaire, Thomas Findlay—an orphan who had created his own wealth from nothing but cunning and determination, she could not settle for intolerable circumstances. She would not.

"But we live amongst the haute ton," Flavion had told her. Had she truly expected his undying love and flattery to continue indefinitely? "You ought to be grateful to me! You are now the Countess of Kensington, for God's sake. You have duties, my lady."

Impossible.

Absolutely not.

Flavion, apparently, had comprehended to know her no better than she had thought she'd known him.

Despite all the lessons and training she'd received from her governess, her middle-class notions of marriage could not be so easily relinquished. She'd married believing she'd found a love match. Instead, she was the pawn of a horrific business transaction.

She wished her papa had not sailed for America so soon

after the ceremony. He would never have allowed this farce of a marriage to stand.

A gust of wind blew, causing the gauzy curtains to billow out from the panes of glass along the ballroom. Cecily could barely make out the outline of her husband and his lover standing scandalously close to each other. Were they in fact touching one another? By God, they were—from hip to chest.

A man possessed of even a morsel of honor would at the very least have feigned affection for his new wife whilst in public. Instead, Flavion's unrepentant disregard laid her open to scorn and ridicule. And as each day passed, the situation grew more unbearable. Making matters worse, but unable to help herself, Cecily could not pretend to be anything other than a lady scorned. She had fallen from the pinnacle of happiness to the depths of despair. Her dreams were shattered.

She was trapped in a loveless marriage.

Furthermore, in the perverse way of the ton, despite outwardly flaunting his infidelity, Flavion continued to be well-received and even revered. For he was one of them. Our poor, dear Lord Kensington, stuck with a lowborn wife! They'd understood his action to be perfectly acceptable. Their precious earl was a martyr, a hero, a victim! What did Lady Kensington expect?

She'd gotten her title, after all. Good lord, Miss Cecily Findlay had been elevated to the title of countess. Amazing, what money could buy these days!

"You are clenching your jaw again, Cece." Her friend Emily's voice broke into Cecily's bitter thoughts. "You'll grind up all of your teeth if you keep doing that. Here, I've brought you another glass of champagne." And then, turning to follow the direction of Cecily's gaze, Emily sighed. "I know. I saw them leave, too. He ought to have two horns and a tail instead of well... looking like such an angel, rather."

Cecily dragged her eyes away from the terrace doors toward her friend and attempted a smile. The image of Flavion with horns protruding from his head and a tail shooting out behind him nearly caused her to laugh out loud. But she did not. For if she were to begin laughing, she very well might become hysterical.

The alcohol made her more than a little fuzzy. Since her wedding night, she'd acted with reckless disregard for her reputation. But did it matter? She'd followed the rules of etiquette diligently when she'd first been introduced to Society, and look where that had gotten her. Now, ironically, as a countess, she received the cut direct nearly everywhere she went. No one but her dearest friends ever met her eyes anymore. She was not one of them. She never would be. She wished her father had not set his sights so high for her.

But, in all fairness she could not lay all the blame for this catastrophe at her father's door. For she herself had been swept up in the intoxication of Flavion's romantic declarations.

When she'd said, "I do," returning his loving gaze, she'd thought she had finally found her happily ever after—her fairy tale prince. But, nay, that had been a fantasy.

She had become a countess, but she'd also become an object for ridicule.

Thank God for Emily, Sophia, and Rhoda, (short for Rhododendron). The three of them had been marginalized to the periphery of the ballroom by diminutive dowries; Cecily by low birth. The bonds of mutual rejection were apparently stronger than one would have thought.

In spite of their respective parents' disapproval, the small group of friends had stood by her through it all.

They'd rejoiced with her when they thought she was making a glorious love match with Flavion, they'd cried with her when she left her wedding breakfast, and then they'd cried with her again when she broke the news to them that it had all been a charade. He only needed her money.

Since then, daily and with unabridged enthusiasm, her three friends now concocted elaborate plots for her to escape her despicable marriage. Alas, all they had been able to come up with to date were methods for murdering him. The law did not allow a woman to divorce her husband. This being the case, their suggestions encompassed poisonous herbs, carriage accidents, and outright shooting the louse through the heart.

And eventually, they'd succeeded in making her smile again.

Fixing her gaze on a distant candle, Cecily wished for the thousandth time that her father was still in London. He would hopefully receive her letter soon. And then, return to England on the next ship. The last time he'd crossed, it had taken thirty-two days to do so. He would likely be unable to return to London for another month—or longer. But even then, could he do anything to help her? His wealth had gotten her into this marriage; surely it could buy her way out of it.

"Perhaps you could get Flavion to divorce you!" Sophia sidled up beside Emily. "You could do something so very terrible that he could not help but begin divorce proceedings." With Sophia being the most timid and shy of her friends, this suggestion came as a bit of a surprise.

Emily pushed her spectacles up higher onto the bridge of her nose and grimaced. "It would have to be truly horrible. The cost of a divorce is exorbitant! He would end up spending a huge part of your dowry on legal fees. And if he divorced you, Cece, your reputation would be beyond repair. The scandal would be horrendous."

By this point, Rhoda had returned from the ladies' retiring room and picked up on the last part of the conversation. As the four had continuously discussed methods to free Cecily from her marriage for several days now, she had no difficulty in picking up on the train of thought. "What could possibly make him angry enough to do that? Cece's dowry was his sole purpose for marrying her after all."

Cecily closed her eyes and pressed her fingertips to her temples. She could barely organize her champagne-muddled thoughts. After a few moments, she picked up the idea again. "He is growing quite angry with me for locking my chamber door at night. Despicable man. I'm not sure how much longer I can hold him off. I find it reprehensible that he still expects for me to... that I will... well, that I would present him with an heir—the lying, snake-in-the-grass, scum-sucking rat."

"You could make him into a cuckold. Present him with another man's child," Sophia suggested breathlessly.

Three sets of widened eyes turned on her at the same time.

"That's perfect!" Rhoda said.

"She'd be an outcast," Emily stated.

A shiver ran down Cecily's spine as she imagined Flavion's reaction to such a scandal. "I'd be free," she whispered. "But how would I go about doing such a thing? I know nothing of seduction, and if I did, who on earth would I seduce?"

In that moment, a commotion arose by the doors where a man bearing an eerie resemblance to Flavion Nottingham stood. Instead of being fair and blond, this man's skin was bronzed and his hair more of a tarnished golden color—but the eyes were the same, the features nearly identical. And as several ladies swooped in on him, it quickly became apparent that he also possessed the same lethal magnetism.

"What about him?" Emily asked with a wicked glint in her eyes.

*I*T HAD BEEN over eight years since Stephen Nottingham had last set foot in a London ballroom. He'd left England at the age of one and twenty with a resolve to find his own place in life, and had finally returned, having done so. He'd established a fortune, a rather convenient set of circumstances, considering the letter he'd finally received from his cousin. News was that the family coffers were in dire need of funds. Stephen vowed this would be the last time he would bail out his cousin, now the earl. He only hoped he wasn't too late. As the second in line to the earldom, and having been virtually raised by his uncle, Stephen felt more than a little responsible for the family estate and holdings.

He was in a position to save it, and save it he would. But there would be conditions. He would not offer his assistance without oversight.

Upon the death of Uncle Leo, Flave had most likely relinquished full control to the stewards who had worked under his father for years. There would have been no control, no guidance, and no innovation.

Stephen tried to ignore the niggling of guilt that assaulted him whenever he pondered his uncle's death. He had not returned home for the funeral. He'd stayed away intentionally, still feeling the sting of his family's betrayal. He had left Flavion to cope alone.

And Flavion had always been a spendthrift. Who knew what had transpired over the past five years or so? Nothing lucrative, for certain.

Stephen would be damned if he would sink his hard-earned funds into the properties and then allow them to be mismanaged. Flave must learn to put in some effort.

Narrowing his eyes, he scanned the ballroom, hoping to locate his erstwhile, younger cousin. But he wasn't quick enough. Before he could take more than a few steps, he found himself surrounded by an army of mamas and debutantes. Oh hell.

"*H*E MUST BE Lord Kensington's cousin. The resemblance is eerie," Cecily said as she warily watched the familiar, yet not familiar, gentleman attempt to extricate himself from the more aggressive Mayfair mothers. The man's similarity to her husband was uncanny, and yet... not. Whereas Flavion drank in adoration greedily, this man looked irritated and a bit uncomfortable. He pulled at his cravat a time or two and scowled.

Handsome, indeed, drat him.

Cecily attributed the zing of awareness flowing through her to the man's likeness to her husband. Until her wedding night she'd thought herself in love with Flavion. Of course, a man who looked so much like him would cause her heart to race. Wouldn't it?

"I think he's even more attractive than Flavion," Emily said. "Sturdier, manlier somehow."

Emily had the right of it. Cecily did not believe, in truth, that she could seduce any man, let alone this one. He seemed far too worldly, untouchable—almost. Her friends' outlandish ideas were getting more and more preposterous.

Sophia shook her head, her blond ringlets dancing about her petite shoulders. "He doesn't look like he would be as fun as Flavion is—was," she said with a pout. "He seems overly serious."

"Could you do it, Cecily? Could you seduce your husband's cousin?" Rhoda asked daringly.

Cecily thought about the kisses she had shared with Flavion during their courtship. The compliments, secret smiles, and elicit touches. It had all been coldly calculated to lure her into falling in love. And she had believed in him. He'd made her heart dance. He'd caused the sun to shine inside of her on the rainiest of days.

None of it had meant anything to him.

And now she felt more powerless than she had in her entire life.

Her father hadn't raised her to be an empty-headed miss, well, not until the last couple of years, anyhow. As a child, she'd sit with him in his office while he made decisions affecting hundreds of people. He'd allowed her to remain in the room during sensitive negotiations and then later explained his strategies and techniques. Although a female, she had been, nonetheless, his favorite protégé. He'd expounded the importance of knowing every detail, no matter how minute, before entering any contract. "And always remember," he'd told her, "once money has exchanged hands, consider the deal final." Cecily could not deny the direness of her situation.

For the payment of her dowry, had indeed, been delivered in full.

If she were going to free herself, she would have to do something drastic.

Could she do it? Could she seduce her husband's cousin?

Her cold anger turned into a steely resolve. "If it will make him angry enough to divorce me," she said through clenched teeth. Perhaps then she would stop feeling so mad all of the time. Perhaps her hurt would go away if she could hurt him. She tamped down the part of her conscience that told her it wouldn't work, it wasn't right. But the scars of betrayal were now a part her. He had done this to her! She handed her empty glass to a passing waiter and accepted a new one.

AFTER LITERALLY PUSHING himself free of the clinging debutantes, Stephen strode across the ballroom, scanning the guests for his cousin amongst the crowd. In doing so, he saw a some vaguely familiar faces. He merely inclined his head toward the few who managed to catch his eye and moved onward. Where the hell was Flavion? Having just arrived from the Continent, Stephen had first presented himself at his uncle's townhouse, Flave's now. The servants had told him that the earl and the countess— surely not Flave's mother?—were out for the evening attending one of the Season's more elaborate balls. Rather than cool his heels at Nottinghouse, Stephen felt compelled to clean up, don his eveningwear, and seek out his cousin to discover what the devil he'd been up to. It had been nearly two days since he'd had any sleep, however, and his temper frayed.

Stepping onto the terrace, he immediately spied his cousin, only partially hidden by ornamental shrubs, in a passionate embrace with a dark-haired, sweet little English rose. Stephen ought to have guessed. Ever since the age of twelve, Flavion had single-mindedly developed this particular skill with unusual persistence.

"Flave!" he said firmly.

The younger man took his time looking up, but once his eyes lighted upon Stephen, he pushed the young woman aside and rushed over with both hands outstretched.

"Cuz!" he exclaimed before pulling Stephen into a tight hug. "Where have you been? Oh, it's good to see you! I've been trying to track you down for years. Did you not receive my letters?"

"Not until recently." He shot a meaningful glance in the direction of the lady Flavion had abandoned so casually.

Flavion laughed heartily, oblivious to his slight. "Well, the joke's on you! I have taken care of matters myself and married an heiress! Largest dowry of them all." His cousin's blue eyes twinkled as he toggled his eyebrows.

At this point, Stephen turned and made a slight bow to the lady who held herself back, arms crossed in front of her. "Felicitations, my lady. Won't you introduce me to your wife then, Flavion?"

At his words, a hard glint appeared in the lady's eyes, and she tittered into her hand. Her giggles caused the curls about her head to bounce somewhat comically.

Flavion ducked his face before grinning back up at Stephen. "Ah, well, about that... We'll have to go back inside the ballroom to find her." Tilting his head with a shrug, he added, "A man must do what a man must do."

Stephen squeezed the bridge of his nose to ward off what he was sure would become a massive headache. Somehow, he'd known the matter of Flavion getting married would not be a simple one. "Exactly when did this wedding take place?" His imagination conjured up all sorts of women who would have happily purchased the title of countess... incomparables, widows, antidotes, conniving bitches. In almost all of the scenarios, Stephen knew there would be complications.

There were always complications when a woman was concerned.

Flavion furrowed his brow and appeared to be counting back mentally. "A few weeks now, what does it matter? My pockets are flush again!"

"Perhaps I ought to escort your, er... friend, back inside to her chaperone, and then you may introduce me to your fortuitous bride," Stephen suggested, already fearful that Flavion had walked into a disaster of his own making.

"Not necessary. Is it, sweetums?" Flavion said, looking back at the lady he'd been thoroughly absorbed with only a few moments before.

Sending him a worshipful look, she shook her head and gazed back at him. Flavion placed a quick kiss on her lips before turning her, patting her bum, and shooing her away. She did just as he asked without any protest whatsoever.

Ah, nothing had changed.

After she'd disappeared, Flavion looked over at Stephen. "Er, yes, I suppose you ought to meet the old ball and chain." Then he paused. "But Stephen?" He shuffled his feet, looking at the ground like an overgrown schoolboy who knew he'd misbehaved.

Stephen feared Flave's next words. "Yes?"

"She's rather out of sorts with me at the moment. A temporary matter, I am sure, but I am currently not one of her favorite people."

"A lover's quarrel?" Stephen asked already knowing it could not be that simple.

"Well, rather more than that, I'm afraid. You see, she didn't take it very well when I told her that I married her for the money."

"You did what?"

"Well, after I had, ah, finalized our contract, so to speak, I couldn't really have her hanging off me and whatnot. You know, expecting me to carry on with all of the doting and fawning. Daphne wouldn't like that at all."

"I'm not following. Daphne, your wife, wouldn't want you to remain a doting husband?" Stephen asked, confused.

"Oh, heavens, no. Daphne is not my wife." Amusement took over his demeanor. "I'm in love with Daphne. My wife is Cecily." And with a wink he added, "Daphne is that fine bit of muslin I had in my arms a moment ago."

"And by 'finalizing the contract' you mean...?" Could Flavion truly be that stupid? Oh, hell, could he have been that insensitive? Of course, he could!

"Well, I couldn't give her cause to seek an annulment. Her dowry will keep me in blunt for years to come! I couldn't risk losing that, now could I?"

Feeling as though he had waded into quicksand, Stephen asked, "How much is this dowry?"

Jerking his chin up, Flavion responded, "Over one-hundred-thousand pounds!"

Stephen took a deep breath. "And who, might I ask, is her family?" Any lady with such a large dowry would be from a well-known and successful family.

"She's middle class, I'm afraid, rather low birth, actually. Her father is a rags-to-riches sort of fellow. Mr. Thomas Findlay. Not even a gentleman, really, let alone nobility."

At that particular name, Stephen flinched. Findlay Shipping and Manufacturing was one of his own company's largest competitors. And Thomas Findlay was known to be ruthless. If Flave's wife took her grievances to her father, Stephen wouldn't put it past the industrial giant to put a violent end to his cousin's life. Lucky for Flave, Stephen knew that Thomas Findlay had left for America on business a few weeks ago. He must have left right after the wedding.

"Have you already invested the dowry?" Stephen asked, his mind straightaway working a mile a minute.

"It's sitting in the bank, Stephen. Well, most of it anyhow. I've been celebrating lately, as anyone would do! Not every day a man creates such a grand windfall for himself."

Flavion's words reverberated around Stephen's head. Only a complete and utter idiot would allow that much money to languish in the bank, uninvested. Before he could complete that thought, Stephen wondered exactly how much of it Flavion had already frittered away. "We need to review your marriage contracts, Flave. Meanwhile, why don't you introduce me to this new wife of yours?" Then, after further thought, he added, "Do make an attempt to be doting, Flavion. Your life may very well depend upon it."

Flave glanced at him with a surprised look on his face.

Stephen merely grasped Flavion's arm and said, "Lead the way, cuz."

Buy *Hell Hath No Fury.*

Read More by Annabelle Anders

Devilish Debutantes Series
Hell Hath No Fury
Hell in a Hand Basket
Hell Hath Frozen Over *(Novella)*
Hell's Belle
Hell of a Lady

Lord Love a Lady Series
Nobody's Lady
A Lady's Prerogative
Lady Saves the Duke

Not So Saintly Sisters Series
The Perfect Debutante
The Perfect Spinster (coming in 2019)

I love keeping in touch with readers and would be thrilled to hear from you! Join or follow me at any (or all!) of the social media links below!
Amazon: amazon.com/Annabelle-Anders/e/B073ZLRB3F
Bookbub: bookbub.com/profile/annabelle-anders
Website: annabelleanders.com
Goodreads: goodreads.com/Annabelle_Anders
Facebook Author Page: facebook.com/HappyWritingGirl
Facebook Reader Group: A Regency House Party:
facebook.com/groups/AnnabellesReaderGroup
Twitter: @AnnabellReadLuv
www.annabelleanders.com

Hell Hath No Fury
(*Devilish Debutante's, Book 1*)

To keep the money, he has to keep her as well...

Cecily Nottingham has made a huge mistake.

The marriage bed was still warm when the earl she thought she loved crawled out of it and announced that he loved someone else.

Loves. Someone else.

All he saw in Cecily was her dowry.

But he's in for the shock of his life, because in order to keep the money, he has to keep her.

With nothing to lose, Cecily sets out to seduce her husband's cousin, Stephen Nottingham, in an attempt to goad the earl into divorcing her. Little does she realize that Stephen would turn out to be everything her husband was not: Honorable, loyal, trustworthy...Handsome as sin.

Stephen only returned to England for one reason. Save his cousin's estate from financial ruin. Instead, he finds himself face to face with his cousins beautiful and scorned wife, he isn't sure what to do first, strangle his cousin, or kiss his wife. His honor is about to be questioned, right along with his self-control.

Amid snakes, duels and a good catfight, Cecily realizes the game she's playing has high stakes indeed. There are only a few ways for a marriage to end in Regency England and none of them come without a high price. Is she willing to pay it? Is Stephen? A 'Happily Ever After' hangs in the balance, because, yes, love can conquer all, but sometimes it needs a little bit of help.

Hell in a Hand Basket
(*Devilish Debutante's, Book 2*)

Sophia Babineaux has landed a husband! And a good one at that!

Lord Harold, the second son of a duke, is kind, gentle, undemanding.

Perhaps a little too undemanding?

Because after one chance encounter with skilled rake, Captain Devlin Brooks, it is glaringly obvious that something is missing between Lord Harold and herself... pas-sion... sizzle... well... everything. And marriage is forever!

Will her parents allow her to reconsider? Absolutely not.

War hero, Devlin Brookes, is ready to marry and thinks Sophia Babineaux might be the one. One itsy bitsy problem: she's engaged to his cousin, Harold.

But Devlin knows his cousin! and damned if Harold hasn't been coerced into this betrothal by the Duke of Prescott, his father.

Prescott usually gets what he wants.

Devlin, Sophia and Harold conspire to thwart the duke's wishes but fail to consider a few vital, unintended consequences.

Once set in motion, matters quickly spiral out of control!

Caught up in tragedy, regret, and deceit Sophia and Devlin's love be-comes tainted. If they cannot cope with their choices they may never find their way back once embarking on their journey... To Hell in a Hand Basket...

Hell's Belle
(*Devilish Debutante's, Book 3*)

There comes a time in a lady's life when she needs to take matters into her own hands...

A Scheming Minx
Emily Goodnight, a curiously smart bluestocking – who cannot see a thing without her blasted spectacles – is raising the art of meddling to new heights. Why leave her future in the hands of fate when she's perfectly capable of managing it herself?

An Apathetic Rake
The Earl of Blakely, London's most unattainable bachelor, finds Miss Goodnight's schemes nearly as intriguing as the curves hidden beneath her frumpy gowns. Secure in his independence, he's focussed on one thing only: evading this father's manipulating ways. In doing so, ironically, he fails to evade the mischief of Emily's managing ploys.

Hell's Bell Indeed
What with all the cheating at parlor games, trysts in dark closets, and nighttime flights to Gretna Green, complications arise. Because fate has limits. And when it comes to love and the secrets of the past, there's only so much twisting one English Miss can get away with...

Hell of a Lady
(*Devilish Debutante's, Book 4*)

Regency Romance between an angelic vicar and a devilish debutante: A must read if you love sweet and sizzle with an abundance of heart.

The Last Devilish Debutante

Miss Rhododendron Mossant has given up on men, love, and worst of all, herself. Once a flirtatious beauty, the nightmares of her past have frozen her in fear. Ruined and ready to call it quits, all she can hope for is divine intervention.

The Angelic Vicar

Justin White, Vicar turned Earl, has the looks of an angel but the heart of a rake. He isn't prepared to marry and yet honor won't allow anything less. Which poses something of a problem... because, by God, when it comes to this vixen, a war is is waging between his body and his soul.

Scandal's Sweet Sizzle

She's hopeless and he's hopelessly devoted. Together they must conquer the ton, her disgrace, and his empty pockets. With a little deviousness, and a miracle or two, is it possible this devilish match was really made in heaven?

Hell Hath Frozen Over
(Devilish Debutantes, Novella)

The Duchess of Prescott, now a widow, fears she's experienced all life has to offer. Thomas Findlay, a wealthy industrialist, knows she has not. Can he convince her she has love and passion in her future? And if he does, cans she convince herself to embrace it?

Lord Love a Lady Series

Nobody's Lady
(*Lord Love a Lady Series, Book 1*)

Dukes don't need help, or do they?

Michael Redmond, the Duke of Cortland, needs to be in London—most expeditiously—but a band of highway robbers have thwarted his plans. Purse-pinched, coachless, and mired in mud, he stumbles on Lilly Beauchamp, the woman who betrayed him years ago.

Ladies can't be heroes, or can they?

Michael was her first love, her first lover, but he abandoned her when she needed him most. She'd trusted him, and then he failed to meet with her father as promised. A widowed stepmother now, Lilly loves her country and will do her part for the Good of England—even if that means aiding this hobbled and pathetic duke.

They lost their chance at love, or did they?

A betrothal, a scandal, and a kidnapping stand between them now. Can honor emerge from the ashes of their love?

A Lady's Prerogative
(*Lord Love a Lady Series, Book 2*)

It's not fair.

Titled rakes can practically get away with murder, but one tiny little misstep and a debutante is sent away to the country. Which is where Lady Natalie Spencer is stuck after jilting her betrothed.

Frustrated with her banishment, she's finished being a good girl and ready to be a little naughty. Luckily she has brothers, one of whom has brought home his delightfully gorgeous friend.

After recently inheriting an earldom, Garrett Castleton is determined to turn over a new leaf and shed the roguish lifestyle he adopted years ago. His friend's sister, no matter how enticing, is out-of-bounds. He has a run-down estate to manage and tenants to save from destitution.

Can love find a compromise between the two, or will their stubbornness get them into even more trouble?

A betrothal, a scandal, and a kidnapping stand between them now. Can honor emerge from the ashes of their love?

Lady Saves the Duke
(*Lord Love a Lady Series, Book 3*)

He thinks he's saving her, but will this Lady Save the Duke, instead?

Miss Abigail Wright, disillusioned spinster, hides her secret pain behind encouraging smiles and optimistic laughter. Self-pity, she believes, is for the truly wretched. So when her mother insists she attend a house party—uninvited—she determines to simply make the best of it...until an unfortunate wardrobe malfunction.

Alex Cross, the "Duke of Ice," has more than earned the nickname given him by the ton. He's given up on happiness but will not reject sensual pleasure. After all, a man has needs. The week ought to have been pleasantly uneventful for both of them, with nature walks, parlor games, and afternoon teas on the terrace...but for some inferior stitchery on poor Abigail's bodice.

And now the duke is faced with a choice. Should he make this mouse a respectable offer and then abandon her to his country estate? She's rather pathetic and harmless, really. Oughtn't to upset his life whatsoever.

His heart, however, is another matter...

Lady at Last
(*Lord Love a Lady Series, Book 4*)
Penelope's Story